Midlife
Senior Moments

at the Danville Center

Jean Young

Renton, Washington

Front cover photo © chaiyon021 / Fotolia.
Edited by S. C. Moore, C. E. Moore, and Emily Goldman.

Published 2014, Moonlight Garden Publications,
an imprint of Gazebo Gardens Publishing, LLC.
www.GazeboGardensPublishing.com

978-1-938281-45-7   (paperback)
978-1-938281-44-0   (e-book)

Library of Congress Control Number: 2013950830

Printed in the United States of America.

I dedicate this book to my children,
all of whom had a hand in my writing.

✢ CHAPTER ONE ✣

I drove past the Senior Center twice, missing it the first time. It was an old, false front building that looked rather like a saloon in a cheap western. Going around the block, I began to realize how nervous I was. Stupid, juvenile, idiot forty-five year old. What in hell was there to be scared about just showing up for a volunteer job?

Around the corner, an oldish-looking man carefully staggered up the steps of Danville's old hotel. I wondered if he went to the Center. I hadn't thought before about what kind of people would go to a senior center. Maybe nice, white-haired women like Mom's bridge group ladies. Cookies and cards would be nice. With my luck, it would be full of smelly drunks and ex-sailors who'd spit and pinch.

I pulled into the dirty parking lot. Nervous? I was scared spitless, even after all my brave talk to my group at Widow's Counseling. I'd volunteer for a while, somewhere, then look around and get a job. I was a woman of the 90s, yet here I was, too frightened to get out of the dumb car, ready to go home just seeing the place.

Come on, Annie, go on, get out, and at least talk to them. It's that or talking to the walls at home again. I got out.

The door was splintered plywood, painted khaki brown, and heavy. I had to shove with my shoulder to get it open. How did all of those little old women I hoped to find ever

1

manage? I stumbled in. Always graceful.

Four ladies, all white haired with glasses, stared at me from a card table. I stared back at them and the room. A pink, no, rose, no, fuchsia rug sort of vibrated on the floor. It seemed to be sending shimmers of roseate light up the hot pink walls.

When all of the ladies turned pink, I realized it wasn't the rug blinking, but a revolving light from the next room. They seemed to be ignoring it, so I did, too.

A lady whose hair was more iron gray than white, held in Marcel waves by a yellow net, got up and said, "Welcome to the Danville Senior Center. May I help you?"

"Thank you. I have an appointment with Mrs. Paige." Jeez, I'd blown it already. All that rehearsal, Ms. Paige, Ms. Paige...I'd no idea what she was, Miss or Mrs., 20 or 90. She'd sounded forty-ish on the phone, which was certainly a chancy guess. The nice old lady bellowed, "Royal, a lady to see you!"

I stared some more. What a voice, and she wasn't very big. I looked at the corner at which Mrs. Hairnet had yelled. A door opened and a really tiny lady stuck her head out. I stared again. Boy, wouldn't Mom jump me for my lousy manners, but her hair was the color of the rug, unless she'd picked the rug to match her hair.

"You must be Mrs. Farley?"

I nodded.

"Do come in. Now watch your head. This door is rather low." She disappeared.

I ducked, and then nearly fell into the office. There was a step down—sixteen inches at least.

Ms. Paige was already seated at a huge, gunmetal- gray desk. It dwarfed her. She gestured at one of those folding lawn chairs that are supposed to look like a director's chair. It was gray, too. So were the floors and the walls. After all the pink, it was rather restful, but dark. I sat down and tried to quit looking around and pay attention to Ms. Paige. I'd bet anything the office had most likely been a janitor's closet. *Pay attention, Stupid. Want to get turned down on a volunteer's job?*

"Now, dear," Ms. Paige was saying, "what can I do for you?"

"Uh, well, as I said when I called you, I heard on TV— that the Senior Center could use volunteers, and as I live close, and wouldn't have to drive far..." *Moron, don't bring that up, they probably want you to drive fifty million seniors up and down the freeway. Don't tell them you can't manage freeways. Just con them into having you do something else.* I smiled and tried again. "Since I do have time, I'd like very much to be of help."

She beamed at me. "There, I knew it was something nice. I wrote your name and the time down on the calendar, but I must have gotten distracted and didn't write down what we were meeting about. Well, let's see, what can you do?"

Oh, God, she'd asked. I knew she would. Why couldn't she just say she needed somebody to type, or pour tea, or make coffee, or sort magazines, or read to the blind, or whatever she needed? Why the hell does she have to know what I can do? Because I don't know. I can bake bread, cook a family meal, plant a garden, sew like mad, herd Girl Scouts around, nurse dying husbands, but what can I really do?

"Well, let's see. I have office skills, but they're a little rusty." *Only a million years rusty.* "I have taught crafts, especially sewing." *Textile's the word now remember, stupid.* "And nutrition." Taught sounded good, of course, it was to Scouts, Brownies, and 4-H-ers. "And then..."

"Well, isn't that just perfect? I knew the good Lord would do it for us."

I blinked. What was perfect?

"We were so lucky last month and were finally given a nutrition grant. We'll be able to put on three hot lunches a week now, and I really need someone who has had nutrition experience to manage it."

Now I beamed. That I could do. After all those thousands of church suppers, potlucks, and company picnics, I could put on hot meals for seniors.

Ms. Paige went on. "Let's see, when can you start? Dear John will be so pleased I have you. He has been just the littlest bit worried, because we are supposed to have the first meal next week. That doesn't give us much time, what with getting some appliances and dishes and a caterer."

I'd be pop-eyed yet. "John?" *That's good. Don't ask the most important questions—first meal next week?!*

"Yes, dear, the mayor. The Senior Center is under the control of the mayor's office. He's a very nice man. A little nervous at times, but all the seniors love him. Now let's see. How is your memory?"

"Memory?" What did she mean? *That I can't forget Terry coughing and coughing, or that I can't seem to remember what day it is, or where I've put anything? Where were those damn rings?* "Well, average, I suppose." I smiled.

She smiled. "That's good. I'm seventy-five, you know, or I suppose you didn't really know—no one ever guesses. It's mostly my hair. I dye it. It really helps, not that being young is important, but I think giving an aura of being younger is reassuring to the seniors' families. But, I do occasionally forget things, and you can help me remember."

That would be the day!

"You know, as young as you are..."

"Forty-five."

"You'd be surprised how cute you'd look with your hair dyed, maybe a medium chestnut. Well, I mustn't waste your time. I'll just call John and get him to pop over and get all this settled. While you wait, why don't I have Hilda show you around? You can ask her anything you want to know. She's been here ever since the Center opened. HILDA!"

Wow, maybe I'd learn to project my voice like that if I were down here much. Terry always said I couldn't be heard across the table, let alone across a room.

As I stepped up—the one giant step—and ducked—hey, great exercise—I heard Ms. Paige saying, "John, come on over, I've got a nutritionist for us."

Holy hell, I'm not a nutritionist. I'm not anything official.

Hilda said, "You'll want to see the kitchen."

How did she know, had she been listening to us? Her three card game partners watched us with interest, their hair turning rose and white. What was with that light?

The kitchen was behind a tall counter that separated it from a dining area. I wondered if the counter had been a real bar at some time. It was chest-high with a black Formica top and black quilted vinyl sides. Hilda led me behind it. Yipes, another step. This one had a three-inch rise from the rose monstrosity to a cracked concrete floor.

"This here is the old stove. Royal's got money for a new one. This one's oven don't work very well and only three of the burners, and anyway, the oven door falls off if you ain't careful." She gave it a little jerk, and it fell off.

"Uh, can I help you put it back on?"

"No, don't bother. Phil will do it. He fixes all the stuff down here. My husband helps, too, but Phil, he does most of it."

"Mmm, yes."

"Now this here is where Phil said he'd plumb in the dishwasher when you buy it."

"Me?"

"Sure. And me and Phil's wife, that's Emma you know, we were suggesting Phil put the cupboards here where those boxes are, and we'd put the garbage cans down at the end, and then you'd have a place to put the dishes."

I would? And where would *I* be getting those dishes?

"We know it'll take a while to get all that stuff, but we can use paper plates a while and that plastic silver like we do at the potlucks. Course that caterer will have pans and stuff."

"Uh, does Royal have a caterer? My GOD, who's that?"

There was a woman on the floor at the end of the bar.

"That's Helen. She likes the lights. I think Royal got a list of caterers out of the phone book."

I stared at Helen. She was sitting on the floor, almost in the fetal position, rocking—no, sort of weaving with the revolving light. I could hardly see her—black pants, black tee shirt, and lots of long black hair.

"One of those caterers has their shop right here in town. The mayor's wife's brother-in-law runs it. They turn out real good food. Now, Helen, you get up off that cold floor. You'll get pneumonia again."

Helen got up, gracefully. I'd have been as stiff as a board sitting like that. She'd be great at Yoga.

"Come here and meet Mrs. Farley She is going to get us our hot meals."

Unnerved, I held out my hand. "How do you do?"

She clasped my hand. Hers were small for such a tall woman, and very soft. She looked into my eyes and said, "Five and seven-eighths." She patted her hair, pulled her shirt down, and walked slowly out of the Center.

"Is she ill?"

Hilda went over and turned off the revolving light, and the big room became dark and dingy. "Well, sort of, I guess. The mental health people said she was...what's the word...a split personality?"

"Schizophrenic?"

"Yes, well sometimes she's pretty good, and then she gets spells. Royal lets her come in, and we kind of take care of her—see she eats something. If she gets noisy, Royal calls John over, and he sends her home. She gets awful noisy sometimes, but usually she just talks funny and turns the dancing light on and watches it and watches it. Poor lady. You want to see the storeroom?"

"Yes, please."

The storeroom took up most of the end of the building. It had another giant step down. Rough wooden shelves lined four sides. An incredible array of things filled the shelves, all neatly arranged and tagged. Crepe paper, plastic flowers, punch bowl and glasses, and three agitators from old wringer washers; one red, one white, and one blue.

Faintly, I heard Royal bellow, "HILDA!"

"I imagine that John is here. Come on."

The mayor was gorgeous. Curly white hair, tanned, looked like he was a sport nut, wiry thin, maybe forty. It was a shame he wasn't bigger. He might have been an inch taller than I, but not more. We assured each other we were glad to meet. I took the director's chair, and the mayor got the telephone table. I thought he looked a little harried.

"Mrs. Farley, Royal thinks you'd be a good choice for a nutrition supervisor. Do you have a resume?"

A resume for a volunteer job? They were getting picky. "Yes, I do, but first, I think there has been a misunderstanding. I am not a nutritionist. I've had experience in nutrition and in putting on group meals, but my training is not in nutrition." Who'd believe English major?

He took my resume, puffery that it was, but neat however.

"Well, we didn't expect a professional for seven an hour."

"Seven *dollars*?"

"That won't do?"

We stared at each other.

"No, I mean yes, that's fine."

He put my carefully typed resume in his pocket, said Royal had all the necessary papers, and hurried out.

An hour later I was home—employed three days a week and almost manic with excitement.

❧ CHAPTER TWO ❧

I was at work at eight the next morning. Only one other car was in the parking lot, but the Center was unlocked.

I could hardly see through the gloom. No lights were on except for a thin line that shown through the crack in the door of the cupboard-sized office. Feeling a little let down after the excitement of trying to get to work on time, I carefully crossed the dark room and stepped down.

Royal looked up. "Good morning, Mrs. Farley. I'm getting out all of the details I have on the meal program for you. In the meantime, would you make a pot of coffee? Use the large pot and make it the way you like it. Half will think it too weak, half too strong, so you might as well enjoy it."

"O.K., I'll turn the lights on, too—and please, call me Anne."

"No, don't. Lights are a sort of signal—Anne. The Center really doesn't open until nine, but the seniors know I'm here and come in if the lights are on, and I need this time to get paperwork done. Hilda and Conner come in at nine, and she'll turn the lights on."

I edged back through the gloom. That fantastic rug managed to send up a few pinkish glows. I got to the bar and finally found the kitchen lights. Coffee pots were under the sink and coffee on top of the refrigerator.

With the coffee brewing, I went back to the office. Royal's desk was covered with papers.

"Now, Anne, I'll give you the information, and you spend all the time you need going through it. We'll have to find you a place to work."

I hadn't thought of that. How in God's name could another desk fit into the tiny office?

"I told John you'd need a desk, and he said he'd send one over when we decided where to put it."

"Maybe outside the door?"

"No, seniors talk! You'd never get any work done."

The phone rang. Royal swiveled her chair. "Danville Senior Center. Yes, Willie, we'll take your name for the lunch. I'll let you talk to the nutritionist."

She handed me the phone. Totally out of my league, I said, "Good morning."

A tiny, sweet, female voice with a heavy German accent said, "I come to lunch next week. I come Wednesday. What you got to eat that day?"

"Well, it isn't quite settled yet." That was a real understatement. Just then Royal handed me a pen and clipboard with a sheet of yellow legal paper titled NOON LUNCH. "Willie, what is your last name?"

"Wyoming."

"Wyoming?"

"Yes. I come for lunch at noon, Wednesday. Goodbye."

We hung up. I looked at Royal, "Wyoming?"

"Willie married a farmer when she came to the States. She says she doesn't know how he came to have Wyoming as a last name. Evidently he never even saw the place. He's been dead for about five years now. I never knew him."

We both began to hear sounds through the door. There were voices and bumping noises in the front room. A tall aristocratic looking man ducked and came into the office. He looked a lot like the pictures of Prince Charles, if Charles were seventy and wore a billed cap. He was beaming.

"Good morning, Royal. Hilda told us last night that the lunch lady..."

I grinned. *That's me, and lunch lady is more like it. This nutritionist stuff has got to go.*

"Anyway, Hilda said she was coming today and we knew she'd need a desk."

"How nice, Gordy."

"So I got out the old desk Janet had when she was a girl, and I cleaned it up. Phil brought it over in his camper this morning." He pushed the door open.

A woman I recognized as one of the card players, and a man—Emma and Phil, evidently—stood in the door, a tiny apple-green desk between them. Phil and Gordy came in as Royal and I flattened against her desk.

"Now, Royal, you and the lunch lady go out for a while. Phil and I are going to move the file cabinet over into the corner, then we'll turn your desk sideways and put Janet's up to it."

I didn't understand how Emma and Phil were going to do it, but it was obvious they thought they did. And it was apparent they were regular volunteers at the center.

Royal picked up the phone and took it out the office door. "Come along, Anne, we'll try to work out here for awhile." She took the papers off her desk and we climbed out.

Emma was shuffling cards in the dark at the same card table she'd sat at yesterday. Royal turned on the lights and we took another card table. In the next half hour, I signed nine more seniors up for the lunch. *Jeez, what'll I do if I can't get a caterer?* Then I went through the papers Royal had gathered.

As well as I could tell, it was mainly lists of phone numbers, names, and prices. There didn't seem to be any system or method of telling what prices went with what or whom. My left ear prickled, confirming my anxiety.

At nine, Hilda walked in, looked around, and began to

straighten chairs, empty ashtrays, and line up the card tables. Phil and Gordy came out, took the phone from me, and went back into the office with it. I followed.

The desks reminded me of a gray whale with a green calf, but they had fitted it all in. The phone rang. It was someone named Lillian. She knew who I was, and she said she was putting a copy of the grant in our basket for me, and that she'd remind Royal to pick it up.

While I pondered that and thanked the two beaming men, Hilda came in and emptied the waste paper basket. Maybe she worked for the Center, too.

By noon I was really scared. Royal was a dear, sweet lady, and had an excellent way with every senior who walked in on us, but she didn't seem to have a clue about what needed to be done for the meals we were starting. She was especially vague about how much money would be available.

Lunch distracted me. It was fun. Royal got Borscht, left from "Soup Day," out of the refrigerator. Emma produced a loaf of homemade wheat bread, and Hilda and I heated the soup and set the table. They had a remarkable collection of Goodwill type plates. Hilda's husband, Conner, came out of the back room and we all ate together.

The talk was about other seniors and which ones were going on a trip. Scattered about the room, six other people were eating sack lunches or hamburgers from McDonalds. A lot of remarks went back and forth. I liked the atmosphere. I turned to Phil. "Is this the usual number who come in?"

Emma said, "Well, this is sort of a quiet day. More will be in after lunch. Conner's going to show movies."

Phil nodded.

"How many usually come to potlucks?"

Hilda looked up. "We had forty last week. What was you planning to fix?"

"Fix?"

"Thursday, that's our potluck day. Royal, she said we'd have them for a while till we see how the lunches go. She said you'd be in charge of them."

God, why hadn't she told me all this? I'd found out more from them than from Royal all morning. I looked at Royal. She was looking, carefully—*why was I sure of that*—at Conner.

"Then I'm to do potlucks?"

Emma and Hilda nodded.

"What do you usually fix?"

"Sometimes Royal gets a roast beef or a ham. We've even bought Kentucky Fried Chicken if everyone is real busy," Hilda noted.

"So, the Center does the main dish?"

"That's it."

They seemed pleased with me.

"Then all of us bring the rest. It's a dish or a dollar. Why don't you get a ham and have the meat man slice it up. I'll put it on for you."

The lunch broke up before I learned how to pay for the ham. I tried to corner Royal, but she hurried out, something about going to City Hall.

I went back to the office.

A stocky woman was at Royal's desk. She said, "I'll do the phone for you while Royal's gone." She pulled Plato's *Apology* out of a knitting bag and began to read.

Well, "Plato", I can't think of a damn thing intelligent to say, so I'll get to work.

When Royal came back, I'd come up with a three-page list of things that probably needed doing before we could serve a meal. I was opening my mouth to demand facts and figures from her, when she handed me a document. She said it was the grant, that she had to shop for the birthday party, and that Hilda and Conner would lock up.

13

The Plato reader and I read on. By the middle of the first page of the grant, I was ready to trade with her. It was written in legalese.

At four o'clock I knew three things. There was fifteen hundred dollars available for appliances, unspecified, but with intimations of torture if they were not used for the proper program. There was an additional five hundred for kitchen furnishings, which I gathered meant dishes and silverware, and sixty-five hundred for my salary. That fascinated me. I was trying to multiply three days times seven dollars in my head when Plato handed the phone to me.

"Anne, this is John. Can you come over to the office now? I'd like to go over the grant with you."

Thank god, I thought. "Of course, I'll be right over." Then I told Plato—*I must get her name*—that I would not come back after talking to the mayor. She nodded and turned a page.

As I walked down the block to City Hall, I felt rather exhilarated. Two days ago I had been an unemployed housewife. Today I was going to a meeting with the mayor. It would look good in my next letter to the kids. Let's see, I'd write, "Hi all, just a note, as I'm rushed today. New job is fascinating. Had a conference with the mayor this afternoon, charming man, so distinguished..."

I came out of my daydream in front of the charming man's office. A nice looking woman, late thirties, took me in to the mayor's office. She seemed to know who I was. Lillian, perhaps?

The session wasn't bad at all. Lillian brought us coffee. It was black, and it was time I learned to drink it that way.

John—he said to call him John—took me through the grant, step by step. I scribbled notes. It sounded simple enough now, but it was a little difficult to understand much between John's explanation and the legal jargon.

When he finished, he asked me what my plans were. I took a deep breath, refrained from saying, "God only knows," and handed him the notes I'd put in a manila folder.

I was pleased with myself. It gave my compulsive list making a rather professional touch. Maybe he thought so too, because a slow, pleased smile appeared. He was delightful, though I felt he also looked relieved. About what?

"Look, Anne, I think you are on top of this, but time has gotten extremely short, and I'm not sure I see where you have put your priorities."

"The caterer is number one, of course." I glanced at my lists. Oh boy, there it was, top of the page, unfortunately followed by, -*flowers?*

"Get on the phone tomorrow, get a caterer committed for a trial, one month say, and insist someone come out with papers. Don't—now listen to me—don't get yourself tied up driving all over looking at stuff, too."

Too? "I understand there is a caterer in town, a relative. Is he any good?" I asked.

"I haven't the faintest. The relationship is distant enough so that is no worry, and it is the policy of the City to try and give contracts to local firms if prices are competitive. Make sure you get quotes from at least three, preferably five places on this, and get them to put it in writing, but rely on phone prices."

I wrote, -*three to five quotes in writing*, on my sheet.

"Now check with me about this time each day. If I'm not free, tell Lillian. I want those meals settled by tomorrow…"

God, so did I.

"…and anything else you can get going."

"Uh, the three days a week…can I work every day for a while?"

"Oh, I should have made that plain. Of course. He built that in."

He?

"Work as many hours as you can, up to forty a week. I realize you probably have home responsibilities and were expecting only part time…"

I blurted, "I'm a widow. I have lots of time." *Oh, please, please, don't let me cry now.*

"I see. Recent?" I nodded.

"You're wise to get busy. I know. My wife died last year."

I was going to cry. Frantic, I bent over and picked up a scrap of paper, managing to blot my eyes on my skirt. Knowing I looked a complete fool, I dropped the scrap in his ashtray. He had gotten up and was at the file cabinet.

"Very good. Work every day then, until the meals are going. Later on, maybe you can plan to work an extra day now and then to give Royal a break. Your salary is hourly."

We shook hands, and I was home by five-thirty. Mother had been over. My bed was made, a casserole was in the oven, and the table was set for one.

❧ CHAPTER THREE ❧

I was restless Tuesday night. I kept waking, thinking about the Center and dishes and milk, and what if no one wanted to come.

Feeling less than perky, I arrived at work the same time as Royal Wednesday morning. She drove the luxurious, big, old Buick I'd seen in the lot on Tuesday. I seemed to be the only one with a newer, small car. The seniors had big sedans, with lots of fins and chrome. Along with lots of dents and crumples. A few pickups were interspersed with the sedans.

I started to make coffee. There was a neatly tied stack of *National Geographic* and *Readers Digest*s on the kitchen counter. Whose were they? I stuck my head into the office. "Royal, there's a bunch of magazines in the kitchen. Where'd they come from? Should I put them out?"

"Who knows who brought them, Anne? No one can stand to throw away magazines, so they bring them to us. Secretly. Sometimes I think the whole town donates them. If they're new, I put them out in the lounge. Oldies I sneak into the Goodwill box. If I have the energy, I lug them to the recycle center magazine box.

I checked. The age of the magazines varied. Most were over ten years old. None were under three. The *Geographics* were gorgeous. Maybe the…No. Resolutely I took them to the Goodwill box, adding a four-year-old *People* I picked up off the couch on the way.

At my desk, I laid out mine and Royal's lists, the phone book, and started searching for a caterer. McCloud's was the only one in town, so they should be the first choice.

I dialed. One of the deepest southern accents I'd ever heard answered. She seemed to have me mixed up with someone else, as she told me Mr. McCloud was expecting my call, but had gone into the kitchen. She'd have him call me right back. If she didn't know what she was talking about, I figured I could call them back later. I put together a list of seven other possibilities and started calling.

Royal interrupted. "I'm going over to City Hall, Anne. Take messages, please."

I reached Acme Caterers. They had never done anything like regular meals. They usually did parties and such. However, they were willing to send me a selection of meal menus and costs. When I asked, they hazarded a guess that each meal could be done for $3.50. I gulped and asked them to mail the information.

Donaldson's "Fine Meals, Fine Deals" suggested I talk to McCloud's, but agreed to send some figures when I finally told them I had to have several bids.

"Farquahr and Sons" sounded like a possibility. They said they furnished meals to five senior centers in Seattle and promised to send out a bid. I breathed a big sigh of relief. If McCloud's didn't work out I still had a place to get the meals.

I was dialing "Martha Washington's Exquisite Cuisine" when the front door slammed. Figuring it was Emma or Hilda, I waited for Martha to answer the phone. A woman on the line was saying, "Martha Washington's..." when a deep baritone voice in the hall yelled, "Where are the damned lights?" Then there was a crash and a string of swear words. I hung up on Martha, sprinted out, and turned on the lights.

A plumpish man was tangled up with a card table. I pulled the table off him and helped him up.

"I'm so sorry. We don't really open 'till nine, so the lights weren't on yet. Are you hurt? Can I help you?"

"I told Ms. Paige I'd be here at 8:45. There is no excuse for you not being ready for me. Take my bag into the foot care area."

I automatically took his bag.

"Foot care?"

He glared. "Who are you?"

"I'm Mrs. Farley, Meal Program..."

"Do you or do you not have an area set up for this morning's foot care?"

"I'm not sure. I haven't heard about any foot care." Feeling guilty, I edged around and looked into the dining room. Nothing different. "Please, I think, well, maybe..." I started again. "What do you need?"

"Look here, I'm too busy to play games at the Senior Center. If I'm to do foot care, I expect everything to be ready. Pull that table over to the wall for me, then set up six chairs in a semi-circle."

I took hold of one end of an eight-foot table and started to pull. He stood there watching. I finally got it dragged against the wall.

"They didn't hire you for your brains, did they?"

"Now see here!" I was furious. "There is no..."

"There has to be a screen so the patients can have some privacy. Put it up and then go get the soaking pans out of my car."

I could hear the phone ringing.

"It's the black Caddy in your lot. Lock the car door afterwards."

I double-timed it to the phone. It quit ringing as I got there. Of course. Should I try and get hold of Royal or run errands as ordered?

The Caddy was parked behind Royal's and my car, blocking us in. What a sweetheart! I carried in six plastic pans, dropped them by the chairs, and headed back to the phone. I had to find Royal.

The man stopped me.

"The *screen*," he demanded.

How could two words have so much venom? "Doctor," I began. What was his name? "I'm going to the office to call Royal. I know nothing about a foot care program. I do not know where there is a screen. I think we will both save time if I get Royal."

I heard something that sounded like "total incompetence" and started to pick up the phone. The ring beat me to it.

"Danville Senior Center."

"McCloud here. May I speak to Mrs. Farley?"

"This is Anne Farley, Mr. McCloud. Please, may I..."

"Good. Now, about meals. I understand you want to start next week?"

The doctor appeared in the doorway. "Please, Mr. McCloud. There is sort of an emergency here. May I call you back? Oh, God!"

The doctor had misjudged the crazy step and was on his knees, swearing.

"Honest, I'll call you back." I hung up. I'd never get meals ordered. The doctor was pulling himself to his feet. I knew he was going to kill me.

I dialed City Hall. "Lillian, this is Anne Farley. Is Royal there? I've got to talk to her."

"She just left. You sound upset."

Boy, you can say that again. "Yes. Was she on her way back here?"

"I don't think so. What is it?"

"Well, this doctor says he's supposed to do foot care, and I don't know where things are, and I can't help him *and* order dishes, and there aren't any seniors in for food care, and..."

"Hey, slow down. I think he has the wrong day. I typed the newsletter and, yeah, it's next week. Look at your newsletter."

I set the phone down. "She says foot care is next week. I mean, no one has come in, and look, here is the calendar."

"Good God, how can you all be so incompetent? We agreed on the third Wednesday."

Even I knew this was the second Wednesday.

"Call your foot care list. I'm not going to waste the entire morning."

"This is the second Wednesday." He ignored me. "Doctor, I've got work to do."

Luckily I heard the outside door slam and voices in the lounge. I edged around him and nearly threw my arms around Emma and Plato. "Do either of you know anything about foot care? There is a doctor here, apparently a week early, and he wants the list called." I was ready to go home.

Plato said, "Again? I'll call. Emma, get your feet done first and help Anne."

I followed Emma into the dining room. "It's all right, Anne. He's done this before. Most of the foot- care people come in anyway. I'll get some water for soaking and then be the first patient. It's time I got my corns fixed anyway. You'll have to sign the others in and take their money. As soon as Hilda comes, she'll take over for you."

"How much is it?"

"Five."

Plato was on the phone. She handed me a clipboard with a list of seniors who had evidently signed up for foot care next week. I moved a card table over by the office door and put the list and a pen on it. Emma dashed in and gave me five dollars. "Get a bread pan, Anne, to put the money in."

Two pool players came in and eyed my setup.

"You're in the way."

I shoved the table a little farther from the pool table. I had to get back to McCloud, but Plato was on the phone with foot care. We'd never be ready by next week!

I ran to the kitchen and pawed through the cupboard. Down on the bottom shelf next to the stove I found a pile of ancient bread pans. They were stuck together. I got down on my knees, felt my pantyhose split and the slight tickle of a long run down my leg. Damnation, they cost money.

I pulled the pans out and tried to pull the top one off. It came apart with a jerk, and I stared at the second pan. It was crammed with money. In a bread pan? Well, why not? That was what I wanted one for.

I started to count the money, but the doctor yelled, "Farley, get the next patient in here to soak."

I ran back, put the money on my desk, and took five dollars from a lady who said her name was Astrid.

Plato came out. "I've called everyone on the list. Six can come. Let me sit here while you call McCloud."

McCloud himself answered the phone and took off from where I'd stopped him. "Anne, I understand you want your first meal next Wednesday. I've got a cycle of menus to show you. Are you going to order your paper products from us? Will your subsidy pay for it?"

Oh, boy. "Mr. McCloud, I don't know. I'll have to look at the grant again."

"O.K. Now, I'll be able to include your coffee, sugar, creamers, and margarine patties for $1.53, but not things like foam cups or soup bowls."

Oh, God.

"If you order your paper products from us, I'll include them at cost. My donation to the seniors."

"That is very kind of you. I do have to have other bids, but so far you seem to be the closest to meeting our needs."

"Sure, there's no one else that can do it except maybe Farquahr. Our prices would be the same, but he'd have to add on a bigger delivery charge. You get your bids, and I'll be out to see you tomorrow with menus, right before lunch. We'll set everything up."

The doctor was bellowing again. It seemed he wanted a cup of coffee, cream, and sugar. A screen had appeared from somewhere.

Oh, Lord, I hadn't finished making coffee. Luckily, someone had, probably Hilda. I made sure the cup was very hot—maybe he'd burn his tongue off.

When I sat down at my desk again, I felt sick, vaguely so, sort of like I'd eaten a huge meal and it just sat there. I was tired of feeling sick. How dumb to get so mad. Maybe I would put poison in his coffee. Then they'd put me in a nice, quiet cell, and I'd never have to be polite and cheerful all the time and do five things at the same time again. Thank God while watching my husband die, Terry's doctors had all been human beings. I'd have gone bonkers, totally, if they had been like Doctor Foot Care.

I got out the phone book and looked up kitchen supplies. Nothing. With inspiration I finally found them under Restaurant Supplies. Royal's list had three names. Bennett's was starred— so I decided to call the other two first. No way could we handle their prices, but I asked the second salesman, "Do you have any used dishes or silverware?"

The warmth dropped out of his voice. "We have some camp kitchen stuff. It's been sorted so that it will meet health department standards. I wouldn't suggest it though. Heavy and not very attractive.

"What would a set of, say, a hundred cost?"

Almost as if he could read my budget, he responded,

"Five hundred for dishes and silverware."

I got both companies to send prices in writing and called Bennett. It was a repetition of McCloud's call.

He knew all about me and swore, "I have just the thing for you. An airline is redoing their whole service. Changed their color scheme and design. They are going first class. I took all of their old stuff as part of the deal. Now I'll be able to fill your order at very little cost to you."

"Sounds wonderful. How much, and can you bring samples out so I can decide if I want them?"

"Hey, Anne, I'm not going to make any profit on this and can't afford to come out on such a small order. You whiz over this afternoon or tomorrow morning, and I'll fix you up."

"Please, Mr. Bennett. Couldn't you come out? I'm swamped trying to meet a deadline." *Inspiration.* "The mayor has asked that I not waste time by doing any more looking."

"I suppose for the old folks I could drop by. I've got a meeting out your way tomorrow. How about after lunch?"

I agreed, and we hung up. I put Bennett on the calendar after McCloud.

Where was Royal? I had to talk to her. I was crazy to go on doing all this stuff without checking with her.

Plato came into the office. "The doctor wants to talk to you."

"Oh, no, not him."

"I'm sorry, Anne, it's important."

There were about twenty people in the lounge. Three women had seen the doctor, but still had their shoes and stockings off, and seemed to be comparing toes. One woman's feet were horrible—swollen, mottled red, lots of broken veins, toes bent and gnarled—the only word that fit.

The doctor was on his knees before his last patient. "Farley, Royal back?"

"No."

"Then you'll have to do it. Bob here has to get to the hospital right away. I'll call over. They'll be ready for him. Take him now."

"But..."

"Farley, this man is in trouble. I've talked him into going, and I think we can save his foot. He doesn't have a car. Get going."

I turned on my heels, got my purse and keys, and yelled, "Someone answer the phone while I'm gone. I'll bring the car up front."

I stopped short in the parking lot. Dr. Foot Care's car still blocked mine. I strolled back in and told him, "I can't get out. You left your car behind mine."

He pulled his keys out and threw them in my general direction. I didn't have a chance to catch them. I had to crawl under a chair for them.

A small, fat man at the pool table said, "Butterfingers."

I moved the Caddy to the tightest slot I could find and grinned as I squeezed out the door. I gave the doctor's keys to Plato, which reduced the chance I might try and kill him, then helped Bob into my car. He looked awful, sort of damp, and greenish gray. Luckily, the hospital was only five blocks north of the Senior Center.

Bob quietly told me, "Doc said go to the emergency entrance."

I pulled in. A nurse and an attendant were waiting for us with a wheel chair. They helped Bob out and waved me on. I went around a couple of blocks to give myself time to calm down. When I thought of it, Dr. Foot Care was a caricature of all the egotistical doctors on TV.

By the time I got back, the main room in the Center was packed. Just as I passed the pool table, the short fat man ambled over in the general direction of the waste paper basket and spat tobacco juice all over the wall.

With my dumb stomach, I was afraid I'd be sick, so I hurried out into the dining room. I took one look at the mess the doctor had left—and just made it to the restroom. I drank cold water until my stomach settled. Three kids and I still had a queasy stomach.

The doctor's pans were still on the floor, empty now. The screen had vanished and Hilda was sweeping up the grungy mess of toenails, calluses, and pieces of corns.

Being careful not to look, I started putting the table and chairs away.

"Hilda, who is the man—short, real fat—at the pool table?"

"Tiny?"

"It could be. He chews."

"And spits!"

"You're so right. What should I do? He left a mess."

"I'll clean it up."

"No, no, I didn't mean that. Shouldn't he be stopped? That wall is ruined."

"We've been talking about it. We get real tired of cleaning up after him. So, we're going to go get that there garbage can by the back door and put it in the poolroom. Then put plastic wrap all over the wall. Let him miss that!"

"Great idea. Let's do it."

Hilda wouldn't let me help. She and two friends started scrubbing and Phil was already bringing in the garbage can.

In the office, the phone rang and rang. Every time I tried to call about milk for the potluck, it rang again. To hell with the milk.

I told most everyone who called that I'd have Royal call them back. *I* didn't know if the Soroptimists were meeting at our Center for breakfast in April. *I* didn't know if we wanted to subscribe to *Fortune Hunters Weekly*, or if there was a great need for adult diapers. *I* had no idea if we were going to have a health fair, take a trip to the Capitol, or if we wanted to see

"The Sound of Music" at the local dinner theater. Feeling fantastically stupid, I wrote a zillion memos for Royal.

I stared at the memo notebook, my mind wandering, then stopped and thought, *of course.* My rings were in the notebook in the bathroom. I had used it for Terry's med schedule, and I'd shoved my rings in the notebook pocket. Last month. Maybe.

Anyway, I'd been going through all the old pill bottles, and my rings kept slipping, so I'd shoved them in the notebook to keep them from going down the drain. What a relief. Maybe my mind was coming back.

Royal popped in and out. She said she had to go back to City Hall, and would I close and to not forget to call John. I updated lists and started some files. When I called the hospital about Bob, I got nowhere. I didn't know his last name, and it wasn't on the foot care list.

Finally, I called John and told him I had set up meals—more details tomorrow. I stretched things a bit, said dishes were settled, and that tomorrow I would finalize the milk order and appliances. I heard a big sigh over the phone.

"That's great. 'Fraid we were stretching it thin. You've accomplished a lot. Remind me to buy you a drink."

Right at five, everyone started to leave. I locked up and was almost out the door, when I remembered the bread pan money. I pulled it out of the desk, put the money in an envelope, and placed it in Royal's drawer. I wrote on the envelope, "When, how, where, what is this? Found in bread pan. Do you or do I do something with it?"

At home I went straight to the bathroom. No notebook. How in hell could I remember so well seeing it there? It had been there. In fact, I had seen it there yesterday. That's right. Mother had been over—helping again.

❧ CHAPTER FOUR ❦

Thursday morning started quietly. Royal and I put up tables for the potluck and made two pots of coffee. She went back to the office, and I dashed over to Safeway as soon as they opened and bought a ham. Just as Hilda recommended, they sliced it for me with no objections. The ham took the last of my money for the week.

At the Center, Hilda took the ham from me and refused my help, so I went back to the office. "Royal, the ham cost $15.98."

"Pay yourself out of the fish envelope."

"The fish envelope?"

"In the file drawer. The envelope marked 'fish.' For the Derby next month. Just pay back the fish after the potluck."

Wondering why not wait and get the money after lunch, I took out my $15.98, got down to work, and called Jonah's Dairy. I was connected through to a Tim Jonah, maybe Jonah Junior from the sound of his voice. I didn't have to explain a thing. He said after Mr. Wilde had called, he'd done some figuring, and since they could deliver on the way to school, he'd be able to let me have the milk at the school price, being a City order and all. I managed to break in. "Mr. Wilde, who? You said he'd called you?"

"Gordy Wilde, on your Board." He continued on. They'd deliver around about 10:00, and he imagined twenty half-pints would do me at first.

Since I agreed, I had no other contributions to make to our conversation except to say I wanted 2% rather than whole milk, a gesture to watching the seniors' cholesterol.

Our final exchange was about money. He said, "I'll send Lillian the bill, she'll set up the purchase order. Do you want a copy of the bill?"

I agreed I'd like one, not that I knew what I'd do with it, and he said he'd put a copy in with Lillian's for me.

Feeling wildly efficient and virtuous, I took out my master list and headed for the storeroom to see if any of the things I might need were there. No sense calling about appliances. It would save time if I checked with Gordy Wilde first.

As I went back, I discovered there were more people in the Center than I'd seen so far. My God, were all those people coming to lunch?

Emma bustled up. "Anne, there's an awful lot of people come in. There's thirty already signed up, and I know some of the ladies in the kitchen aren't on the list yet, and the pool players never do sign 'til the last thing. What should we do?"

Oh, God. I edged into the kitchen. "There are forty-five slices of ham. Did anyone bring baked beans?"

Hilda opened the oven. Of course, the door fell off. At the sound, I saw Phil leave the pool table and start for the kitchen. Bless him.

"We've got two big dishes of beans."

"O.K., one of you please get the sign-up sheet and get everyone on it so we know where we are. Then make sure we catch everyone else who comes in. At a quarter to twelve, we'll see how many are here. If necessary, we can cut up the slices of ham and give everyone some of the baked beans. Emma, maybe you'd better plan to serve the ham and beans. We can let everyone help themselves to the other stuff."

Everyone seemed satisfied with that decision. As I left the kitchen, I noticed a big woman I'd not seen before had already cut the ham slices into fourths. Phil and Conner had set up two more tables. They'd already had it worked out, so why did they bother to ask me?

In the storerooms I found lots of paper napkins, paper cups if needed, vases, sugar bowls, but no cream pitchers, tablecloths, or placemats. Now what? The tables were a mess, so beat up and scarred, it would look better if they were covered somehow. Back in the office I asked Royal about placemats.

"There's no money for placemats, dear. But we do have tablecloths. I think Willie took them home to do up. She'll bring them back. By the way, Gordy's looking for you."

Well I was looking for him too. "Prince Charles" was sitting in the big platform rocker in front of the TV and beamed at me when I came in. I took the footstool and felt a little as if I should bow. He still had a billed hat on. This one said "Mechano's Cream."

"Good morning, Anne, how nice you look today. That blue blouse is especially becoming."

I beamed back. It was my favorite blouse.

"Anne, Phil and I were talking about the tables."

You were, were you? Have you got it all figured out, and how about my new stove and dishwasher?

"Tablecloths are nice, but it would be too hard to get them washed and ironed for each meal. Now, the City's got a lot of old ledger sheets from the billing office. We thought we'd get a bunch of them and cut them in half. That would be just the right size for placemats. The backs are a blue color and should look all right with those dark blue airline dishes."

So the dishes were blue? I hadn't thought to ask!

"Now the paper's got some printing on one side, but that wouldn't show, and the City's just going to throw them out. If you want them, I'll go over and get John to give them a call, and we'll have a bunch ready by Wednesday. I'll bring you a sheet so you can see if you'd really like them."

That's nice of you, "Charlie," 'cause I bet I get them anyway.

"Then Phil and I planned to get some of the guys together and start refinishing the tables. Could do them one at a time so you'd always have enough tables to serve lunch..."

Thorough. "Thank you, Gordy, it sounds like it should work out fine. Now, about the meals. Mr. McCloud, I guess you called him, and while I appreciate it..." I couldn't go on, he was looking so pleased with himself. "...Uh, everything is working out, and Mr. Bennett is bringing dishes out for me to see today." *I couldn't resist.* "Have you seen them? Maybe you'd like to come look when he comes."

"That would be mighty nice, Anne. Not that I care what they look like, though I suppose some of the women do. Oh, Phil and I thought when you buy them, we'd go down in his pickup and get them for you. If you have to wait for Bennett to deliver, it'll be next month before we get those dishes. Anyway, we can check them out and make sure they are all right."

I looked at him in awe. All the bases were covered, and I wouldn't have to cope with the freeway. "Well, that's settled. Have you any advice on appliances?" I was dying of curiosity. Did he have them all arranged too?

"That's a problem. I don't really know. He only allowed fifteen hundred."

I tried to interrupt to ask, "He who?" But Gordy continued on.

"That makes it pretty tight because you've got to have a dishwasher that will have a power boost to get the temperature up to health code standards, and there is no room and not enough money, of course, for a commercial machine. You'd better get a self-cleaning oven because it will get so much use. Other than that, you'll probably want as simple a stove as possible. You won't need a clock or anything.

Refrigerators are expensive though, so we thought we should put the old one in the storage closet for backup."

"Gordy, how do you know all this? Sounds like you've done so much work on it already..." *And since you've done so much why didn't you do it all? What do you need me for?*

"Well now, Anne. We've been thinking about this for a long time. Course we thought it might be better to wait 'til they got the new Center done and do it up right. But he went ahead and started it this March and..."

"Who, Gordy?"

Gordy stared at me.

"The mayor? Someone else?"

"Of course not the mayor. Bertram. So, of course a bunch of us talked it over, and Mary, she used to work in the school kitchen, she had all sorts of ideas, and we've kind of been thinking what might work. If Royal hadn't found you, Mary might have had to get it going."

"Mary? Bertram?"

"You were in the kitchen with Mary. White hair, glasses, sort of heavy."

I thought back to the women in the kitchen. Every single one of them had white hair and glasses. So, who? Oh, the heavy lady who'd already cut up the ham. O.K.

"You don't mind that I sort of called around, do you, Anne? The time is getting pretty short, and the ladies are dead set against having to use paper plates and that dang plastic silverware for our meals."

"No, of course I don't mind. You've been a lot of help."

Especially if you'd let me know what you're up to before you do it. Guess it didn't matter. I had to get those bids for the mayor anyway. Wonder if John knew my work was all done. A pat setup. "Have you checked into the appliances, Gordy?"

"Michael's, right next door, is the place for you. He's Washburn's nephew. Real fond of his uncle."

I didn't try to find out who Washburn was. He probably had white hair and glasses, too.

"Anyway, you got to phone around and get the bids the City needs."

"Yep."

"But Michael will come in at your budget. Now, Mike said he'd plumb the dishwasher in if we'd get the spot ready. So, Phil and Conner are going to rip out the old cupboard right after the potluck's over. We'll save the boards."

I'd better get out there. In theory, I was in charge. "It sounds wonderful, Gordy. I'll get the calling done this afternoon, soon as Mr. Bennett goes." God, it was almost noon. A thought struck me. "Is all this O.K. with Royal? It's all right to take out the cupboards and stuff?"

"Oh, we wouldn't bother Royal with this kind of thing. She's way too busy, and frankly, she can't make heads or tails out of a floor plan."

He chuckled and walked out.

Did Royal know a damned thing about their ripping the kitchen apart? Though he was probably right, and it didn't matter. They were going to do it anyway. Maybe we'd all go to jail for defacing government property. Did they do that to people who trashed City stuff, or was that only for the Feds?

✳✳✳✳✳✳✳

There were exactly sixty for lunch and a huge assortment of food. No green salad though. Oh well, lots of vegetables anyway.

I eyed the meat. *It should stretch. Let's see, forty-five pieces cut in fours made... NO, not that way.* There'd be three pieces for sixty. Well, it would be enough if Royal and I didn't eat any. Would a calculator help? Nope, not unless I could first figure out what to divide or multiply into what.

My stomach lurched. Figures. Income tax. God, I still had to find all those figures Terry's accountant said he'd need—in that desk. My rings—and where the hell did all our money go? Fifteen dollars left for the week. Thank God, a real salary. Jeez, I'd better find out when I would get paid. *Come on, Annie, get to work. Earn the salary.*

Hilda brought me back when she said, "Here, we filled a plate for you 'cause you've got to wait in the office for that dishes man."

I stared at the heaped plate. Fatsville! Oh yeah, the dishes man and McCloud. He hadn't shown up yet with those menus. When I went into the office, Plato got up and put a marker in her book, *Zane Gray*, and she went off to lunch. I used the time waiting and worrying about Bennett and McCloud to call appliance dealers.

Sure enough, Michael's had the best deal. With a senior discount, tax, etc., he figured he could have a dishwasher, stove, and refrigerator for us tomorrow—*hallelujah*—installed, and ready to go; unless, *ominously*, I was particular about color. I assured him color was of no concern.

Gordy had forgotten only one thing. Mike wanted to come over and look at the kitchen. He said he'd amble over tomorrow at nine and bring papers to sign. Somehow, I'd have to glue Royal down and find out how to pay the bills. I'd just hung up when McCloud breezed in. He said he'd forgotten about a meeting of the Royal Order of the Buffaloes. Well, a meeting that sounded something like that anyway. That was why he was late.

Wasn't it the "Flintstones" Fred and Barney who belonged to the Buffaloes? Oh well.

He tossed a sheaf of papers down on my desk, sat down on the telephone stand, and smiled at me. I began to be suspicious that the Buffaloes had met at the bar.

"Now, little lady. We've got you all fixed up. Got a real good meal for your first day—ham, those old folks like baked ham, and we've added a special dessert, apple pie, to give you a good start."

Old folks? Ye gods, and ham again.

"And here's the contract for John to see. Now, little lady..." I sat up straighter, "my buddies and I thought it was time we did something for the old folks. We've got a benevolent fund. Usually give it to the kids, but we decided that this year we'd split it. Fifty to you and fifty to the kids."

"Uh, that's very nice." *Percent or dollars?*

"I'm chairman of the benevolent fund committee, and I've got it all fixed up. You give us a list of the things you need, and we'll get them for you. Some of the brothers can probably get things for you at cost."

"Uh, what sort of things did you have in mind?"

"Why, anything you want. You make out a list, and we'll see what we can come up with."

"That's really lovely. I'm sure Ms. Paige will be thrilled, and we'll get a list to you right away. Oh, I'm not sure I quite understand. You said fifty, uh, dollars?"

"That's right. Glad to be of help. Now, call me anytime you've got questions or problems. We'll deliver next Wednesday, no later than ten, and pick up the pans Friday when we bring the second meal. We charge eighteen for lost pans, so keep track of 'em."

He walked out.

You twit. Anything we want. Fifty dollars. *Wonder what you guys just spent on your bar bill?* Oh, hell, it was probably nice of them. For equipment every bit would help. I added *-list* to the list, and then Bennett walked in. More like staggered. He'd evidently been with McCloud at the bar and stayed longer.

He grinned, called me "little lady," took over Royal's

desk, and pulled bowls and cups and saucers out of his briefcase. They were pretty for plastic. Yep, dark blue with white on the eating surface.

"Are they dishwasher...?"

Screams came from the main room. Someone shrilled, "It's Bill! Royal, it's Bill! He's dead! Call the ambulance, Royal, Royal!"

I was up and out the door while Bennett was still trying to get out of Royal's chair, his mouth open. The meeting room was in chaos, a knot of people around a card table, all shouting.

Plato whispered in my ear, "Royal's gone over to the drug store."

I pushed through the crowd. A tall man lay with his head on the table, his cards still in his hand—a full house. Maybe the excitement had gotten to him. I felt sick and shaky, but I put my hand on his throat. There was a slow, faint pulse.

"Everyone, please stand back. Conner, could you stay here, see that he doesn't fall off his chair. Please, everyone else, get back, give us some room." I sounded like a soap opera to myself. "I'm going to call the aid car. Someone stay at the door to hold it open."

At the neighboring card table, four women began dealing out a new hand.

Bennett was still at Royal's desk when I entered the office. He had a flask out. *Hell on wheels*, my hands were shaking so badly I could hardly dial. Thank God 911 was on the speed dial. The operator said they'd be there in a minute and a half. Plato came in and took up her usual position beside the phone and said she'd call Bill's son. Bennett handed me a sturdy tot, and I drained it then went back out to Bill.

The fire department and aid car must have shaved a few corners. Within seconds they were checking Bill over.

Five minutes later they carried him out on a stretcher, eyes still open and unblinking, breathing slowly, thank God. Everyone settled down quickly. As I went back to the office, one lady jerked my skirt.

"Is Bill going to live?"

"I don't know. I think so."

"That's good. I don't want him to die."

I started to say, "Of course not," when she went on.

"If Bill dies, I'll be the oldest one here. I don't like that. I'm ninety-seven."

She went back to dealing out solitaire—and I guess that was probably as good a reason as any not to want someone to die.

"Mr. Bennett," I sat down, I'm sorry for the interruption." He'd calmed down and was beaming again. "The dishes are very nice."

He'd also brought a plain white plate. Guess the airlines didn't serve off regular sized plates. The silverware was stainless, a little small, but adequate.

I ordered a hundred plates, soup bowls, sauce dishes, cups and saucers, and the silverware. To my great pleasure, it came to only two hundred fifty dollars. Bless the airlines and their changing image.

Bennett said, "Little lady, you show me your kitchen, and we'll see what else you need."

Royal came in, met Bennett, and admired the dishes. She didn't even raise an eyebrow over the flask.

The three of us went out to the kitchen. Helen was there, the floor awash with water. Evidently she thought she was mopping.

She stopped mopping, glared at Bennett, and shrieked. He froze. She shook the mop in his face, splattering his blue pinstriped suit, and he backed up fast. She shrieked again, and he left, running. I didn't know what to do.

Royal said, "Now, Helen, you know you can't yell here."

Helen threw back her head and howled, looking delighted.

Royal said sternly, " If you don't behave, I'll have to get John."

Another shriek.

Feeling I was sort of Bennett's hostess, but not wanting to leave Royal alone with Helen, I stood, indecisive. Helen had the water running full force in the sink. Feeling like an idiot, I tried, "Helen, remember me? I'm Anne. I met you earlier this week." She stared at me, but she didn't yell again.

Royal whispered, "Sometimes she'll eat."

"Do you want some lunch?"

She glanced at the refrigerator. "The floor was dirty."

"Yes, probably from the potluck."

"And I am thirty."

"Oh." You couldn't prove it to me. "Would you like some lunch?"

"That man was flirty."

"And now he's dirty." Oh, God, she'd think I was laughing at her.

Helen beamed. "Lunch."

I opened up the refrigerator.

Helen reached a long arm around me and took a platter of chicken and a lone piece of pie. She slammed the door hard and walked out, leaving a trail of wet footprints across the dining room floor.

I turned off the water, and Royal and I sloshed back to the office.

"She's gone," I told Bennett. *What a day.*

Bennett patted my hand. "You are running a real three-ring circus here. Have to confess I was really shaken for a time. I was wondering if I should call the police. Real brave of you to get her out of there by yourselves."

Yeah, us and the chicken. I wondered whose platter she'd gotten.

"Now, Mrs. Farley, Ms. Paige, I think it would be a good idea if I took you out and bought you a real drink. You both look like you could use one."

Well, you don't, Buster.

Royal said, "I'm sorry, I can't leave the office, Mr. Bennett, but Anne has had the brunt of this. You take her along."

I was still protesting as I was being herded out. Royal leaned over and whispered, "I've got to get over to the hospital and see how Bill is. Get him out of here. I'll check on Bob, too."

Bennett hustled me around the corner to Danville's best bar, right across from City Hall. I wanted a big sign saying, "This isn't my idea. Royal made me." I debated ordering the most expensive drink on the menu, but stuck to my usual 7 High.

It wasn't a bad fifteen minutes. Bennett told several stories about the impossible kitchens he had rescued with advice and equipment. He mentioned neither our impossible kitchen nor Helen.

It was nearly five when I got back. The Center was empty of seniors. The kitchen floor was dry and the old cupboards were gone. John was at my desk looking at my latest list. For God's sake, I'd forgotten to check in with him. I took Royal's chair.

He said, "Had quite a day?"

I nodded.

"Royal filled me in. She's still over at the hospital and she called me. She's seen Bill."

"How is he?"

"The hospital says he's fine. The way Royal sounded when she first called me, I thought he was dead, or nearly so."

"So did I. Sorry about not calling you. It got hectic."

"I hear Bennett was in. Royal showed me the dishes. Are they sturdy enough?"

"I hope so."

"Did you try and break one?"

"No." Cripes, I'd probably fouled the whole deal.

"Oh, well. If they stood up to the airline's treatment, they'll likely stand up to our ladies washing them to death. Anyway, Bennett stands by his stuff. How are you going to spend the rest of the money?"

"I don't know. I'd like to wait 'til we've served a few meals and see what we need the most. I think we'll need some really big kettles. There's only one ten-quart pan. The rest are home castoffs. By the way, some group that Mr. McCloud, and I think Bennett, belongs to, have voted to give us fifty dollars. I think I'd like to ask for some of the kitchen stuff from them. Then fill out the rest with our money."

"You don't seem too thrilled."

"No. It was the way they did it, and besides, I bet they'd spent more money at the bar deciding to give it to us than the amount they offered."

"Think it through, Anne. Maybe they were condescending, or whatever got to you, but at least now they are aware we exist, and that the program is running and in need of approximately a million things. Once they understand that, we may stay on their books, and fifty a year isn't to be sneezed at."

"I know. Guess I was really mad at being called "little lady" at least a hundred times, and besides, they gave us fifty dollars that they usually give to some kids organization. So some other group has had their budget fouled up."

John stared. "McCloud? The Royal Order of something or other?"

"Yes."

"Oh, no. I'll have to learn to get off the soapbox and quit

preaching. That bunch has been giving the park's soccer team a hundred a year. Pays for some equipment replacement. Now we'll have to dig up the money somewhere else. Out of your budget maybe, Anne."

"Never. But that reminds me, how long do I have to spend the equipment budget?"

"Until January. Anne you look really beat. Lock up now, and I'll buy you that drink I promised."

"Oh, no, not tonight. I…"

"Come on. Do you good."

And then I found myself, back at the bar, having my third drink of the afternoon.

❧ CHAPTER FIVE ❧

Friday started out sanely enough. I helped Royal get ready for the Pinochle tournament that afternoon. While we wrapped prizes, she talked about the next month's calendar.

Every weekday had to have a special event planned, and she was trying to come up with someplace to take the seniors on a trip. She wasn't interested in my suggestions of Hawaii and Disneyland.

"It has to be a one day trip Anne, less than twelve hours, preferably under eight. It should be interesting, not too much walking or stairs, with a good inexpensive place to eat, and someplace we haven't been to for at least a year."

"Spring flowers at Mt. Rainier?"

"Too early. Also, hard to find a place to eat. We'd be out in the wilderness around noon."

"The loop road and lunch at the dam?"

"We do that in October for the fall colors. The lunch is too expensive up there. We stop at the dam for coffee and then eat at the shopping mall.

"Boy, any more requirements? How do you ever find a place?"

She grimaced.

"Don't you ever go on longer trips?" I asked.

She shook her head. "It's too hard for me to get away for more than a day at a time."

"Why not do the arrangements and let them go alone?"

"It doesn't work. You'll see. Someone has to be in charge."

Was she planning to send me on a trip for her? I'd better tell her about the time ten first graders and I got lost at the zoo. I shuddered. It was not my favorite memory. Speaking of which...

"Have you been to the zoo?"

"I want places they can't go to by City bus. Though during the summer, I do plan a couple of local trips a month by bus. We call it 'City Scenes.' We go to the zoo, the locks, Chinatown. Places like that."

I promised to think about it and went back to shuffling my papers. Maybe I could write a paragraph about food for the newsletter calendar. Like about eating green salads.

At ten, Royal went over to City Hall and the deliveryman from Michael's arrived, so I took him to the kitchen. It looked like we had been invaded.

Conner and a man I didn't know were putting together shelves out of the old cupboard materials and were working across from the old stove. Or rather, where the old stove had been. It sat out in the dining room.

A lady in lavender slacks was cleaning the stove while Mary cleaned the place that it had come out of. Every once in a while, she and the man I didn't know bumped rears as they bent over to work, but they never stopped or looked around.

Phil and Gordy had the back door propped open and were bringing in boxes of dishes. They must have started out early to be back already. Emma and Hilda opened the boxes as fast as the men brought them in. Tiny had a table to himself and was hacking some pretty blue paper in half with a paper cutter. He was chewing again—every place mat would have to be checked. Besides, he wasn't very careful, and a lot of our new placemats were sort of trapezoids, but he sure was fast.

The guy from Michael's looked a little bewildered, but he yelled, "Hey, Wash, come show me where the new dishwasher is going to go."

Conner's helper dodged Mary and came out. We all went around the kitchen bar and looked at the hole Phil and Conner had made yesterday. I suddenly realized it wasn't really the greatest place for the dishwasher.

We'd have to drag the rinsed dishes from the sink, across the floor. Of course that wasn't far, but they'd drip all over the place. However, I couldn't see that there was any other possible place. Jeez, real foresight. I should have been out in the kitchen the first day on the job checking where things would go.

One thing for sure, something had to be done about the sink cupboard and the mess of cleaning bottles and rags and what looked like junk in there. Maybe the best thing was to wait until most of the seniors had gone home, and then go out and go through everything.

All the men except Tiny were now draped around the spot for the dishwasher and talking plumber-ese. No use trying to get involved there, so I went over to Tiny.

I had some vague idea about suggesting he be a little more careful and maybe not chew while he cut the place mats. He already had a pile that looked like enough for a couple of years. Most of them were weird shapes. He looked up as I came over, smiled, and pinched me—hard. I gaped at him, my mouth open, too startled to yell. He reached out for another pinch, and I raised my fist. I almost took a punch at him when, luckily, he hesitated, and I had a chance to think.

In my head, I could hear Terry say, "For God's sakes, Anne, if you ever really take a punch, don't hold your thumb like that, you'll break it, sure as hell." That was the time I'd tried to hit him when he kept tickling me after I'd begged time out. Anyway, that had nothing to do with Tiny, and I decided it wasn't a good policy to hit the customers.

Feeling mad and stupid, I went back to the office. I got there just as the phone quit ringing. I realized I'd left the office thinking it would run itself. I'd gotten used to Plato always picking up the slack and wondered where she was today.

I set to work trying to plan what still had to be done. Mainly, figure out how many people would be needed to work in the kitchen, talk to Royal about how to recruit help, and divide up the work. So I started a new list. Finally something I was competent at. I'd done this a million times for church and the PTA.

Royal came back and we both went out to the kitchen.

"What's going to be done with the old stove?" I asked.

"The seniors are having a rummage sale next month. Phil said he'd store it until then."

"They'll never sell it."

Rummage sale. An incentive to go through Terry's clothes. I didn't want to. Then there were all his tools and his computer. I was not going to have a garage sale. It would be like selling my husband. Hell, I didn't have to think about it now. Probably the girls' husbands would take what tools they wanted and I'd learn to use the computer.

I went back to the kitchen. Only Michael's guy and Washbourne were still in the dishwasher hole. Mary and Lavender Slacks were through cleaning and were watching Conner and Phil put up shelves. Tiny was gone, permanently I hoped.

The dishes were stacked neatly in their opened boxes. I went over to put the placemats away, but Hilda came over and took them away from me.

"I'll do that, Anne. Me and Emma are going to look through these and kind of trim 'em up. Gordy will take the paper cutter back."

The phone rang, and I sprinted for it. It was John.

"Anne, tell Royal, that Lillian just saw Agnes in the bar. She may want to do something."

I thanked him, and repeated the message to Royal.

"Oh, dear, what a shame. I'd hoped...Well, I suppose it was bound to happen. I didn't notice. Was she here yesterday?"

"I don't know who Agnes is, Royal."

"Of course you do. She's been here every day."

"Sorry, I don't connect that name to anybody. What does she look like...?"

Royal came back with the ritual, "Gray hair, glasses, stocky. You've talked to her. She answers the phone and runs the whole place for me when I'm not here. She's covered for you, too."

Light dawned. "You mean, Plato? No one introduced us, and I never asked her name. She hardly says a thing."

"You'd be surprised," Royal quipped.

I'd learned more new names this week than I had in years. It was stupid to be so reticent about asking someone's name just because they knew mine.

"Why on earth did you think her name was Plato?"

"I didn't. It's just that she was reading *Plato* when I first came, and I got to thinking of her as him and gave her the nickname. Yes, she was here yesterday. She was reading a novel."

"Oh, my, that's a bad sign. I wish I had noticed. But there's not much I can do."

"I don't get it, Royal. She's at a bar, and the mayor wants you to do something. Does she drink, or does she make like Carrie Nation?" Drinking sounded like a way out idea. Tiny, maybe.

"She drinks. Does real well for weeks, sometimes months, then something seems to happen, and she goes on a spree. Her reading a novel is a pretty definite sign. If I notice, I can sometimes get her to go over to Mental Health, and once in a while that helps."

A drunk? That nice lady who seemed to know more about the Center than even Royal? "What are you going to do?"

"I usually go over to the bar and see if I can get her to go home. I guess I'll give it a try since you're here. If she goes home, I'll have to go with her, or she'll just go out again."

"Is she likely to leave for you?"

"It's hard to tell. The worst of it is, when she sees me, she sometimes insists on coming over here, and then she upsets everyone. I have a terrible time settling them down and getting her out of here."

"She's so quiet. What does she do here when she's drinking?"

"She reorganizes the whole place, and turns the TV off and tells everyone it's the invention of the Devil and weakens their minds. Some of them get real mad when they can't watch their soap operas. "Then she insists they help her clean out the library, and she throws out all the detective stories, romances, and the *Reader's Digest* condensed novels. It takes us forever to put them back. Once the garbage man came before we got them rescued." She looked at me. "I suppose it sounds funny, but it is tragic, really. Everyone gets upset and they lecture her, so she comes in the office to hide and tries to help with the filing. Then it takes me days to get things back in shape. Don't laugh."

"I'm sorry, Royal. I know it's not funny, but you've got to admit it does sound like a comedy. But sure, go ahead. See if she's still there. I'll be here."

She left and Michael came in from the kitchen and nearly fell down the step. I gave him Royal's chair, and we exchanged pleasantries. He was really fond of his uncle. He told me, "Wash practically raised me. My dad was in the service and gone most of the time. Mom had to work. I'd have had a hard time of it if it hadn't been for Wash and Aunt Sal."

"Your Aunt Sal, does she come in to the Center, too? I don't seem to know everyone yet. I hadn't even met Mr. Washbourne before."

"Aunt Sal's dead. Died about five years ago. Nearly did Wash in when she went. They didn't have any kids, except me, sort of, and I thought he'd go nuts, he missed her so. That was what made me quit the shipyard and come here to Danville to work. My wife wasn't sure she wanted to live in a small town, but I just had to do something to help Wash, and she likes him too. He wouldn't come live with us. I guess that doesn't usually work out so good, but we wanted to give it a try.

"Anyway, we found a home a couple blocks from him, and I went to work at the shop next door doing their repair work. Bought the owner out last year, and now I'm the boss. It's been good for Wash. He comes in and helps out when I need it. Gives him something to fill the time—though I haven't seen quite so much of him lately." He gave a big grin. It made him look like a nice kid instead of forty or so. "I think Wash has a lady friend here. He never says anything, but he's been coming to the Center a lot more lately, and we saw them having dinner at Denny's Sunday."

The grin faded. "You know, if I understand Wash, he's going to be kind of sensitive about going out with anyone but Aunt Sal. I hope nothing messes it up. Gosh, he just needs someone to go places with, have some fun. We'd take him with us anytime, but he's always afraid of intruding, and we can't get him to come very often. This Senior Center is a Godsend for people like him. He sure was excited about my being able to get your appliances for you."

He stood up and stretched. "I've been talking your arm off,

but Wash is special, and you know, maybe you can help get those two together."

He left it at that, and I decided I'd better ask Royal who the lady friend was.

Michael said he'd bring the appliances over early Monday, and we could give them a tryout before lunch. He had one more idea. "How do you expect to heat everything in one stove, especially if you get a crowd?"

"It will be a problem. We'll only be able to get two of the caterer's pans in the oven at a time, perhaps three if we stack them. Usually it should work out because we can heat vegetable and gravy on top of the stove. When there's a crowd, we'll shuffle." God forbid we'd have a crowd for a while.

"Well, look. We've got a roaster over at the shop—paint chipped and the lid dented, but it works fine. I'll bring it over, too. That will give you a place to heat one more pan or your rolls. Part of the whole deal, no extra charge."

"That's wonderful. It would help. Are you sure? I don' want to impose or make you lose money."

"Not me. I'm not making much on this deal, or maybe nothing counting the time, but I'm not losing money either. It's mainly for Wash, but for the Center, too. It's one place the City is doing a good job."

He left me still fluttering thanks.

The main room was empty. Everyone seemed to have gone home. I wrote, -*thank you note, to Michael*, on my list and began to look over Wednesday's signup sheet. I'd have to phone McCloud's and Jonah's with a firm count Monday morning.

Looking at the list, I realized I couldn't use it, as it was, to do a simple count job. Some names were crossed off and maybe added in again, and I found some were down twice. Tiny was written down three times, once in my writing, then in Royal's, and finally in Plato's. So, I alphabetized the list roughly and counted. I was aghast. I had forty-three names already, and there were two more days to go. I'd been figuring on forty at the most. My name wasn't on the list. That was forty-four if I ate, and Hilda and Mary's names weren't on the list either. Of course there was the trip coming up. Maybe no one else would sign up.

Just to prove me wrong, a Mrs. Griffith called and registered for herself and her husband. Forty-six—really forty-eight. Well, like every group meal there would be either too many or too few, and while I could have wished for too few, I didn't have to decide until Monday. I added to the list, - *ask Royal when I should cut off the sign up for lunch.*

I looked at the empty jars in the kitchen. A shame to throw them out, but there was nowhere to put them. I wrote on my paper, -*get can for glass recycling.* There was a banging on the back door and of course the phone rang at the same time. I yelled, "Front door is open!" and ran for the phone. One more woman signing up for lunch.

I hung up as an indignant voice said, "I can't find my hat. Someone stole my hat."

I couldn't believe it. It was Bill. "I thought you were in the hospital."

"I can't find my hat. Why was the door locked?"

My God, I'd made him walk all the way around the building, and him looking dead yesterday. "I'm sorry, Bill. I was all alone, so I locked the door. What does your hat look like?"

He looked at me reproachfully. "I don't see my hat."

I decided he didn't hear well. I could see aides in both ears. I lowered my voice and tried to strengthen it. "Do you remember where you put it?"

Maybe he got that because he said, "I put it on the shelf in the closet."

There were six hats on the shelf, but none seemed to

be his, so I started looking around the room. I'd have to add closet to my housecleaning list.

A very pretty brunette, about my age, came in. "Aren't you ready to come, Granddad?"

He just kept on looking.

"I'm sorry, we still haven't found his hat. If you'll tell me what it looks like, I'll ask Royal and we'll see if it turns up. I hate to keep him up like this."

She sighed and stepped in front of Bill. "Grandpa, your hat is home. Dad took it home yesterday. Why didn't you tell me it was your hat you wanted to stop here for?"

Bill said, "What?"

She yelled back, "Your hat is home!"

When he started to search again, I moved in front of him and tried a basso profundo voice. " Your hat is at home!"

He looked at us both and said to his granddaughter, "Then come on, I want to get home for the news."

We looked at each other. She shrugged and started out after him. "Is he all right? I couldn't believe they let him out so soon."

"He's fine, or would be if he could hear. The doctors don't know what happened, but he's as good as ever now. We're supposed to take him back for some tests, but I don't think he'll go. Thanks, he'll probably be back Monday."

I went back to the kitchen and finished up the refrigerator. I combined four dishes of butter and threw out some dead-looking sandwiches and the remains of the soup. The carrot sticks were dubious, but I wrapped them up. They'd do for soup, maybe.

The phone rang. It was Royal. She said she'd given up looking for Agnes and that John was out of the office, so how about I give Lillian my report, close up, and come on over to City Hall. She and Lillian were going to go out, have a drink and dinner, and celebrate the end of the week, and I should join them. I agreed to meet them and had her put Lillian on the phone. I told her about the appliances, the gift of the roaster, and the number of people coming to lunch, I hoped. I sort of missed talking to John. His questions usually gave me ideas of what to work on next.

I locked the files, pulled the shades, emptied and washed the coffee pot, and looked the room over. It was rather messy. Funny. How did the rooms get so tidy every day? Did we have janitors? Maybe they came in during the night. I turned the lights off, locked the door, and went over to City Hall.

I was just going in the door when I stopped. What a fool I was. Almost no money left, and I was going out for a drink and dinner for which I would be paying. Oh, hell, I could have a beer and a hamburger and worry about the budget tomorrow. A paycheck was coming, and maybe I could go to Mom's for dinner on Sunday.

๛ CHAPTER SIX ๙

On Saturday I woke up slowly. Ten o'clock—unbelievable. I hadn't slept that late since before Terry got sick. In fact, maybe after the kids came. It must have been the work week, and I had been more tired than I had known. It certainly hadn't been the one beer last night. It was great to sleep like that. The day would not be so long. *Oh hell.* I realized the old depression had settled in again. It had been good to be free of it, or almost free, all week. *Come on, Anne, get busy. Lying around brooding won't help.*

I got up, showered, and put on old jeans and a sweatshirt. It was a gray, rainy day out, not good for working in the garden. I made coffee, lit a fire in the den, turned the radio on, loud, and started to clean Terry's desk. Slowly, anger grew. He had no right to leave such a mess. It wasn't that he was stupid, or didn't keep track of all the bills, or pay them. It was just the constant sheer mess. No rhyme, no reason. How in God's name had he ever managed to work in this chaos? Hell and double damnation, there was still that box of things from his desk at work.

This was doing no good. I got some more coffee, sat on the couch, and looked at the fire. I was doing this to myself. I'd lived with Terry and his capacity to work happily in the midst of disorder for twenty-five years. I'd ignored it, or picked up after him, all that time. Why was I having a tizzy about it now, this last time?

I felt frozen. That was probably it. Another last time. That on top of all the usual screwy feelings of being deserted, mistreated, betrayed. I knew most widows went through all of this, but, God, how I wanted to be clear of it. I wanted to be happy again.

How long was it since I'd been happy? I straightened. I'd been happy, well, in a way, all last week, at least, when I hadn't been scared stiff. That silly little job. That crazy pink Center—and they'd be there Monday. There were just two days alone again to get through. I knew enough tricks to get through two days.

I went back to the kitchen for more coffee. I knew I shouldn't drink so much of it and that I should eat breakfast. But no, I was going to do things I liked, and not try and do everything just right. I took my coffee and the garbage can and went back to have at the desk.

Like most jobs I kept putting off, it wasn't all that bad. By noon I had the receipts piled together, tax records corralled, and the garbage can half full of scrap paper, doodles, old cigarette wrappers, and about fifty pencil stubs. I stared at the piles. There were pictures to be put in the scrapbooks some day, and lots of weekends coming up—but, what to do with it all for now? It was time to start a system I could use, so I went into the sewing room and got the file I'd started when Terry had finally had to quit handling the money.

I realized I had made advances. I was better. I hadn't worked in the study since Terry was sick from his chemotherapy treatments, and it had been our favorite spot in the house. We'd had coffee there together by the fire almost every morning since we'd bought the house the year Carla had been two and Elizabeth four. It didn't seem possible. Anyway, I'd had coffee there this morning, lit the fire, done a lot of work, and no ghosts had walked, not very hard anyway.

Time to give myself a break. I got a bowl of cereal and called Thelma, my friend from WICS. Her daughter said she'd gone shopping with Gwen.

Betty didn't answer.

I thought about going through the hedge and seeing my neighbor, Jo Anderson, but Greg would be home and he was always bored stiff with woman talk. Maybe I should call and see if she'd like to come over for tea later. I didn't call. They probably had plans.

I dialed Mom. She was home, just back from the grocery store. Funny, she still shopped Saturday morning, just as she and Dad had done every Saturday until he'd died that day, sitting on the sun deck. I shook my head. I was really overdoing the nostalgia bit.

Mom told me about her bargains, and I listened and ate my corn flakes quietly. I told her about my week. She didn't think Tiny was funny at all. I guess I didn't either, but I didn't tell her about the pinch. Sometimes she acted like I was twelve and couldn't take care of myself.

There was no invitation to dinner on Sunday. She was going over to Ruby's for dinner and bridge. She refused my suggestion that she should come over to the Center and have lunch Wednesday or Friday.

She said, "Who'd want to sit around with all those old people?"

We hung up on that. My God, Mom was seventy-five, no, seventy-six herself. When was old?

I got some boxes from the garage, boxed all the piles, and labeled them. I kept the stuff for the accountant in the study and put all the rest on the top shelf of my closet. My heirs could decide what to do with them. By then I'd had it and decided Terry's things from his office desk could wait 'til Sunday.

As long as I was being so efficient, I decided to try and

deal with money again, not that there seemed to be any real answer. I got a piece of paper and a pen. The insurance payment was in the bank; I'd figured out how much I could use every month until I was 65. What was left of our savings, after I'd paid the hospital and funeral home and stuff, was for emergencies and after the insurance ran out.

My ear burned—my little warning system—and I rubbed it slowly. I just didn't trust the stocks and bonds Terry had bought. Those dumb checks for twelve dollars. God, the advice I'd gotten about them. Sell, transfer them all to Mutual Funds, buy real estate, buy Boeing stock, buy gold. I'd left them just as they were when Terry died. Again, I reminded myself to take a course in investments for women. Anyway, I wasn't sure how much they brought in. I'd put that on the list to find out. Probably the accountant would know, but I was sure it wasn't enough.

Hell, it was all so stupid. Compared to the income of most of the widows I knew, I was rolling in luxury, but it wasn't enough. It was way less than half what Terry had earned. The taxes on the house and the utility bills kept coming, and I had less than seven dollars left for the month and not much food in the house.

O.K. I'd get paid pretty soon and stock the freezer then. What I probably needed to know was what it was costing me to work. Gas, things like last night's outing. I didn't need any clothes for quite a while. I'd planned to get a new coat, but the old one would do without having to listen to Terry's fussing about my needing a better one.

Crap. All this could wait. I'd give it a year, like they advised, before I decided about the house—whether I'd sell it, get an apartment, buy a condo, or invest the money in land. What did it matter? There were disadvantages and chances either way. I'd see how the money went each month, and in December, I'd do something.

It was still raining out. I started a batch of bread and got out one of Carla's Georgette Heyer's books that I hadn't read in years. I had hot bread and salad about ten that evening, and went right to sleep after I finished the book.

Back to the old 6:00 wake-up schedule on Sunday. It would be a long day. I made myself get ambitious and fixed cinnamon toast and a boiled egg. I crawled back in bed while I ate and read the Sunday paper. I decided I still didn't like breakfast in bed. Maybe something besides a boiled egg would work better, but even coffee was a bother. Terry used to love it. He said it was the only advantage to being sick. As far as I could see, it didn't even save on fuel, as I couldn't eat and keep the covers around my shoulders.

I gave it up and decided to save the paper for evening. I took a long bath and did my nails, getting ready for the next week. Still, it was only eight a.m. Well, it would be a good time to go back to church.

I dashed around getting the housework done, put on my tweed suit, and was at church by 10:45. I walked in with the Baxters, and after they asked how I was, we talked about the weather. Strange how embarrassed people are about death. I always got the feeling they'd rather not deal with me.

I sat beside them during the service. My unholy ability to tune out any long talk took over and I switched the minister off. He was new. Can't say I liked his style, it sounded adenoidal to me, and I hadn't the faintest idea what he talked about after he read the passage about the meek inheriting the earth.

I was probably one of the meek, and no way did I want to inherit the earth. Who'd want all those problems? I sort of shook myself and told myself that wasn't what it meant at all, but still managed not to hear a word of the sermon.

Terry used to try and bet me that I'd attended more sermons I'd not heard than anyone else. I'd assured him that was why all the Ministers liked me. I was so free to discuss the sermons, I agreed with everything. That, and my homemade loaves of bread. I'd have to send some to the new guy. He looked sort of scrawny.

The Baxters told me how good it was to see me and dashed off. While I was waiting to get out of the pew on the other aisle, I watched them talk to the Polsens and Graziks. I could tell exactly what was going on. I'd probably asked them a thousand times, or been asked by them, "Come on home for Sunday brunch."

Why the hell did people have to treat widows like lepers? Widows still had to eat, didn't they? And I still liked to talk. I shook the minister's hand and started making my way toward the car, being careful not to get near any of them. If I were a widower, they'd ask me in a flash. Somehow, men were supposed to be unable to feed themselves when their wives died.

Well, Anne, what now? Going to go home and sulk because you didn't get asked to lunch? You're not the only single person here. You can speak to strangers. You've taken new people home from church a million times. So I walked up to a tall woman standing alone by the porch railing. "Hi, I'm Anne Farley. Aren't you new here?"

She stared at me solemnly. "No, I'm Mrs. Macintosh, the minister's wife."

I coughed. The taste of foot did it, choked me every time. "Oh, well, I, well, I've been unable to attend for some time..." I paused, hoping she'd straighten it all out. She kept looking coolly down the porch, "so I'm afraid I haven't met you. Anyway, would your husband, and..." *Did they have a family? What had I read in the church bulletin?* "...family come home with me and have Sunday brunch?" Lists of hot bread, soup, salad, and hot fudge sundaes swirled through my head while I kept up that sincere, bright, social smile.

"No, thank you, I have dinner on at home. I always cook a good, nourishing meal for William and have it ready as soon as he can get home." She drifted down the porch. William was through shaking hands.

So I slumped out to the car. *You're being supersensitive,* I told myself. Like hell I was. That battle-ax had no manners, and she'd better learn some or her husband's next parish would be in Timbuktu, and soon.

To my satisfaction, there were no clusters of eager parishioners walking with them. They were leaving in solitary splendor. Old Mr. Osmund and his wife had always taken at least an hour to get away, so many people wanted to talk to them. I slammed the car door and went home.

I sat in the car and stared at the place. How was I supposed to get the yard in shape if it continued to rain all year? I stomped in, put my jeans and sweatshirt back on, got into my old raincoat and boots, and got the hoe. It took three hours, but I got the vegetable garden weeded. Luckily we'd decided it was too big last year, and Terry had only gotten half of it sodded.

I saw the Andersons come home and waved. Greg looked loaded. Wonder where they'd been? Today wouldn't be a good day to go over.

When I went back in the house I was in a better mood. I took another long, hot bath, uncomfortably reading the new *National Geographic* balanced on the edge of the tub. Finally I got out, the magazine finished, and put on a long warm robe.

I stared at myself in the mirror. I wondered if Royal was right. How would I look with chestnut hair? I'd been a blonde. Terry had nicely called it a honey blonde, but it had really been dishwater blonde.

My hair had darkened each year, and as I had begun to gray, it had turned mud-colored. I hated it. Gray would be O.K., but who wanted muddy hair? I pondered, but the decision to color or not color would have to wait for the improvement of the budget.

I couldn't help giggling as I brushed my hair. What on earth did Royal use to get that sort of fuchsia she sported? Per usual, my curls did what they wanted instead of the casual, short pageboy I'd spent thirty dollars having cut. All the women who'd said to me how lucky I was to have curly hair—they never knew how exasperated it was to have hair that never went the way you wanted it except the day you had it done, and it never was in style. It wasn't even curly enough for the little Orphan Annie rage this year. Still, I was glad. I don't think I could have stood fighting corkscrews all those years.

I'd just dumped the office box on the floor when Jo stuck her head in the back door. "Where are you, Anne?"

"Hi. In the study."

She yelled back, "If you've got the time, I'll put on the pot."

"Sure." I went to the kitchen with her and got out the tea and my porcelain cups. "Hey, nice to see you. Lousy day, isn't it?"

"Graysville. Are you nuts? Saw you out in the yard. It's a miracle you didn't wash away."

I laughed. It felt good to have company. I sliced some bread and got out butter and honey. Oh, yipes, I hadn't opened up Terry's bees this year. Another job to do, and one I hated. I was convinced the bees knew it. They always behaved like miniature golden angels for him and as if I were a pillaging bear.

We made the tea and took it into the study. "What have you been doing all week, Jo?"

"Oh, the usual. Trying to get the place cleaned up. Greg's having the office in next Friday."

I grimaced with her.

She asked, "But where've you been all week? I saw you rushing out real early several times."

I stared at her. I hadn't even told Jo about my job. I'd not had time to tell anyone but Mom. "I've got a job!"

"A job?"

"A real, honest to God, paying job." I shared. "Well, it's only part time. Three days a week. But until I get things organized, I'm working every day."

"But, Anne, where? What are you doing?"

"You are looking at the new Meal Supervisor at the Danville Senior Center."

She wasn't terribly impressed, but Jo was nice about it, and glad for me. She didn't know about all my money troubles, but I knew she'd probably guessed at a lot of it. We'd raised our kids next door to each other and had a pretty good idea about each other's financial state. She hugged me. "Anne," she said, looking serious, "won't it be awfully depressing?"

"Oh, Jo, not really. Mostly it's fun."

I told her about the rug and Royal and some of the things the seniors did around the Center. I wasn't sure she was convinced, but she ooh'd and aah'd in the right places, and I relaxed and poured her more tea. I often accused her of being addicted to tea, though I was not one to talk with my coffee fixation.

I made myself ask. There had to be a reason she was over here on a Sunday afternoon. "How's Greg? Still working lots of overtime?"

To my horror, her mouth quivered and tears filled her eyes. "Anne, what am I going to do? Greg got drunk over at the Baxters' brunch. *That damned woman.* "And I had a horrible time getting him to come home. When I finally did, he was mad at me for nagging, had some more drinks, and passed out on the couch."

I patted her, got Kleenex, and poured more tea. These sessions about Greg had become more and more frequent the last three or four years, though she'd not said much the year Terry had been sick. I guess I hadn't had much time for anyone. "Was today worse?"

"No, I suppose not. It's just that it keeps happening more and more often. He never comes straight home from work anymore. He's never sober when he gets here, and more often than not, he's completely looped."

"Lord, Jo, I don't know what you can do. You've talked to your doctor?" She nodded. "You've been to Mental Health, and God knows you've talked to Greg."

She grimaced.

I don't know how many of those "talks" Terry and I had heard clear through our houses and yards.

"The latest thing is he's carrying a flask, and I'm pretty sure he's having a drink before he leaves home in the morning."

"Is the company complaining?"

"Well, if they are, I don't know about it. One thing's certain, he's not being sent on many trips, so I suppose they know. Anne, I've got to do something."

"You can leave him."

The last time I'd talked about them separating, she'd talked about how she loved him and not spoken to me for two weeks. "Jo, a lawyer would know what to do."

"It's not the legal stuff. It's Greg. If I walk out or make him leave, he'll go on a binge that'll make all the rest look like tea parties. Then where'd we be? No paychecks probably, and there's still the mortgage and everything else."

We'd gotten our mortgage paid off five years ago. They should have too.

"But, Jo, you don't know that. Maybe it will knock some sense into him?"

She stared at the table. "I sort of tried, last winter.

When I told you I was going to see Mother. Well, I did—see her, that is—but I told Greg I was leaving. I came back when the doctor called. Of course Greg promised he'd never touch another drop, but instead he keeps harping on my having deserted him. He makes it sound like his drinking is all my fault. If I leave again, what good will it do? Instead of being just miserable, I'll be broke and miserable."

"Get a job. Stay here and get yourself ready in case he does blow it financially."

"Hah, me, a job. Don't be dumb, Anne. I'm forty-eight. I can't type. I've never worked. Not even in a drive-in in high school. Can you see all the people waiting in line to hire me? I don't think I could even get baby-sitting jobs. Anyway, I've had it with bottles and kids." She got up. "I didn't mean to cry all over your shoulder, Love, but I seem to have a need to spout off. I'm really glad about your job, but don't make yourself so scarce." She went to the door, opened it, hesitated, and looked back at me. "You know, Anne, I guess you're the lucky one," she said, and went out.

That hurt. I think in our way, Jo and I really loved each other. It hurt that she was so damned sad, that my being a widow sounded better than her marriage. So there I was, as blue as yesterday. I couldn't face it. I put Terry's office stuff back in the box, got a coat, and went over to the Austins'.

Brad and Myrtle were in their seventies. They had lived in the same house ever since they'd gotten married over fifty years ago. Fifty-two, in fact. They'd had their golden wedding anniversary two years ago during the Christmas holidays. That had been a bang-up affair. They were home, and Brad's sister, Lila was there. They had a gorgeous coal fire going in the fireplace. No one else I knew had coal fires. I knew they had a hard time getting the big lumps now. The kids and I used to get Brad to give us some smaller pieces now and then and we made fairy crystal gardens with bluing and salt. I didn't like the pink ones as well, where you put mercurochrome with it.

They took my coat and gave me the rocker, and Myrtle brought me cocoa and her fruitcake. I knew I was going to slosh after all that tea, but I adored her fruitcake. Every September she made huge batches, enough to last all year. Carla and Elizabeth used to help her shell nuts and cut up fruit. At least, they thought they were helping. I suspect they ate more than they helped.

I told them about my job and they even knew about the Center. Brad said he went there and played pool now and then. Myrtle added she went down when they braided rugs. With Lila, we had enough for a good game of Spite and Malice. Brad and I were partners and we won. We always did because he cheated like mad. Lila and Myrtle were too nice to call him on it and I always encouraged him.

About eight o'clock, I said I had to go home, but they insisted I stay for supper. Myrtle and I made a fruit salad and Lila put together sardine sandwiches. Brad made a scotch and soda for himself and one for me. Myrtle and Lila had a thimbleful of their homemade Dandelion wine—horrible stuff but awfully pretty.

I went home at 9:30, replete. I shocked myself when I went to bed and bawled and bawled. Finally, I cried myself out around eleven.

❧ CHAPTER SEVEN ❧

Monday and Tuesday went by fast. I was nervous about the first meal, though not too much. When I tried to talk about kitchen help and show Royal the breakdown for the jobs, she looked it over briefly and said to talk to Mary.

Mary was crocheting granny squares for an afghan—pink, purple, lavender, and cream—and watching a card game. She took my lists and we went back to the kitchen together.

I might have known. She had it all planned out, though she looked at my lists with interest. "My, that looks, efficient," she said. "We thought Phil, Conner, and Gordy would put the tables and chairs up about nine. Then Sylvia, Florence, and Rose, they'll set tables and help me do the cooking, and we'll serve. Butch and Tom will serve coffee. Hilda, Emma, and I'll clean up. Of course, we expect everyone to scrape their plates and stack them, like at the potluck. What do you think, Anne, shall we set up for fifty-five?"

I agreed. It was as good a number as any.

She went on, "You'll probably want to take the money yourself."

"Well, no. I thought I'd be needed in the kitchen..."

She swept on, "That way you'll get to know people and can keep track of numbers for us. Now, I've got other crews for Friday and Monday, and everyone's agreed to work once a week. Maybe you can make us some lists, and if people can't come, they can phone in, and we'll get someone else. I got several to say they'd help out occasionally."

She sure had it under control. Who was I to argue about it? I went to the office, called McCloud's, and ordered for fifty-five for lunch on Wednesday.

Each night when I went home, I found it hard to remember what I'd gotten done that day, because it seemed so little, but my lists got whittled down and time passed quickly.

On Wednesday, I went in proud of myself. No butterflies in my stomach, no headache, and I was happy about the whole prospect. Maybe at forty-five, I was growing up. I sat in the parking lot for a minute and looked around. Already I wasn't really seeing it. I parked every day in the same spot and hurried in. It was part of the job, and I no longer thought about the cracked cement, weeds, and old signs plastered on the building and power poles.

****

By eight-fifteen, all the seniors going to the ocean were milling around and had drunk all the coffee Royal had made the night before. Boy, I hoped there was a toilet on that bus.

At eight-thirty they all piled on, arguing viciously over who got what seats. Royal wore a smart black pants suit and an orange flower in her fuchsia hair. I waved as they drove off.

I made another pot of coffee, got out ten dollars worth of change, and put it in an envelope. Oh, hell, now how had I figured I could take money from the seniors for lunch and also run the office? I hadn't even given it a thought. Wonder if Mary had. Foul up number one for the day. Why couldn't I ever remember everything?

At nine, the work crew marched in, and at nine-thirty, Agnes came into the office. She took her place by the phone and pulled out her book, *Zen and the Art of Motorcycle Maintenance.* I tried not to stare. As far as I could see, she looked perfectly normal. She wasn't pale or anything.

Greg always looked sick as sin for days after he tied on a good one. I couldn't think of anything normal to say, but then we'd never really talked, so I got down to business.

"O.K. if I'm in and out? You'll handle the phone? I'm going to go and take money at eleven." She nodded. I asked, "Want some coffee?"

"I'd rather have tea."

"O.K." I managed to get near the stove and made tea for her. I took my coffee and the tea back in the office and we both worked in silence. I wandered out to the kitchen every once in a while, but they didn't need me. The food came and everything was fine.

On the second trip out, a white-haired woman—Rose?—took me aside and said, "Do you want one or two sets of salt and peppers on the tables?"

"Why, probably just one. Makes a little less work and it should be enough."

She nodded.

On the third trip out, I noticed there were two sets on every table. Rose came over. "Mary said to put two sets on."

"That's fine. Doesn't matter."

"I told her you said one."

Oh, God in heaven. I went over to Mary. "About the salt and pepper..."

Mary said, "I'm sorry about that. I had two pairs on when Rose said you wanted only one. I'll get someone to take them off."

"No, I mean, it's O.K. the way it is. I didn't see they were already on. Rose wanted to know how many to put on each table. I don't really care.'

"That's Rose. Gets an idea in her head and then works

to find someone who'll tell her what she wants. I'll leave them and next time she asks, tell her two pairs. Oh, and Mike hasn't come with the milk yet."

I looked at my watch. Ten thirty. "I'd better call and check on it."

I called Jonah's. The Secretary said she'd check. When she came back, she said the driver had already come back for his second load, so milk should have been delivered. Had I checked the back door?

I put her on hold and ran back to the rear door. There was the milk, gently warming in the spring-like March sun. I marched back to the phone. "The milk is here. It was to have been delivered by ten. Why is it sitting outside?"

She didn't know, but said the driver had a heavy schedule so he probably had to leave it before we opened.

"Please have the driver pick it up, and tell him to be sure to talk to me when he comes," I instructed.

She said she'd leave the message.

She certainly didn't seem very interested in my problems. The milk felt lukewarm, so I went back to the kitchen and told Mary to leave it outside. We decided we'd not serve any. I could go buy milk, but didn't want to tangle with health regulations. I dug the can of Tang out of the back room and asked Mary to mix some of that up in case someone swore they'd die if they couldn't have something to drink besides tea or coffee.

I began to get ready to start taking money for lunch when Emma and Phil came into the office.

"Anne, Phil here made you a box to put the lunch money in. Be faster this way."

Phil handed me a beautiful wooden box. It was surprisingly heavy. Oak or cherry? I didn't know woods. It had places for bills, fifty-cent pieces, quarters, dimes, nickels, and pennies. He'd even carved a small design of flowers around the edge. It was a real treasure.

"Phil, thank you. It's beautiful and will be so useful."

He nodded, once.

Emma added, "That's nice of you, Anne. I've got a table and chair ready for you."

Together we carried my lists and the money out. About fifteen people were already lined up waiting for me.

It wasn't too bad. Most of the seniors told me their names without my asking, and I found I knew a lot of them. One, Barbara, kept trying to find her name on the first page because she insisted she was the third to sign up, and her name should be third on the list.

"Barbara, we've alphabetized the list," I told her. "Here's your name. Lunch is one twenty-five." She paid me but went away still muttering about being third on the list. Her friend patted her on the shoulder, winked at me, and took her into the dining room.

Mary came over and looked at the list. Forty had paid for their lunch in the first fifteen minutes.

"You know, Mary, everyone seems to be going in and sitting down. They're going to get tired of waiting. Maybe, after this, we'd better keep the doors closed until quarter of twelve. They'll die of boredom waiting until lunch."

"No they won't, Anne. They're all eating their dessert and the bread and butter and having a cup of coffee. I've put on another pot."

"But, Mary, that's the third pot today. That's 225 cups. They can't, well, they shouldn't drink all that coffee. And why do they want their dessert first?"

"Something to do, I guess," she said.

"Maybe we shouldn't put the dessert out until we've served the meal."

"That'd take longer," she explained, "and we'd need more help, too. They're happy."

"I'll think about it." Just then, Tiny came up to the table. I'd hoped he'd stay home.

"I ain't eating today. Don't like ham."

The menu had been posted for days. He'd known what we were having, if he could read, that is, or bothered to look.

"Give my place to Zeke, here." A round little man with a beautiful drift of silver hair, rosy cheeks, and sparkling eyes followed Tiny. No glasses! I glanced over my list. I couldn't remember any Zekes.

"Thanks for letting me know, Tiny. Zeke, I'll put your name on the waiting list. I'm sure we'll be able to get you in. I'll let you know if I get another cancellation or someone doesn't come."

Tiny glared and shoved his face close to mine. "He can have my place," he yelled.

"Tiny, I'm sorry. I've got two other names on the waiting list. They come first, but I'm sure there'll be no problem. Zeke, what's your last name? You'll probably get lunch, but I can't say absolutely for sure right now."

Tiny's jaw came out at a threatening angle, and I tried to slide further back in my chair and sit up straighter. Several people were watching with interest.

"I ain't eating. My friend Zeke can have my place."

"No, I told you..."

"You dumb woman, just like all stupid females. Can't understand a thing. Zeke wants lunch!" He was bellowing now. Everyone in the building watched. "You fix it up or I'll call the mayor."

God, I hoped he would. What in hell could I do?

Conner drifted over. "Tiny, you and Zeke got time for a game of pool?"

I looked at Conner in deep gratitude as the two men followed him to the pool table. I noticed that Gordy and Mr. Griffith had vacated the table and were headed for the dining hall. Saints and angels.

At eleven-forty, all fifty-five on my list were signed in and I had five on my waiting list, including Zeke. My ear burned like mad. I gestured Mary out of the kitchen and showed her.

"Well, the vegetables and dessert will stretch, and probably the rolls," she said. "Lots of ladies won't want them. Don't know about the ham, though. I counted the slices. They sent us exactly fifty-five."

Could we get away with cutting the slices up again? No. This wasn't potluck; there were no casseroles to fill up the plate. "O.K., could you get one of the men, with a car, to go to Safeway and buy a canned ham? A little one." I handed her a ten from the cash drawer. God knows how the money would be repaid. "We can start heating it as soon as he's back, and then the people on the waiting list can eat last and have the canned home."

Mary headed for the kitchen and in a minute, Phil came out, got his hat, and left.

The door had barely closed when it opened again and the mayor breezed in.

"Hi, I thought I'd eat with you. I really want to thank you for all you've accomplished. I was afraid we'd never get everything done and be able to serve a meal today."

I resisted the urge to tell him we still might not and signaled Mary again.

She greeted John like a long-lost son and said she was having two card tables set up. "I've saved a table for the kitchen crew, Anne. You and John can eat with us. I'll take a plate into Agnes."

I told John, "That woman is a treasure. She thinks of everything."

John nodded and wandered off to talk to the seniors. Politicking maybe? He seemed to know them all.

Phil rushed back in and I breathed easier until Rose

rushed out of the kitchen.

"Anne, it's not fair. Tiny and Zeke are sitting at a table, and Zeke is on the wait list. He's eaten his cake already, and Tiny's had two rolls. You've got to make Zeke wait. My sister's on the wait list and she's sitting out there waiting. Zeke has to wait too."

I could just see me trying to separate Tiny from his faithful friend. But, fair's fair. "Stay with the money, Rose. I'll be right back." I went to the kitchen, having the feeling John was watching. Sure enough, Zeke and Tiny were at the first table, which seemed to be a table of pool players. If Rose was right, Tiny was having this third roll.

I found Mary and asked, "I can't see any way short of war of trying to get Zeke out of here. I'm going to let the rest of the latecomers come in to the card tables. Now, when Zeke comes up, give him a plate with the canned ham on it."

She grinned and nodded.

I went over to Tiny's table, keeping out of his reach. I took the plate of rolls away from his end, and said, "One roll apiece," and practically ran for my money table.

Rose was putting the bills in order. I told her it was all fixed up and told the four people waiting they could go in to eat. "The card tables are set up especially for you."

John came over. "Must be time. Got your speech ready?"

"Speech?" Sheer horror.

"Sure, you've got to say something about the first meal—give thanks to everyone who's helped."

He had to be kidding. "I don't think that will be necessary, John. Royal didn't say...anyway, you're here. They'll expect you to say something."

"Of course. You take the mike. Do the pleasantries, introduce me, and I'll have my say."

"They all know you. Shouldn't you...?" Oh bloody hell. He wasn't smiling. "I'll take the money into the office and be right back out."

Now knowing how a prisoner on death row feels as he's marched to the electric chair, I led the way to the microphone, clutched it desperately, and blew on it. Nothing. I clicked the switch off and on. Blank. The plug was in. The whole room gazed expectantly at me. Still holding the mike, I shrilled, "The mike doesn't seem to be working. I hope you can hear me."

Over my soft attempt to get my voice to carry, I heard Bill say, "That damn doctor told me that I was in the best shape he'd ever seen for a man my age and he'd not seen many, I bet." The rest of the table shushed him and pointed to me.

I tried to deepen my voice. "Good morning. We want to welcome all of you to the first of the regular lunches..." Suddenly, the mike went on, and everyone jumped as I boomed, "at the Danville Senior Center."

Phil came out of the supply closet. He must have done something.

I lowered my voice. "We will be serving lunch every Monday, Wednesday, and Friday from now on. There is no way I can thank everyone who has helped in making these lunches possible and who has done so much work. I am not going to try and name names, but to each of you I say a special thank you. I hope you know that these meals could not be put on without you."

"Now I want to introduce the mayor." My God, I couldn't think of his last name. "Without his help, advice, and guidance, this day could not have been accomplished. The Mayor." I handed him the mike, hoping I'd made sense, and tottered over to my table. Tiny was buttering a roll as I passed by.

I was still so nervous I didn't hear much the mayor said. He mentioned Royal, the City Council, and me. There was a faint clapping at that point. Was that good or bad? He got a real hand when he finished.

Mary started serving, with a table at a time going up for their plates. Hilda took a plate over to a lady in a wheelchair, and Phil carried two over to a couple in the back of the room that had canes hooked over their chairs.

John said, "How are you serving the milk? I'd like a glass."

"There was a foul up. It was delivered early and no one saw it to bring it in. It was warm when I found it."

"What are you going to do about it?"

"I called and asked the driver to come and pick it up and see me."

"That won't do. Call Jonah. Give him hell and tell him they aren't to charge for it."

"But, John, it was the driver. Shouldn't I deal with him?"

"Look, Anne. You made your arrangements with Jonah. He knows the terms. Get arrangements to straighten it out."

That would be lots of fun, I was certain. "O.K., I think it's our turn. We'd better go get our plates."

Mary had a plate ready for each of us. The mayor had been given a special helping of pickles and a big serving of ham. The kitchen crew filled their plates and joined us. The food wasn't bad. The string beans were way overdone. I'd have to talk to Mary about that. All in all, it was a good first effort. I looked at the clock. They'd served all of us in just sixteen minutes, and even for those of us at the last table, the food was hot. Marvelous.

After lunch I went back to the office. John followed me. Agnes closed her book and took her empty plate back to the kitchen. I'd have to do something about that. She couldn't be expected to eat in the office every day. John perched on the corner of Royal's desk and said, "Phone Jonah now."

"It's lunch time. I'd better wait 'til after one."

"Anne."

I picked up the phone and found the number on the clipboard.

John added, "I happen to know he eats at his desk."

Praying he was wrong and Jonah would be out until John left, I dialed and asked for him. The receptionist wanted to know Mr. Jonah the younger or Mr. Jonah? Thank God, from somewhere I dredged up, "Tim," and unhappily for me, she said he was in. "Mr. Jonah," I said. "This is Mrs. Farley at the Senior Center. Through some mistake, the milk was delivered early and I felt it was unsafe to use." I glanced at the Mayor. "I want the milk picked up, the charges removed from our bill, and your assurance it will be delivered at ten as agreed."

Much to my pleasure and surprise— seldom had I encountered businessmen who were very obliging—he promised to pick it up and agreed there would be no charge. He said he'd talk to the driver and get back to me about the delivery time.

John got up, said, "There, that wasn't so bad, was it? Have fun counting your money," and left.

Glad I didn't have to make a fool of myself while trying to balance the money in front of him, I set out to count it. Two hours and eleven phone calls later, I seemed to have $78.28, after I returned my $10.00 in change and deducted the canned ham money. While that was better than having less than the money I should have had, I couldn't figure out where the extra change had come from. I'd known all along I wasn't the one to make change. I finally got an envelope from Royal's desk, put the money in it, labeled it "Extra," and put it in my bottom drawer under the cash box.

I got out a sheet of lined paper and started trying to figure out what sort of records I'd need. I decided that could wait and went out to the kitchen. It was all cleaned up, though a couple of loads of dishes still remained to be put through the dishwasher. Hilda came in with the garbage can. I could see she had washed it. "You'd better quit now, Hilda. It's been a long day for you. I'll finish up the dishes."

"I'm just going to mop the floor. Then the dishes will be done. You go on back to the office."

"But, Hilda, you shouldn't work so hard. Don't you want to go play cards or something?" She must have been in her seventies. She'd kill herself. I'd have to talk to Mary about getting others to share in the cleanup.

"I'd rather work. It makes me awful nervous to sit around. I've got to keep busy."

She started mopping, so I grabbed the box of dirty dishcloths and towels and went around the counter. She snapped, "I'll take those home and do them up tonight."

"That's too much, Hilda. You can't go home and still have to do the Center's work. I'll do them."

She put down the mop and took hold of the box. "That's my job. I've been doing the towels ever since the Center first opened. Conner and me and the Wildes are charter members and no fancy young lady is going to take my job away from me."

Boy, she wasn't fooling. "Of course not. Not if you really want to do it."

Followed by her glare, I slunk back to the office.

Getting smart, I called Lillian and asked her if she knew what sort of records were needed. I found out I had to know how many males and females ate each day, how many were sixty-five and over, and how many were under sixty-five. *How am I supposed to find that out?* And how many minorities? Unfortunately in Danville that was easy. None.

With her help I devised a form I thought would work. I started a sheet and filled in what I could, but I'd have to talk to Royal tomorrow.

The Center was empty when Royal and the tired travelers returned around five from the beach. A few came in and drank the rest of the coffee. Royal sprawled at her desk rubbing her feet. "I swear each time, Anne, I'll never take another trip."

"Tired?"

"Frazzled and mad. I've walked my feet off."

"Something wrong?"

"We lost Amy AND the bus driver. I walked miles trying to find them."

"Evidently you did find them. What happened?"

She sat wiggling her toes. "The bus was supposed to leave at three to come back. I got there at five of. Everyone was back except Amy, the driver, and Percy. Well, I know Percy, so I went to the corner tavern and told him the bus was leaving. He finished his beer and we went back to the bus. Still no Amy or driver though. No one remembered seeing them or had even had lunch with them. I made everyone stay on the bus while I looked. I looked in every bar, at the hotel, and the movies. I even walked up the beach to the waterfall. To make a long story short, they still weren't at the bus when I got back. I had just decided I was going to call the police when they came hurrying up together."

"Where had they been?"

"You'll never guess."

"Come on. Tell."

"They'd been fabric shopping."

"The bus driver, too?"

"Yes. Wait 'til I get my hands on Finisterre."

I knew Finisterre was the bus company.

"Where does he get these idiots? Seems that character sews, of all things, and he and Amy had gotten together when they both wandered into the same fabric store. They'd had a marvelous day and lost track of time. I was so mad I didn't dare say much."

I couldn't help laughing, but it was obvious Royal had had it. I shoved her out of the Center and locked up.

❧ CHAPTER EIGHT ❧

I woke up about midnight. My god, Jonah's hadn't called back and I didn't know if they had picked up the milk. I hadn't even looked. Hell and damnation, it would be just my luck that some reporter from the local weekly would see the milk sitting there, rotting, and write a real sob story about the Center letting food spoil while the old people went hungry.

Danville's paper was really good at stuff like that. What could I do? With no enthusiasm, I considered driving down to the Center and putting the milk inside. It took me no time to decide not to do that.

Not only did I not like being out alone at night, I could only too vividly imagine the patrolman coming along just as I stepped out the back door of the Center. Besides, the place probably had a burglar alarm. I'd have to ask Royal about that.

I lay there, miles away from sleep. Probably best to get down there ten minutes early tomorrow, put the milk inside, call Jonah's, and scream bloody blue blazes at him. Lord. Better get up at six then, not six-thirty. I wanted to put a load of clothes in the washer and had planned to vacuum before I left. Breakfast, dishes, pick up, shower. Nuts. I hadn't washed my hair this morning so I'd have to tomorrow, no, today.

Well, anyway, I'd shower, throw the load in the washer first, breakfast, dishes, pick up, and vacuum. Oh, plants would need watering. I'd never make it. Plants after work, no, wash after work. They wouldn't get so wrinkled sitting all day. I'd have to leave at seven-forty, maybe seven-thirty to be sure.

I got up, put Terry's old robe on, and went into the kitchen. It was going to be one of those nights. I got a glass of milk, hesitated, poured a slug of brandy in it, and sat at the table and sipped at it. I never really liked brandy. Well, I might as well go whole hog as long as I was dissipating. I put two heaping spoonfuls of brown sugar in it and a splash of vanilla.

I got up and wandered around the house, slowly drinking my mixture. Why was I awake like this? I knew damned well I could get all of the stuff done in the morning. It just sounded impossible late at night.

Sighing, I got a piece of paper and a pencil. I made a list, thought a while, and added, "Take papers to recycle." I took my glass back to the kitchen, filled the teakettle, and watered the plants. I crossed that off my list, took the list and pencil with me, and went back to bed.

I woke at five-thirty, and dashed out and got to the paper. I read in bed for half an hour. I saved the funnies for breakfast. Everything was done by seven, so I started a letter to Margie. Funny. We hadn't seen each other since college, but I wrote almost every month and called several times a year. I still thought of her as my best friend. I was telling her about last week's potluck when I finally remembered Thursday. It's potluck day.

What meat should I serve today? I grabbed the paper and looked at the ads. Glory be. Albertsons had chicken advertised. Could I get enough in the oven? Well, bless Michael. The roaster could take the overflow. If I shopped at nine, the chicken could start cooking while I screamed at Jonah.

I made it to the Center by seven forty-five. I went out the back door. No milk. Hilda hadn't lugged it in. Evidently the driver had quietly picked it up. All that midnight turmoil for nothing.

79

I got the coffee going and opened the office. Royal was late. It was nearly eight-thirty when she came in.

By then I'd marked my calendar with circles for potlucks and squares for lunches. Maybe I'd remember next week. I'll have to try for different meat next week, different and easy. How about Hamburger Stroganoff? Then I went through the guessing game with Royal. We decided on forty-five for potluck, thinking fewer would come than for our first lunch.

Royal said, "We've got to think of something to call the meal. Something snappy and attractive that will do for publicity. Oh, that reminds me. The paper is sending a reporter over tomorrow afternoon to talk to you about the meals."

This simple job seemed to have several unpleasant sides.

"John and I will be with you, but you should be ready to talk about what you think the meals will accomplish and what the seniors think about them."

"Royal, it would be best to have one of the seniors talk about that."

"Good idea. We'll see if Mary can be here, too."

"You don't really need me then, do you?"

"Of course we do. Besides, the paper has already done stories about the Center with John and me. They want someone new."

Evidently there was no way to get out of it, so I shut up. I'd have to rewash and set my hair tonight. Maybe, just maybe, I'd try a rinse. Oh, hell, of course not. Wouldn't it be wonderful if my hair turned purple? I'd leave it for when I had more time.

Royal approved of the chicken, and I went over to the Albertsons to get it. Four servings in a package, so I needed twelve. It would give me a slight margin. A woman in front of me in the checkout line looked at my pile and sniped, "Don't you think you should leave a few for someone else?"

I considered not saying anything, but knew I should keep up good public relations.

"It's for the Senior Center potluck.

She didn't seem embarrassed but looked even madder. "Just like every government agency. Wasting money every time. Sheer laziness. Have you considered buying chicken on sale rather than spending all that money?

Wow, she was really on her high horse.

"A little planning is all that's needed. Besides, it's criminal to use public money catering to a bunch of ne'er-do-wells."

I was furious. She looked about the age and type to put her mother in a nursing home, never go see her, and scream about expenses. I restrained myself.

"It's your turn, the checker is ready for you," and I couldn't resist adding, "besides, the people at the potluck pay for the food, not the government."

Luckily, the checker had added up her cigarettes and Hamburger Helper, so she left before the fight could go on.

I was angry. It felt like my own family had been jumped on.

The checker said, "She's always bitch-, uh, complaining about something. I think the Center's worth it. My Aunt Rose, she goes over there. Do you know her?"

I nodded.

"You been a member long?"

Aghast, and a bit hurt, I stared at her. I finally managed, "I work there." I paid for the chicken, parked the cart by the door, and ran back to the drug section. I bought a medium, chestnut brown hair rinse and went through a different line.

When I got back and had given the chicken to Hilda, I called Jonah's. Of course, he was terribly sorry he hadn't called back. He assured me the milk would be there Friday at ten sharp, and every Monday, Wednesday, and Friday after that. I made a note to tell John it was straightened out.

Royal went out prize shopping for the fishing derby and said she'd be back for lunch. I worked on the sign-up sheets for Friday. Not as many had signed up as had for Wednesday. Spaghetti was on the menu. Sort of a comedown from the ham, but placing a bet against myself, I called McCloud's and ordered 45 meals. At least spaghetti was easy to stretch.

I'd just hung up when Hilda came in. "Where do you want me to put the milk, Anne? The fridge is full."

"What milk?"

"Jonah's just delivered a bunch of milk. Said to tell you it was ten o'clock exactly."

"My God, that driver's got a screw loose. Right time, wrong day."

I dashed out to the kitchen. Sitting in front of the refrigerator was an awful lot of milk. I counted. That benighted man had brought forty half-pints. A real mixture, too—2%, whole, skim, chocolate, and one strawberry. I'd never heard of strawberry milk. And Hilda was right.

There was no room in the refrigerator. I got one of the seniors to help, and we piled it into the dishpans and buckets. I put all the ice we had on it and covered it with a ton of newspapers. Then I stormed back to the office and called Jonah's. I had the number down pat, now.

"Tim, this is Anne Farley again." He sounded a little apprehensive. "Your driver just delivered milk, right at ten o'clock as he was careful to point out, but I'm afraid he was a day early."

Groans came over the phone.

"Also, he brought 40 cartons, not 20, and an assortment, not 2%. What do you want to do about it?"

"Anne, I'm terribly sorry. I can't imagine where the foul up is. Can you get rid of it some way?"

"We're having a potluck tonight. I think they'll drink it." I was learning. "But I have no budget for it."

"Oh, no. I understand. Consider it a donation. I'm sure there will be no more trouble."

We thanked each other and I hung up. I crossed off the notation to John and wrote in, "Explain about milk."

I went back to typing Friday's list. I was working at my top speed of about forty words per minute when a woman came in. Her silvery hair was done in a perfect French roll and she had on a beautiful mink. "Can I help you?"

"I'd like to talk to the director, please."

"I'm sorry, she's not in right now. I'm Mrs. Farley. Can I help you or perhaps take your number and have her call you later?"

"I don't know. It's...it's about my check."

"Please. Sit down." I gave her Royal's chair and got a piece of paper for notes. I didn't let myself glance, even once, at the mink. "What seems to be wrong?"

"I don't think I really know. It's become so complicated." She sighed.

I realized she looked, well, best I could think of was awfully tired, or sick. "There's plenty of time. Would you like a cup of coffee or tea? Or maybe I can tempt you with some milk?" I sighed too. "We've got an awful milk of milk by mistake."

"Thank you. I don't want to take too much of your time," she said.

"I usually have coffee about now."

"Great." I went out and asked Emma if she would bring us coffee and a milk.

"Now, hasn't your check come?"

"No. I called the DSHS."

I must have shown my confusion.

"The Department of Social and Health Services. They suggested I wait a few days in case it was delayed in the mail. However, it hasn't come and I've called several times and nothing happens. Now they don't even return my calls."

"Is this the first time this has happened?"

"This is my first time to get checks. I've been working."

"I wish Royal were here. I'm new and don't know much about such things. Would you like me to call and see if I can get some information, or should I give the details to Royal?"

"Please, will you call? I don't want to be a bother, but I can't manage without the money. You see, my food stamp authorization and Medicaid coupons should have come too." She looked so white I was frightened.

"Suppose I try. Do you have the name of anyone I should talk to?"

"I've talked to a Mrs. McCaully, who seems to really try to help. She was out of the office last week."

I dialed the DSHS. I got a recording that the lines were busy and was put on hold. I kept the receiver to my ear and asked, "Where did you work?"

"At Nordstrom's. I did alterations."

I nodded. That didn't go with the mink. "Mrs....my god, I didn't get your name or address or anything." Frantically I handed her the paper and pencil.

She had it all written out before the DSHS operator came on the phone.

I identified myself as Mrs. Farley of the Danville Senior Center, asked for Mrs. McCaully, and got put on hold again.

"How long did you work there?"

"Seven years. Not long enough to get much Social Security."

"I see you live in Danville."

"Mother is in a rest home here, so when Jack died, and I had to sell the house, I moved here. Then when I got the job, it was easier to stay here where I could see her each evening than move closer to work. The bus..."

A voice in my ear said, "Vivian McCaully. May I put you on hold while I finish with a client?" and back on hold I went.

"Sorry. I had Mrs. McCaully for a second. I didn't hear what you were saying."

"Oh, just that the bus service is so good. They certainly need more phones or help at the DSHS. One day I was on hold for an hour, all told."

But Mrs. McCaully came back. I told her who I was and asked about Mrs. Nemmers' check. I got a long sigh.

"Mrs. Farley, I know how improbable this all is, and I'm sorry the Center has had to become involved. I really tried to call Mrs. Nemmers this morning after I sorted through a week's worth of messages. I've been on vacation."

I murmured understanding.

"I'm afraid nothing has been found. I've sent through tracers but Olympia hasn't responded yet."

"I don't think I understand. If the check is lost, can't it be replaced?"

"It isn't that simple. It can take up to three months to replace a check, but no one can locate Mrs. Nemmers' records. Her papers don't seem to be in the files."

"Would you like us to send her up to fill out the papers again?"

I'm beginning to think that would be best, but I hate asking her to do it, it takes so long."

"I'm sure you will do all you can to expedite matters. Just a minute, please." I put down the phone. "Mrs. Nemmers, would you be willing to go to the DSHS and fill papers out again?" She looked very reluctant, but slowly nodded agreement.

Mrs. McCaully said to have Mrs. Nemmers come in and tell the receptionist she was expected, and Mrs. McCaully would see her as soon as she was through with her current client. I told Mrs. Nemmers that. She just sat still.

Finally, so softly I could hardly hear her, she said, "I don't know how I can get there."

"You mean you don't know where it is?"

"No."

I realized her eyes were filled with tears.

"I don't have bus fare and I don't really know anyone anymore who'd take me."

God, if she cried, I would too. I grabbed a Kleenex and put it in her hand. "Be right back. Transportation is no problem."

Out in the kitchen I took Mary aside. "There's a lady in my office who needs to go up to the DSHS." Curious how easy an in-vocabulary was developing. "Is there anyone here who could drive her up?"

Mary yelled, "Hey, Butch, come here."

Butch put his cards down and came over.

"Got your car here today?"

He nodded.

She asked, "Can you take a lady up to Welfare?"

"Can after lunch. That be O.K.?"

I thanked him and went back to the office. Mrs. Nemmers was back in control, Kleenex out of sight, but she was still pale.

"Butch, uh, Mr. Ackerman, can take you up after lunch. Will that be all right?"

"Thank you so much. That will be fine. I'll come back at one. Is that all right?"

"Certainly, but why not stay and have potluck with us? I think it's sort of fun, and there's really good food."

She shook her head. "I have nothing to contribute."

"That's O.K. Not everyone does." I almost said a dish or a dollar, but remembered in time, luckily. No bus fare, probably no dollar for lunch. Oh, dear, I'd have to find out somehow what the Center usually did when a senior needed help.

"Maybe you can bring something special to our next potluck."

She agreed, so I offered to introduce her to some of the ladies.

"First, please, Mrs. Nemmers, I don't want to pry, but I've gone through, sort of, what's happening to you. A house to sell, my husband dying, and I know how confused things can get. Do you have any money?"

She stared at me.

"Any food?"

Slowly, she shook her head. Today was the 22nd and checks were supposed to come on the third.

"I know it seems impossible to be so broke, when I'm working, but I am." She sat a few moments again in silence. "I'm not out of food, exactly. I've got oatmeal and flour and some canned goods. I won't starve, but a potluck sounds wonderful. I've been wanting a green salad so badly."

"Well, I'm not sure you've come to the right place for that. This group doesn't seem to have a love affair with salads."

She smiled a bit.

"Look, I really don't know what I can do, but I'm going to put a box in Butch's car and have you take it home. Now—please don't take this the wrong way, but you shouldn't wear that mink up to the DSHS."

"I know. I'll leave it in the car—but I don't have any other winter coat and I'm so cold. Let me tell you why so you'll understand."

"No please, you don't have to."

She shook her head and continued, "My husband died eight years ago. He was an artist. Well, he painted, and wrote, and did pottery. Many things.

"His family had money, and we all lived well. Then when he died, suddenly I discovered there was nothing. No will, no insurance, no Social Security, and the house was mortgaged. The trust fund stopped with Jack's death, and the car wasn't paid for. It was a mess, and it took me forever to straighten out. Then I tried to get a job. No one I knew had a job for me, so finally I did the only thing I knew how to do.

"I'd always sewn, and sewn well, so I went to Nordstrom and did alterations. The job fed me and paid for the apartment, but with Mother ill and me trying to see she gets something extra once in a while, I've not saved anything. This coat and that horrible case of Scotch are the only things I haven't sold or returned to Jacks' family."

"Scotch."

"It's part of a payment Jack got for an ad he did. Still, like so many things, I can't sell it for anything like it's worth. No one ever heard of the brand. Jack didn't get paid very often for his work, and it meant a lot to him. He used to drag it out and laugh about it. The dumb stuff sits under my bed gathering dust, and I just haven't made myself do anything about it."

I sat looking at her. "If I find anyone needing Scotch, I'll let you know. I'm afraid I think it tastes like iodine."

She agreed with me, and I took her in and turned her over to Rose. Maybe not the best choice, but everyone else was either busy in the kitchen or playing cards. Plato wasn't around.

The phone rang. I hoped that it wasn't bad news. Conner was reading, so I asked him to answer it, and I went out to the storeroom.

We really needed an emergency shelf. I hoped what I was doing was O.K. Maybe I could ask Royal if the church would donate some food, then we could keep it on hand for times like this. There was a can of corned beef and lots of dried milk. Finally, I got together a few things that might stretch oatmeal and flour.

I went back, let Conner go to lunch, and Mary brought

me a heaping plate. I asked her to have Butch pick up the box before he left with Mrs. Nemmers.

Royal didn't get back until after they'd gone. I told her about the morning.

"My God, Anne, you didn't send her with Butch?"

"Why not? What's wrong with him? He wouldn't..."

"No, no, Butch is marvelous, but he's the worst driver I've ever seen. He's nearly driven into me twice when I've been coming into the parking lot. He just goes—without looking."

"Oh, Royal. Here I am trying to help, and I've probably murdered her."

She laughed at that. "They're most likely just fine. I think most of the seniors live a charmed life, at least when it comes to cars. But, Butch really shouldn't be driving. A lot of them shouldn't."

The phone rang and Royal sat making commiserating noises into it and horrible faces at it. She hung up and looked at me tragically. "I can't believe it. That woman."

"What's the matter?"

"My painting teacher. She was supposed to do the spring lessons. The class has already been announced in the bulletin and is nearly full. Now she tells me she has been so sick this winter, she thinks she'd better go to Europe right away to recuperate. Where am I going to find a teacher so last minute?"

"Tell me a little bit about the job."

"It's a paid position with a small salary that isn't covered by class fees."

"Well, look. Mrs. Nemmers' husband was an artist. Maybe she is, too, and could teach the class for you. Do you ever have seniors teach for you?"

"Of course, but it's more difficult when they're getting a

Social Security supplement."

"What do you mean?"

"If they earn much money while on supplemental, they aren't eligible and would probably lose their Medicaid. Then it may take quite a while to get started again when the class is over. It's really not worth it."

"Fudge."

"However, if she could teach, sometimes I can arrange it. Shall I ask her?"

"Please do, Royal. And if she can't, she worked at alterations and might be able to teach a sewing class. Besides, if you can't find anyone else, maybe I could do it for you."

"Heavens, are you a painter, Anne?"

"Strictly amateur, but I've taken lessons for years. I could do a beginner's class. I've done them for Scout troops."

"Marvelous. I'd rather have you than Mrs. Nemmers, who I don't know. Let's settle it now."

"Please, no, Royal. If Mrs. Nemmers can, and you like her, let her. She's flat broke."

"All right, but at least I won't have to cancel the class. Can you teach anything else? Knitting, any crafts?"

"'Fraid not. Can't knit, can barely crochet. All my other talents seem to be things like vacuuming, weeding, and such. I've done some cooking demonstrations for kids, but I don't suppose you'd want that."

"We might think about it later. Maybe you could bake bread or make cookies some time. If they get to eat the results, they might like it."

She got back to work and I called John. I summarized the work and sadly told him I thought I needed to work only the three days from now on.

"Tell you what. Work every day next week. Make sure the record system is working, then bring everything in to me on Wednesday, and we'll go over it. I want to make sure it's all set up and that our records are complete."

"All right. Oh, one problem. It's still the milk." I told him the latest mix up.

He groaned. "Why does there always have to be some kind of snafu? O.K., make a memo that itemizes everything that has happened, please. Then if it isn't straightened out tomorrow, write a letter for me to sign detailing the problems."

I couldn't see what good that would do, but agreed. "By the way, John, do you know anyone who wants a case of Scotch?"

"Scotch? You want to sell some Scotch?"

"Not me. A lady who was in today is nearly broke. She's had a case of her husband's Scotch for eight years or so and would like to sell it."

"What brand? And how much does she want?"

"I don't know. I think it's probably an off brand. I don't suppose she knows what it's worth."

"Well, I'll pass the word around. Let me know if you get any details."

"Keep in touch. I hope Jonah's finally got the milk order straightened out."

Just as I hung up, a voice behind me said, "The lady with the Scotch, is she the dame Butch took up to town?" I jumped, and the voice cackled. How long had Tiny been there?

I snapped, "Yes!" and he turned and disappeared out the door. I hoped he didn't start hanging around a lot.

I stopped at the liquor store on the way and priced Scotch, then looked at Terry's bottle. We had Ballentine's.

I fixed a sandwich and took my hair rinse into the bathroom. The dye smelled awful, and I felt like a fool while I wandered around with that plastic scarf on my head while the stuff aged, or whatever it did, for half an hour. Terry would have howled. I brushed my hair dry while I watched

T.V. I stared at myself in the mirror. It was a little hard to tell how much good the rinse did. Guess the color was a little more like it had been when I was thirty, say. My face sure wasn't.

I lay in bed thinking about Mrs. Nemmers. God, I was lucky. I turned and looked at Terry's pillow. Thank God he had done all the things like wills and insurance that he had done. It was horrible of me to be so angry at him because he'd died.

❧ CHAPTER NINE ❧

On Friday morning, I kept checking the back door for the milkman. At ten to ten, I went out and stood waiting for him. At ten sharp he drove up, and I barred his way until I'd counted twenty containers of milk and made sure they were a l l 2%. "It's about time. What on earth happened yesterday?"

He said, "Mrs. Farley?"

I nodded.

"I'm Tim Jonah."

"You're not the driver too, are you?"

"No, your driver's sick. Also several others are out with the flu, so I'm covering a double route. Sorry you can't yell at your driver." He carried the milk in for me. "I should rush, but can I get a cup of coffee and take a short break?"

We put the milk away and I poured him a cup of coffee while Mary got out a cookie. Tim went in and kibitzed a pinochle game while he had his coffee.

Both Mary and Rose were working in the kitchen.

"Mary, you haven't put yourself down to work again, have you?" I asked.

"Why not, Anne? I've got nothing else to do. It'll help having at least one person each time who knows what's what. I like working in the kitchen. Food's food, you know where you are. Long as I don't have to keep records and count money, I'll do this every day."

"Well, great, but don't feel you have to if something else comes up. I feel sort of guilty," I admitted. "I'd thought I'd be in the kitchen, but I seem to have all I can do in the office. I don't mind the records, but I'd like to find someone better than I am at making change."

"Why don't you ask Brenda? She used to cashier at the A&P."

"Which one is Brenda?"

"She's not here yet. Usually comes by bus about 11:00. I'll send her to see you if you like."

"That would be great, thanks, Mary."

When I got back to the office, Royal said, "Shut the door, Anne. I need some privacy to get the calendar ready for Lillian to type this afternoon. Agnes is going to sit outside and answer the phone and keep people out.

"Now, about the painting class. I talked to Janet Nemmers. She can't teach painting, but offered to do a wood carving class. I've been thinking about that for some time. It should attract the men. They're so hard to find classes for. I'll announce it in the bulletin and we can start it on the first of May. But what I want to know is, can I list you as the teacher of the painting class? It meets Tuesdays at 10:00."

Feeling horribly embarrassed, I queried, "Royal, would I get paid for it? I mean, I really want to help, but, well, I won't be working Tuesdays after next week. I'd have the driving and equipment, and..."

"Certainly you'd be paid. The class goes to noon so it would be $20.00 for two hours?"

"That's fine. It's just that it sort of seems to take money to work, and I keep coming up short. So if it didn't pay, I thought I should take the time to work in the garden and stuff like that. It's not that I don't want to help..."

"Nonsense. There's no reason to be hesitant about asking to be paid. Women aren't business-like enough. They have to learn to expect their rights. I'm sorry your salary isn't larger."

I murmured negatives and said how it helped.

"That's not the point. If that twerp had only asked for more salary and more time, you could be my official assistant. Why the City won't fund the position is beyond me. How can they expect one person to do this job the way it should be done?"

My curiosity got the better of me. "Royal, please, who is this twerp, this Bertram? What does he have to do with my job and why does everyone get furious when they talk about him?"

"Didn't I tell you Anne? Good heavens. Well, last summer this smooth-talking college kid comes in and volunteers to help mornings for the summer. He was a junior in Social Work at the U, and he really seemed sincere and had lots of good ideas. John talked to him too, and we agreed he could come. We always need more help. There's so much that could be done if we had the people and the money. There are hundreds of old people who never come to the Center because many of them can't, and we should be reaching out to them too. But that's digressing.

"About Bertram, he was a pretty good worker. He took over the trips for me. Remind me to tell you about the man he lost on the battleship *Missouri* sometime. He played the piano and was nice to everyone. I let him do the 4th of July celebration and he did a bang up job. Skits and a cookie bake. We made $50.00.

"I really had no complains, except he kept wanting to know why we didn't do this, that, and the other thing. I got tired of telling him we didn't have the money. He was obsessed about the seniors not getting enough to eat. I think it was because he loved to eat himself. Probably every woman in here who still cooks baked him cookies. You'll have to taste Willie's.

"Anyway, he didn't seem to understand that I felt I couldn't tie the building up for so many hours for lunches. During the lunch program, Anne, we can't use the room for anything else.

I vaguely felt guilty, as if I were preventing some people from using the place.

She went on, "Thank God we talked a lot about implementing programs slowly, starting small and then enlarging once we saw how it worked and fit in."

"But what did he do?"

"That boy! He never said a word. But he was taking a grant writing class in the afternoons, and used us as his term project."

Light broke.

"He wrote a grant asking for a nutrition program for us. Mind you, I knew he was really interested in our getting meals, but I know the City will never pick the program up when the grant runs out, and I think it's criminal to get people used to things and then snatch them away."

I froze. "How long is the program for, Royal?" I hadn't realized there was a time limit.

"It's three years. It would be an excellent idea if you looked into it so that we could make plans to get the program renewed and refunded if possible."

I nodded. That could turn it into a real job. *How do you find out about stuff like that?* "How did he finally get the money?"

"That's just it. He didn't. We did. What he did was write up a grant *proposal*. I gather he got an A for it too. One of the requirements of the course was that they had to make an actual *application*. Like I said, he never said a word to me.

"Then when the summer term was over, he said goodbye. We had a special potluck for him, and we never heard from him again.

"In the fall, I got this official letter. We'd been awarded a grant to start a nutrition program for seniors three days a week. I couldn't believe it. I took it over to John right away. They also sent a document about the grant provisions, about a hundred pages. John worked on it for nearly a month trying to understand the whole thing. We had to send it to the City Attorney and, of course, the City Council. They voted it in with no trouble as soon as they realized it wouldn't cost the City any money. I'm always so busy, so I couldn't pull it together and John was really getting worried—when you showed up." She looked at her watch. "Lord, look at the time. I've got to get busy."

I made a note to get the complete nutrition document out and take it home to read. Maybe I'd have to take a grant writing class also if it were going to need renewing.

Royal muttered to herself for a while then said, "If you'll just write a brief blurb about the painting class, this planning thing will be finished."

I looked at my watch. I'd have to be taking money in fifteen minutes. I shoved a piece of paper in the typewriter and felt my brains die. Something light and brief. "Come paint with Anne." Bah. "BEGINNING PAINTING—Learn to paint. Tuesdays at 10:00 am. The class will include techniques and use of color, perspective, sketching, and still life. At the end of the term, there will be a field trip to a local art museum."

I dropped it on Royals desk and grabbed the money. Royal crossed out BEGINNING and put it in her folder. What in God's name would I do if I got some advanced painters? Grandma Moses probably. It would be just my luck. And I'd try to show her how to fix up her perspective. Yeah! I took my money out. The table was set up for me again. A slender woman with big gray eyes was waiting for me.

"I'm Brenda. Mary said you'd like me to take the lunch money and I'd like to do it. Want me to start today?"

"Thank you. I'd love to have you take the money, but I think we should wait for you to start the end of next week.

Royal wants me to get to know more people." I had a thought. "Wait, I know. If you don't mind, why don't you take the money, and I'll take the names? That'll save me from fouling up the money, and I can still learn names." We pulled up another chair and started in.

Barbara was third in line.

She looked at me and said firmly, "My name is on top of the second page."

I'd learned my lesson and said, "I remember," and turned the page, put my hand over the top name, and pretended to write, "paid" by it.

She smiled and walked into the dining room. I found her on my alphabetized list and marked paid.

Butch and Janet Nemmers came in together. He bought both of their tickets. Hmmm.

Janet mentioned she was pleased with the idea of teaching a wood carving class. Butch said he thought he'd take the class and they went over to the pool table.

We got everyone in line signed up, and I watched Janet and Butch at the pool table. He was showing her how to play. Then Brenda and I visited.

Brenda told me she'd been a widow for ten years. I was amazed when she said she was seventy. She looked maybe fifty. She had a son who lived south of town, and I gathered she spent a lot of time with his family. We got to talking about how you manage until you can get Social Security. She'd worked at the grocery store until she was sixty-five, then she began drawing on her husband's Social Security.

It sounded as if she were better off than many of the women at the Center I'd talked to. I asked her if she'd missed not working.

"Not really, Anne. Oh, I missed the women I'd worked with, but I was so glad not to be on my feet all day. The last two years I thought I'd die some days, they hurt so, and still

I'd have to smile and be nice all the time. Some of the people were really awful.

"Take the man who used to come with his cart loaded high, and then he'd yell at me to hurry and tell me to jump to it. Then when I'd get it all added up, he'd say he'd forgot something and go off to get a six-pack or some wine, leaving me with his bill on the cash register and not able to take the other people in line until he paid. When my feet would feel like boils, I'd want to throw his beer at him and just go home."

She stuck out a slim foot in low-heeled oxfords. The shoe looked deformed by a large bunion by her big toe. "It still hurts, but I can stay off it now."

"Shouldn't you have it operated on or something? What do they do for bunions?"

"I talked to the doctor when he came for foot care and he sent me to a surgeon. He said I should probably have it taken care of. But I couldn't pay for it. It requires a stay in the hospital.

"But you have Medicare, don't you?"

"Of course, but I couldn't keep up with my Blue Cross, and Medicare only covers 80% of the bills, and usually the doctor charges much more than Medicare will pay."

"What do you mean? I thought Medicare covered everything."

"Oh, no. It only covers 80% of what they call *allowed* costs. Most doctors charge way more than that, and we have to pay that, as well as the 20%. Then the hospital bills are so high, that even 20% is a lot of you have to say for more than a day or two. The doctor thought I'd be in for several days, and I'd need some time in a rehabilitation center."

"I had no idea. I was sure all medical bills were covered, at least all the hospital costs."

"Don't you believe it. If you've got medical insurance now,

make sure it's the kind you can keep when you retire, and do anything, go hungry, rob a bank—but keep it."

"What in God's name do the people do who get that, what do you call it, supplemental?"

"Don't swear, Anne, it isn't very nice."

I could feel myself blushing. "I beg your pardon."

"People with supplemental have Medicaid."

We took money from two more women who'd just come in.

"The government gives that to people on welfare. It pays for everything, but the rules are real complicated, and lots of doctors won't take Medicaid patients."

My head was swimming. I'd have to ask Royal more about it. Just then, Zeke came in. Thank God Tiny wasn't with him. He came up, smiled at both of us, and produced a dollar twenty-five. I knew he wasn't on the list, but made a pretense of looking.

"Zeke, you didn't sign up for lunch. You have to sign up so I'll know how many meals to order."

He nodded and just stood there.

"Please, Zeke, you need to sign up for lunch. Would you like to eat here on Monday?"

"I really don't know, Mrs. Farley. I have no idea what might come up."

I sighed and wrote his name on Monday's list. "Now remember, I can't guarantee a meal unless you sign up. However, I'm sure we'll have room today. I'll let you know by noon."

He smiled even more sweetly, put down his money, and went into the dining room. Hell and damnation. How much did he understand? Should I or should I not see whether or not he'd leave the dining room?

Brenda smiled at me and said she'd get him. How I wished I knew what to do that quickly. About a minute later she was back, Zeke in tow, still smiling. She took him over to the pool table and he began to mark for Janet and Butch. When Brenda came back, I said, "How'd you get him out?"

"I told him he couldn't go in 'til noon when he hadn't signed up."

"But I told him the same thing, sort of."

"I know, but he's used to me. I just took him by the hand and led him out."

"What's with him? Can't he hear?"

"It's not his hearing. I don't know what it is. It's more like he doesn't pay any attention. He used to be the principal of the high school in Ellis. His wife died the very day he retired, and he's been getting quieter and quieter ever since. He's really nice though and everyone likes him and sort of looks out for him."

"Like Tiny?"

She laughed. "Well, not exactly, but Tiny's good to him."

"It's a good thing he's good to someone." *Oh just shut up, Anne. Don't start any gossip. You'd better adore everyone here.*

We got busy again. Pretty soon there were fifty seniors signed in, and then fifty-three.

Brenda went to the kitchen and told Mary. When she came back, she said Mary had it under control and was going to set up five extra spots.

I started to close shop at 12:00, but three women came in. The end of the week seemed to be catching up with me. I didn't even want to try and explain why we had room for two, not three, and why they needed to sign up early. I looked at Brenda and got smart. "Will you handle it? I'll go help put one more plate on. O.K.?"

Brenda was smiling as I escaped to the kitchen. I told Mary we had fifty-six for lunch and that I'd put out one more place while she handled the serving.

I'd gotten out a plate and silverware when Hilda came over and took them from me. She already had a place mat ready.

No good trying to tell her I really was capable of setting the table for one more.

I stood around and then I saw Zeke sitting by the pool table. He smiled sadly at me. My God, I'd forgotten him. I went over and said, "I'm sorry I was so long. Come on, I'll show you your place."

Luckily, I found the only empty spot easily. I left Emma passing him a filled plate and Phil getting him coffee. I wondered how long he would have sat there if I hadn't seen him.

Royal took her calendar over to City Hall as soon as I took the money into the office.

About one o'clock, I came to and realized I'd skipped lunch. I got a roll and a couple spoonfuls of salad. Mary fussed, but I convinced her it was plenty.

The phone was ringing when I got back. It was John.

"Anne, I have two tickets to dinner tonight. A political thing that I have to go to each year. My sister was going to go with me, but her daughter's school called her this morning. Her kid fell off the parallel bars and is at the hospital, so Gena can't go."

"I'm sorry. Is she, your niece, seriously injured?"

"I don't think so, but Gena wants to stay there until all the test results are in, and the kid is pretty shook up, of course."

"Of course."

"What I've been wondering is, would you like to go with me tonight? The dinner will be pretty good, and the speeches don't go on too long. They've got a good orchestra. Maybe we could get in a couple of dances."

"Why, I guess, I mean, it sounds very nice."

"Could I pick you up about seven? It's formal, long dress. Is that OK?"

"Yes, of course." There wouldn't be time to stop and get my hair done, but I could get dressed and get a dip made should he come in for a drink. "I'll be ready at seven."

"Great! Thank you. I hate going alone. Now, Royal and I'll be over in half an hour. The reporter is going to stop here first. Is everything ready?"

I told him I was, but how do you get ready to talk to a reporter when you haven't the faintest idea what they'll ask or what you should say? Still, I felt better about it, and it was nice to have a full evening to look forward to. I got out a sheet of paper and scribbled some notes about low-income, continued need for nutrition, and effects of loneliness on eating. Maybe I wouldn't go totally blank.

Plato came in. "I'll stay in the office, Anne, until your interview is over. Maybe you better go get some extra makeup on. With the lights in here, the camera will wash you out."

"Thanks." How did she know a reporter was coming? The CIA could take lessons from this bunch. I took my purse and went into the restroom. A God-awful place—cement floor, peeling gray walls, pipes, and old, old stains. I'd never been one to lug a lot of makeup around, so there wasn't much I could do. I combed my hair and put on lipstick. Brenda came in and watched.

"You should use some mascara and blush for the pictures."

"I don't have any with me. How did you know about the newspaper?"

"I think Rose told me. Why? Is it a secret?"

"Oh, of course, not. I just wondered. This place has the most effective grapevine."

"I don't know. I hadn't thought about it. Now, wait a minute, I've got an idea." She dashed out and came back with Mary, Janet, and Emma.

Mary said, "I've got a lot of makeup samples, Anne. I used to sell Avon, and I brought all my unused stuff down here for Bingo prizes. You pick out what you want."

She dumped a sack full of makeup on the counter and

they all began sorting and urging all sorts of wild colors on me. Janet took charge. She picked out mascara, eye shadow, blush, and foundation. She was holding out a second eye shadow color when I stopped her. "I'll never wear all that." She argued, but I wouldn't try it, though she put it in my pile. They all watched and criticized as I applied the makeup.

"Now, put it in your desk, Anne, so you'll have it when you need it."

Once I made sure the makeup really wasn't needed as Bingo prizes, I picked out some duplicates for my purse. Maybe I'd experiment a little bit tonight.

The interview was O.K., awful, and funny. The reporter turned out to be a woman about my Liz's age, very brisk and efficient. We sat on the couch while she questioned me. She asked about my background, and I talked about the Scouts and 4-H.

She took a few notes, and John came in with an explanation of the City's need for someone to organize the nutrition program. I thought he was probably making a pitch for funding for the Center. Then she asked me why I thought we needed a nutrition program, and I told her about the small amount of money so many had to live on, and perhaps even more important, that so many hated eating by themselves and practically didn't eat, because they were so tired of being alone.

I told her we'd discovered that some of the women almost existed on tea and toast except for meals at the Center. Then, she surprised me and asked what plans there were to improve the program. I looked to Royal for rescue, but she kept quiet. I took a big breath, rubbed my ear, which felt on fire, and said, "This program will have to be evaluated in terms of cost and its effect on the overall schedule. Then, after seeking the seniors' advice, we may try holding lunches five days a week." She kept looking at me, so I had to go on. "There are many other ways to improve the program, but we want to go in to them slowly."

She asked, "Such as?"

"Breakfasts, some dinners, weekend meals. Then, I'd like to see some real nutrition education and perhaps cooking lessons."

"Would you do the nutrition education?"

"I'd like to do some very simple things, more in line of displays. However, I'm not qualified to do real nutrition work. We'd have to find a professional." There was some more chitchat and then she started to take a few pictures.

All of a sudden, Helen stalked in. She was tearing pages out of a magazine. She'd tear a page out, set it in front of her, step on it, and tear out another and step on that. After every two or three pages, she'd let out a loud moan. We all sat there with our mouths open.

Royal and I got up together. I was thinking about trying to get her into the kitchen, perhaps getting her something to eat, but our movement caught her eye, and she spotted John. She let out three hair-raising shrieks, threw her magazine clear across the room at him, and ran for the back room. Going out the back door, she slammed it so hard I thought it would fall apart.

John and Royal hurried the reporter out the front door. They weren't gone two minutes when Helen came back, peering through the back door before she came in. This time she was quiet and stayed in the dining room. I found a roll and the last carton of milk, but she acted like I wasn't there. She went over and turned on the dance lights, curled up, and stared as they blinked.

God, I felt cold and scared. I went in and got an afghan Mary had crocheted for Bill's favorite chair and put it over her. She didn't move. Helpless, I went back toward the office.

Hilda looked up from her cards and said she'd watch Helen and send her home pretty soon. When I left at five, Helen was gone.

I stopped on the way home and got some cream cheese

and chips. I mixed up a clam dip as soon as I got to the house, turned on lights, and did a fast pickup. I took a shower and re-did my face. I even tried a shadow under my chin. I couldn't see it helped any, but it didn't look dirty or obvious so I left it. The phone rang. I grabbed a robe and answered it. It was Mom.

"Did you just get home, Anne? I tried calling you a little while ago."

"I was probably in the shower. How goes it?" I tried to see the clock. There should be plenty of time, but I'd most likely have to press my dress.

"Fine. I went to town with Olga and Sal. I bought some new towels. What I wanted was to ask, why don't you come over and have dinner with me and spend the night? I've got a good pork roast nearly done."

"Sounds nice, but I'm going out to dinner. Maybe I could come over for breakfast waffles in the morning?"

"That would be fine, dear. Who are you having dinner with?"

I realized I didn't want to tell her. She'd been very fond of Terry, and it wasn't a real date. It was a funny feeling. I'd not gone out with anyone but Terry, nor had I not told Mom what I was up to, for over twenty-five years. "It's a political thing, Mom. Dinner and speeches."

"Well, don't get too bored. I'll see you early tomorrow. OK?"

"Fine, thanks. I love your waffles."

I'd put on my bra and panties while talking to her, so I slid into my dress to see if I really had to press it. My God. I hadn't realized I'd lost all that much weight. It looked awful. Hell and damnation. Now what? And of course the phone rang again.

This time it was Jo.

"Hi, Anne. I saw your lights go on. How about coming

over for dinner and then we'll go to a movie?"

"Oh, Jo, I can't tonight. I'm going out for dinner. Tomorrow night instead?"

She sounded let down. "I'll have to see. Greg's out of town but he might be back tomorrow. I'll call you.'

I said I was sorry and that I had to rush. I skimmed out of my dress and started going through my closet. If that dress was too loose, both the others would be even worse. I'd never needed many long dresses. In despair, I heard the phone ring again. Shit! The clock said 6:30.

This time it was the minister's wife, Mrs. Macintosh. It seemed they were having a meeting at the church Sunday, on aging, and since they'd heard about my job, could I come? I accepted so fast she must have been amazed, and I hung up while she said thank you. Where did I get this compulsion to answer phones? How come I had all these offers to go out now, when I'd been home alone every night for what seemed like a thousand years?

In desperation, I went in and rummaged through Elizabeth's closet. Yep, there was the green peau de soie skirt she'd made in 4H. She'd been skinny then. Thank heaven, it fit. Maybe a little tight...no, not really. I ran back to my room and pulled out the lacy silver sweater Terry had brought me from New York. I had worn it only once. Wow, they looked great together. I added my jade pendant, took off the blue eye shadow, and replaced it with silvery green. The doorbell rang.

Seven o'clock straight up, and it was John. He came in and refused a drink, but said he'd like coffee. He followed me into the kitchen, so I gave him the dip and put the coffee on. While it perked, I excused myself and found my evening bag. That left the coat problem. Nobody wore capes anymore and my leather coat wouldn't do with the satin. Finally I took the lovely shawl Mom had crocheted for me. It would look fine, even though I'd freeze.

John had poured both of us some coffee and had made inroads on the dip. I smiled brightly at him and said I was all ready. He chatted about the reporter's reaction to Helen while we finished the coffee. I turned off the lights and led the way to the front door.

With a really funny look on his face, he looked down and said, "Uh, are you going to put on some shoes?"

I died.

❧ CHAPTER TEN ❧

After I put on my sandals, we got in his car and headed for the hotel in town. I was still so embarrassed, I didn't even worry over whether I should stand around while he opened the door for me, or be independent and open it for myself. I just go in.

The trip wasn't too strained. John told me about the reporter's questions about Helen. After she was over being scared by the scene, she'd scented a story. John said, "I had a hell of a time persuading her a story would only cause trouble all around and not help Helen."

"I don't really know anything about Helen. Shouldn't she be in a hospital?"

"As long as she doesn't hurt anyone, or herself, and can manage to get herself fed and sheltered, there isn't much anyone can do legally, though she's been hospitalized briefly dozens of times. She comes back a little better, but soon she's out of it again.

"Most of the seniors don't mind her coming in, though sometimes I have to go over and send her home. Whether it's that, or something else, she hates me. You saw how she acted today. In a way it's a help—I just have to appear and she leaves."

I didn't tell him about her coming back.

"Kind of hard on the ego, though."

"Do you suppose you sort of stand for someone, maybe in her past? I don't think it's you specifically that she reacts to, though perhaps being sent home every time she sees you doesn't help."

"I certainly upset her whenever she sees me. I was in the hardware store last year when she came in. I don't know what she had intended to do, but when she spotted me, she got out of sight until I forgot about her. Then she came up behind me and poured a whole bottle of floor polish over me. I was stunned. I just stood there while she poured, trying to figure out what was going on.

"When I finally ducked, she took the bottle up to the counter, told the clerk to send it, put three cents down, and left. I couldn't help laughing. The manager was going to call the police, but she'd been pretty straight for a while so I talked him out of it.

"Then, wouldn't you know, some blabbermouth called the paper. Barbara, the reporter before this one, came over. So there I was, the next day, on the front page. She captioned it, 'Mayor Gets Polish.'"

"How'd Barbara explain it?"

"She didn't bother very much. She called Helen an irate customer, and left it pretty vague whether she was mad at the store or the City. Buried in the last paragraph, she said the customer had a history of mental problems. Of course, every guy at City Hall dug at me for days.

"The problem was, Helen's outbreak was the start of her getting worse. She spent the next week causing hell all over town. She scared some school kids, and finally nailed her front door shut from the outside, then went berserk when she couldn't get in that evening. The police had to take her to the hospital."

"My God, that's awful. Have you seen her watch the dance lights?"

He nodded.

"It makes me feel helpless. Hilda does pretty well with her, though."

We got to the King Hotel and went up to the conference room. There was no reception line, so we wandered around. John introduced me to the party fundraiser and we shook hands with the congressman from our district. I'd met him once before at a coffee hour at the church. Then John left me by a palm tree and went to get us a drink.

I was happily clothes watching and feeling pretty good about my skirt and sweater, when Graham Pettijohn pushed through the crowd and came over to me. In typical fashion, he threw his arms around me, kissed both cheeks, and then stood holding my hands.

"Anne, darling, how nice to see you out again. How good you are looking." All the time he was busily sizing up the crowd, probably looking for his next victim.

"I've thought of you often and that sad day I last saw you."

Lord, yes, he'd been at the funeral. He'd kissed me then too and patted my hands for at least five minutes.

"Now that you've recovered somewhat, I'll call and take you to lunch." With that he took off, and probably found some other woman standing alone to shove a little cheer and bull her way.

John came back and gave me my drink. It was good. Weak and lots of ice. "You know Graham?" he asked.

"Sort of. Terry was on a finance committee with him once, and since then, Graham acts like our greatest friend whenever we run into him. I never see him between meetings, though he sends letters requesting donations every time he runs for something. Is he trying for some office again?"

"Not officially. I hear he's after the governor to make him head of a new citizen's advisory committee. Look, I've got to circulate. Let's go get our plates filled, and then we'll start making the rounds."

We went over to the buffet and filled our plates.

"John, you don't need me, and you'd have to introduce me every time you meet someone you wanted to talk to. I'm going back to my palm tree and enjoy the clothes. If Graham finds me again, I'll come over and latch onto your coat tails."

He grinned and started out. He was short enough I couldn't see him as he got into the crowd.

The food was delicious. I was finishing my plate and observing a pink chiffon gown on a dyed blonde when Terry's boss showed up.

"Anne, how nice to see you. I didn't believe it at first. Don't tell me you've gotten interested in politics. It used to bore you. My dear, I am glad to see you."

"Hi, Howard." It was good to see him. He'd always been a nice guy. "No, I'm still not very interested, but my boss had a ticket, and the dinner was worth the speeches."

"You're working?" Then a look of horror passed over his face. "Anne, you don't have to work. Surely? I was certain Terry left you well taken care of."

"It's OK, Howard. I don't have to work, though it helps, of course. It's part time and very interesting." I told him a little about the Center.

He looked relieved, but kept at it. "Anne, I feel like a perfect heel. I haven't checked on you like I should have. Are you through probate, do you need any help? Look, come to dinner tomorrow, and I'll go over everything with you."

"Thank you, Howard, but it isn't necessary. As soon as I see the accountant about the income tax, I'll be completely straight. Anyway, I'm busy tomorrow, and Lala would hate us both, springing a dinner guest on her suddenly. How is she? Is she here tonight?"

"No, she's down at our oldest girl's. You remember Laura?"

I nodded.

"Lala wouldn't have minded about dinner, not for you. Sure you can't make it? I'll buy you a steak."

I shook my head. Bet they'd had another fight.

Lala took off on a "visit" about three times a year. We'd probably had Howard alone for dinner at least ten times as often as the two of them. He hated eating by himself. Still, I wasn't going to face a quiz on the way I'd handled the estate. As long as the company stock kept paying dividends, that was all the mixing business I wanted.

An orchestra began playing in a corner and Howard asked me to dance. We'd danced before and did well together. Thankfully, they were playing nice mellow tunes, no rock. After two numbers I insisted he take me back to my palm.

I had plans to make another go around of the buffet table, but John came back and asked me to dance. Unfortunately, he wasn't a very good dancer, or maybe we just had different styles, but I couldn't follow him. We'd go along for a couple of patterns, I'd relax, and he'd throw in an extra step. I'd hop to catch up and step on his toes. "Sorry."

"No, no, my fault." We stuck it out to the end of the dance and both said, "How about some more supper?"

I giggled. "Love to. The pate's fabulous."

We filled our plates again. I concentrated on the pate and salad. John picked roast beef, chicken, and the smoked salmon, and we snagged one of the little tables they'd scattered around.

I was sorry when everyone began to drift into the auditorium for the speeches. I'd have liked to dance some more, even with John. Maybe I'd figure out his system.

Howard got a seat beside us, so I had to introduce him to John. He immediately quizzed John about my job. I was thankful the speeches started before he could play the Godfather too much.

I didn't really know what the speeches were about. Lots of

big words and clichés that didn't seem to add up to anything. I perked up when our junior senator spoke about the elderly, but it was the usual about helping those on fixed income, nothing concrete, but it did start me thinking.

Under the cover of the applause and change of speakers, I turned and got Howard's attention. "Howard, does the company still give those seminars, specifically the one on grant writing?"

"Yes. A new one just started. Why?"

"They are open to families, aren't they? Would that include me?"

"I could fix that. You want to know about grant writing?"

"I think so. The program I'm on is financed by a grant. Royal, my boss, said I should be thinking about its renewal."

"Well, I don't know, Anne." The senior senator was beginning his speech. "Let me call you tomorrow. I'm afraid our series is too specific and wouldn't help you much."

Hell, so much for trying to get a freebie. I settled back to daydreaming.

John looked like he was listening and enjoying it, so I shook myself and tried to listen, but damned if I could tell whether the senator was saying anything. Still, like John had promised, it was short and over by eleven.

Howard got surrounded so I didn't have to talk to him, though I did get trapped and kissed by Graham, *again*. He and John shook hands, and I noticed Graham massaging his. Evidently John hadn't used the politician's usual grip, or lack of it.

The trip home was pleasant. John turned on the radio, and we drove back to a series of show tunes. He had the heater on so I wasn't cold, but I was tired. I think I understood a little better why Terry always preferred to collapse Friday nights. I wondered where John got all his energy.

I turned down a drink at the Inn, but when John admitted he was still hungry—how could he be?—I said I'd always take a cup of coffee, and we went into the Egyptian. He ordered a double burger, but I insisted coffee was all I could manage.

John must be a night person, because he really began to talk. He told me all about the sewer system planned for the northwest area of town. The waitress knew John and brought us a bowl of nibbles, and we finished them all. I was amazed, but he made sewers interesting. Who'd ever imagine so much was involved?

While we were having our second cup of coffee, I saw Plato. She was at the bar and had what looked like a double bourbon in front of her. God, she looked sick.

"John, look. It's Agnes. She's drinking again."

I'd interrupted him, but he picked her out. "I don't think we can do anything."

"Do you think she'd go home if we offered her a lift?"

"I doubt it, but do you. Want to give it a try?"

I nodded, so embarrassed I nearly cried.

John paid our bill and we went over to her. I realized she had seen us, and she looked as though she hated us.

"Agnes, we are on our way home. Would you like a ride?"

She shook her head no, gripping the bar with both hands.

"Please, you should."

"Go away, Anne."

John put an arm around my shoulders and started me out. I wiped my eyes with the shawl and got into the car.

He asked, "Are you OK?"

"Of course, but it makes me so mad I could bawl. She's really great, you know. I feel so helpless. My friend's husband is drinking too. He's ruining his marriage and himself."

We were at the house. I got out of the car and murmured, "Thanks," and ran in.

John waited until I'd gotten the door unlocked before

he drove off.

I washed my face, threw my clothes on the chair, and set the clock for eight. The bed felt so good, cold though. Maybe I should get an electric blanket or mattress pad.

❧ CHAPTER ELEVEN ❦

The radio music evidently hadn't made much of an impression on me, but the alarm scared me awake. Why couldn't someone design a good-sounding one? It should start off soft and get progressively louder, but still sound good. Lord, I'd slept cold. I felt stiff, like I hadn't moved all night. I put last night's coffee on to heat, started the dishwasher, and threw a load of clothes in the washer. I took my coffee into the tub. I could spend twenty minutes soaking and still make it to Mom's by nine. I dropped some of my good smelling bath oil in the water.

The water was still running when I woke up enough to think. The bathroom was cold. We kept the bedroom cold, so I hadn't really thought about it. I shut the water off. Hell and damnation, the kitchen had been icy too. I put my robe back on. The thermostat was on 60 as usual, but the thermometer read 48. When I looked out, there was frost all over. I went and checked the furnace. Dead silence. I'd gotten the card last month when the oil company had filled the tank, so I should have had plenty.

Now what? I finally found the start button and punched it several times. Nothing doing. Well, first things first. I went back, got in the tub, and luxuriated for ten minutes. When I got out, I put on wool slacks, a shirt, and Terry's ski sweater, then called the furnace company. They said they'd send a man out Monday.

After a long argument and my absolute refusal to stay

home from work all day, we finally agreed the repairman was to call me at work, and I'd give them the address of the neighbor who'd let them in. I slammed down the receiver. God help me, I'd probably have to spend all afternoon trying to find someone who'd be home Monday.

I was ten minutes late to Mom's, and she didn't think I should be running around in Terry's old clothes, sans makeup. Last year Mom had finally quit wearing a hat and gloves whenever she went to town. But her hot fresh coffee cheered me up, and I made her laugh when I imitated the furnace man. Still, I shouldn't have told her about the furnace. I finally convinced her I wouldn't freeze to death if I went home instead of spending the weekend with her, when I let her convince me she wouldn't freeze to death if she stayed at the house Monday and waited for the repairman.

While we ate waffles, I told her all about the food at the buffet and running into Howard. I kept going around and around in my mind. Mom was in her late seventies. Surely it wasn't right that she still did all the stuff for me she did. I should be taking care of her, but except for doing her income tax and driving her to the airport for one of her jaunts, it was all the other way around.

I must have still been tired, but it made me feel good, and yet guilty, to know she'd be at the house all day Monday. She would probably do a million things I never got to, except in emergencies, like ironing napkins, cleaning the silver, and getting the crumbs out of the toaster. Then she'd have dinner ready when I got home.

I shivered. What would it be like when I was suddenly the oldest and had no more Mother to depend on? She wouldn't let me do dishes of course, so I left at eleven. We weren't a demonstrative family, but I kissed her and told her I loved her when I left.

Howard called just as I got the fireplace lit. Yes, the

company course would be open to me, but he felt it wouldn't be of any help. However, with his usual thoroughness, he'd called his instructor and checked the two Community Colleges for suitable classes, and had all the information on time and place. From his insistence that the class at Central was the one for me, I decided it was the bonehead one and told him I'd let him know if I decided to take it

"You do that, Anne. Now if you do take it, I want you to then consider signing up for the company course. If you complete that one, I think we could see if there isn't a spot here for you. If you're going to work, you should have a real job."

I thanked him, of course, and repeated again I wasn't free to have dinner. I hung up and sat by the fire. Lots of mixed feelings were running through my head. A full time job? The secretaries at the company got good wages, insurance, pensions, the whole bit. Why would they consider me? Sure, Howard always liked me, but he'd always acted like I was a lightweight piece of fluff.

Did having a job and talking about wanting specific schooling for a specific reason make him see me as someone— my mind was all muddled—as someone who might be a prospective employee? Nuts, it was just the Godfather bit. He'd always been as paternal as hell to the whole staff and their families. Still, it really was my job that had set him off in that particular direction. Or maybe Lala had been gone for more than a few days and he was beginning to get a little hungry for more than a dinner partner, that is.

I threw another log onto the fire and turned to toast my other side. I'd heard rumors about him and the treasurer's wife. Not from Terry, God forbid, but the other wives talked. I shook myself. One date, and I had begun to imagine things.

I was no sexpot. Guys never even flirted with me. And, where'd Howard get off with his "real job" bit?

I accomplished a lot. I got the house in good shape and the ironing done. My feet nearly froze till I put on wool socks and boots. I fixed a big pot of stew and made a lot of progress with the weeding while it cooked.

I finally phoned Jo. She'd been crying, and said she couldn't have dinner. Greg wasn't back, but he wanted her to join him, so she was catching a 7 o'clock flight. I offered to take her to the airport, but she said she was going to leave her car there, as they'd be back Sunday or Monday. I told her to take care, and hung up.

Now what? She never went on those business trips. It was awful of me to be so suspicious, but Greg must be in trouble with his drinking in some way, and she had to go get him.

I tried not to think about it and went back to the fire, but I kept coming up with all sorts of lurid ideas. Greg in jail. Greg hitting the president of the company, or in the hospital. I finally decided I'd have to have my stew by the fire later. I was almost tempted to call Howard back, and ask if HE was still good for the steak, but knew that wasn't a good idea.

Before I was really feeling sorry for myself, Gwen called, and I dashed off and met her at the Burgermaster. We had super burgers and hot pie and then we went ice-skating— which I hadn't tried for years. I still skated on my ankles and fell twice before I learned to stop again.

Church the next day was great. First, I went to the adult Sunday school class at nine—their heat was on—and had coffee and donuts in the parish hall from 10:30 until 11:00. Then I went to the 11:00 service.

Feeling warm and virtuous, I met with the committee at 12:30, and more coffee and donuts. At first it sounded like they were on the senator's wavelength, all sweetness and light about doing something for the poor, dear older ones, but they didn't have any idea about what they wanted to do, or if anything was really needed.

I'd slunk down in my chair and was trying to be grateful I was warm, when I realized Reverend Johnson—the young assistant minister—was leading them somewhere. It was slow, but as people talked, he began to write ideas on the blackboard, and gradually they got more specific. First, he told us 30% of the church's membership was over 60, and 70% of that group were women. Of the men, 65% were retired.

Some needs seemed evident. There was a group, small but growing, who found it hard to get to church. There was a larger group who wanted something to do. The church needed lots of help, and Reverend Johnson asked for suggestions for how to get them together.

Mrs. Johnson muttered an aside, "If anyone suggests quilts, or arranging flowers for the service, I'll kill them."

"Not very pastor's wife-ish. I pretended I hadn't heard. I wondered what experience brought that on. Sure enough, one woman suggested a quilting party. Mrs. Johnson didn't kill her, but I got brave enough to talk.

"One of the things I've heard at the Senior Center is that Sunday afternoons are the hardest part of the week. They've been family time for most of us, and it becomes a bad time for people who are alone. Maybe our church could sponsor something, maybe not just for the church people, but for other seniors too."

Lots of talk, and then it worked out. Rev. Johnson asked me to tell them about the Senior Center, so I did. Mrs. Quilting Bee asked why the Center wasn't open on Sundays and why they couldn't have dinner there. I told them about the lack of funds for staff and even supplies. Gradually it all drew together.

By the time the meeting broke up, I was authorized to ask Royal if the Center could be opened on Sunday with the church supplying a volunteer staff. They would sponsor a potluck and even make a token donation of ten dollars to cover supplies.

In anticipation that we'd get permission, committees were formed, and Mrs. Grant accepted the position of volunteer coordinator. It turned out she'd been an occupational therapist, and it was obvious she knew what she was doing and would really get busy.

In my euphoria about our accomplishment, I shut the quilting bee lady up by thanking her for her idea, and told her I would see if we couldn't get quilting lessons started at the Center.

Thinking about the heat, I drove over to the Egyptian to eat. The coffee and donuts were sort of sloshing unhappily together. To my embarrassment, John was sitting at a booth at the back of the room.

While I was deciding that I'd better pretend not to have seen him, he waved and pointed to the seat beside him, so I went over and joined him. He didn't look especially thrilled to see me. In fact, I decided he looked a little like he had a hangover.

He said, "Hi, decide you like their coffee?

"So, so. I've been at a meeting at church and thought I'd better settle the coffee and donuts." The waitress came over and I ordered the Spanish omelet, a salad, and milk. "Besides, my furnace is off and I'm cadging places to keep warm." *Hell, he'll think I'm hinting.* "I'm going to go over to the library next, check out a dozen books, and read in that lovely spot they've fixed up next to the Franklin stove. Whoever dreamed that one up was a genius."

He nodded, but I hadn't diverted him. "What's wrong with the furnace?"

"It's a mystery to me. It won't' start. A service man's coming tomorrow." I went on to tell him about the oil company's refusal to set a time. Like my mom, he seemed amused and told me about his tribulations with the telephone people while I ate my omelet and he finished his piece of pie. Evidently being Mayor didn't pull much weight with servicemen. Without thinking, I said, "We both need a wife."

He scowled and said, "A husband for you and a wife for me?"

Oh, boy. Either he'd had his fill of women willing to be number two, or his ego was a little big. "No, no. A wife. Every working person needs a wife, or maybe even better, my mother."

He looked sort of bemused. "Surely you've heard the joke. The women's rights movement probably started it. This world isn't geared to the single working person. It's like trying to get service on nights or weekends. Shopping, fixing food, all that. The housewife has been working a twelve-hour day, seven days a week forever, but now, so is every person with a job." He leaned back and signaled for more coffee.

I managed to claim one, too. I thought he looked a little more relaxed.

"Yeah, guess so. It's daunting to realize I'm not the only one suffering over all these domestic things. It's been a bad weekend."

I nodded and hummed encouragingly.

"I like to work in the yard, but I knew I'd better tackle the dishes. Turned out I'd loaded the dishwasher earlier in the week but forgot to wash them. Had to scrub most of them by hand, so it took an hour to get them washed, and then I still had to load all the recent ones in. By the time I cleaned the counters, threw stuff away, and unloaded the dishes again, the whole morning was gone. Anyway, the condition of the kitchen made me realize the shape the whole house was in. I dithered the whole afternoon away with the vacuum and beds and such. Never got out in the yard, and it's a mess too. Then I had a meeting last night. Afterwards, we all went out for drinks and something to eat, so I got home late, slept in, and wasted this morning."

Uh, hung over. I'd been right.

"I figured I'd work in the yard this afternoon, but I gathered up a load of clothes first and put them in the washer. The damned machine overflowed—suds all over. I had to clean that up. The basement is cleaner than the kitchen, I mop it up so often, and the damned repairman can't find out what's wrong with the machine."

"How do you put the soap in?"

He couldn't seem to figure out how to answer me. He pantomimed sprinkling soap in and muttered, "Through the top, open the lid, you know."

"John, just like you gave me the grant to read, read your soap box. Read the machine's instructions. Never sprinkle, always measure. Use a measuring cup." For one brief satisfying moment, he stared at me as if I were a genius. I began to laugh. I couldn't help it. He kept on staring, but finally laughed too.

"Really? You mean there's nothing wrong with the machine? I've paid all those bills and had the water level device replaced because I've been using too much soap?"

"Probably. Try it." I put my coat on.

"Hey, wait a minute, Anne. Are you busy? The new bike trail is going to open next week and I'm going to walk this end of it today. Keep warm walking instead of lazing at the library. Have your fire too. I'm going to try out the fire pit where the trail crosses the river. The yard will have to wait."

Well, why not? If he'd been a woman, I'd have suggested my getting some of the stew and having that at the fire, but we'd had enough domesticity.

It was a lovely walk. The crushed rock path was dry and firm. Some of the trees were showing green, and even though it was gray, it didn't rain. It took us about an hour to reach the fire pit.

John told me about the history of the path. It seemed the original settler, named Dan, had surveyed this area, and the path followed the old road—one of the first improved ones in the county. It was even more interesting than sewers.

I thought of telling him about the church and their senior program, but figured I should talk to Royal first. I did ask him if there were any alcoholism programs in Danville. He knew about AA, but wasn't up on anything else except the Mental Health program. He said he'd look into it.

Lovely man. He'd brought marshmallows. I cut some sticks while he built a small fire. We had a nice time roasting them, though we didn't wait for good coals. I loved them all burned until the top layer was crunchy and pulled off so the next layer could be burned. I got five layers off my third one. John ate six.

It was definitely getting cooler as we walked back, so we went faster and didn't talk. He asked if I wanted to have dinner, but I told him I had to deal with my own washing. Not really the truth, but I was not going to let him start thinking I was chasing him. Besides, Terry always said mixing business and fun was dangerous. Come to think of it though, we'd always had to do a lot of company social things. He'd meant *singles*—man and woman stuff.

I went to bed early with two hot water bottles, wondering about John's mood. Just before I went to sleep, I had a glorious thought. His moodiness was none of my business. I didn't have to worry about any man's mysterious thought processes. Not anymore.

❧ CHAPTER TWELVE ❧

I was up and huddling over the fire, which wasn't burning very well, when the phone rang at seven. It was John. My first thought was that too much was too much, before I adjusted to the fact that he was my boss, and it was as a boss he was calling.

"Anne, John here. Royal just called me. She is sick—you're going to have to manage today. She gave me a list of things going on and her plans. I want to meet you at 8:00 with the key and go over the day with you."

I agreed, of course.

With lovely dreams of making a huge success of everything, I went into what Terry had called my blitz act and was at the Center parking lot by 7:45, dressed in a good pants suit, makeup on, dishes done, bed made, coffee pot on timer for Mom, note to Mom about the stew, and a tiny bouquet of crocus for my desk. John pulled into the parking lot right behind me and let me in.

I began to realize my dreams of a perfect day and my being the fair-haired heroine weren't going to come true when the lights wouldn't come on and the phone began to ring before we got the office door open. I dug the flashlight out of Royal's desk and gave it to John while I answered the phone. It was Mary. Her brother was sick, and she wouldn't be in to help with lunch. *Lord, why do you hate me?* She said

Hilda, Emma, and Serena were today's helpers. I promised I'd find someone to take her place and hung up the phone.

Of course it rang again immediately. It was some early bird at the DSHS this time. A man I'd never heard of had a lot of questions about Janet Nemmers' missing check. He seemed quite hurt I wasn't willing to have a long talk with him, but finally let me go when I promised to have Janet call him.

The phone was ringing again when John came back, looking disgusted, and still no lights were on. This call was for him. I recognized Lillian's voice. She sounded upset. All I heard from John's end was, "Oh no, oh no, hell. Not today. All right. I'll be in as soon as I get this mess going."

"Not sure I like being referred to as a mess," I murmured. "More problems?" I asked.

"The auditors are honoring us today."

I sat down. "They won't come over here, will they?" Somehow the look of horror on his face didn't seem very funny, but John began to laugh and sat down too.

"Has Royal got some skeletons buried?"

I shook my head. "I don't know a thing about her money system, but I've got a feeling that only Royal can explain it." I resolutely didn't look at the drawer with the fish envelope in it.

John reached for the phone. "Have you had coffee?"

I shook my head.

"Lillian, we've got an emergency here. Get a hold of maintenance. Tell them there's no power at the Center and they've got to be here a half-hour ago. And then call Sandie's and have her send over a pot of coffee and a couple of rolls. We're freezing. Explain the problem to the money guys. See if they don't want coffee or something. You can get them started on the books as well as I can if they are eager beavers."

My mind was whirling. No power, no lights, no heat, no coffee. The seniors would raise hell over no coffee and a fish lunch. My God! Lunch! How was I supposed to heat lunch? No power, no Mary. What had ever made me think I wanted to work?

John queried, "Come on, Anne. It's best I know what the catch is now, not when the auditors *are* here. I know some of Royal's methods, but which one has you in a tizzy?"

Feeling like a third grade tattletale, I said, "The fish envelope."

He nodded.

"A fishing derby envelope. We make change out of it. I don't know where it all came from, who's paid, or where any records are.

He nodded again.

"I'll never be able to explain any of it."

The front door banged open, a man yelled, "Coffee," and the door banged closed. At least someone was working. John went out and brought back a tray with coffee and rolls. They tasted great, though I was nervous about wasting time.

"No problem. If they come over, and if they see it and ask, just tell them you work on the nutrition program and they will have to ask Royal about it."

"Will they ask about my funds?"

"Probably. Though Lil has every day's receipts over at City Hall. Do you have any irregularities?"

"God forbid, not yet anyway." I crossed my fingers.

"Look, I'm sorry to leave you with the power out, but I've got to get back. Here's what Royal said had to be done today. Call Finnistere. Check on how they are coming on April's trip. Do you know about it at all?"

"They're going in to see the spring flowers at the Arboretum and then to a play on campus. Then they'll be shopping on the way back to the village."

He shook his head. "That trip would kill me. Anyway, check, make sure they are moving on it, get times and money, anything you can think of."

The phone rang.

John hissed, "Put it on hold."

Over a lady's protest, I put her on hold.

He handed me a list and hurried on. "Call the race track, find out when Senior Day is this year, and ask for fifty tickets. There's a birthday party this afternoon. Pick up the cake at 11:00 at Safeway. Plans are in a folder in her desk. There's a lady coming at 3:00. Talk to her. Royal will call her as soon as she's back to work. I think that's all. Call me or Lillian if you have any problems. I'll make sure the guys are right over about the lights." He was out the door, running.

Damn. I'd never get it done. I picked up the phone again.

The lady on hold was Mrs. Griffith. She was furious. I explained and explained. She was still furious. She had wanted to sign up for lunch and complained I had told her to sign up early and when she tried, I put her on hold so she couldn't. I couldn't shut her up or get her off the phone.

I finally sat down at Royal's desk and began going through a two-inch thick stack of papers as I listened to her rant. She was still going on, now about how the telephone company kept charging her for long distance calls to Chicago when they didn't know anyone in Chicago. I finally found the party folder. I said "Oh" or "I see" whenever she paused. I found I couldn't read the party folder while she talked. I slid the chair over to the files and got out several blank folders.

I had half the desk cleared off and folders made for the racetrack and the trip when Mrs. Griffith ran down. She'd talked herself out of being mad.

"Loved having a nice chat with you, Anne. See you at lunch, dear," she said, and finally got off the phone. I rubbed my ear and got my neck straightened out. I made my list from John's and added -*Janet* to it and -*get sub for Mary*.

The phone rang *again*. God, I needed Agnes. This time it was McCloud's. Talk about it never raining but pouring.

"Anne, we've got a problem." *You've got a problem? Ha!* "One of our vans is in the shop, and we just discovered the other was vandalized over the weekend. I've got the driver out trying to get wheels..."

"Wheels?"

"Yup, they took all four wheels. I'm sure we'll get on the road soon, but we're likely to be late."

"Oh, wonderful. I'm sorry. I don't mean to sound unsympathetic, but I'm in a mess too. I don't have any power. I'm sure they'll get it fixed soon, but if they don't, could you possibly take the food back?"

"No way, Anne. I'd like to help you, but it wouldn't be acceptable to return it. Look, tell you what. You call me the minute you get electricity. I'll hold your delivery until I hear from you. I'll even run it over in the station wagon if necessary, say up to 11:00."

"Thank you. That would be wonderful. Hey, I hear the maintenance men now. Got to run."

"Anne, Anne, wait a minute. Have you checked your refrigerator?"

Ready to shoot myself, I thanked him and went into the Center. Three big men were clustered around the fuse box with a flashlight. The building was so old we didn't even have circuit breakers. I stood on tiptoe and tried to see while they talked. I finally said I'd be in the office if they needed me, but first I took Royal's flashlight and went and looked in the refrigerator. I'd known what I'd find—a mess, like the whole day.

The freezer compartment had defrosted and a murky puddle dripped into the bottom of the case. When the phone rang again, I closed the refrigerator, leaving the puddle. The lunch crew would have to deal with it.

By 9:30, there were still no lights, I'd answered what seemed like 150 phone calls, and seniors were beginning to arrive. Every single one of them came in to tell me the Center was cold and dark. Five were really upset because there was no coffee, and four demanded Royal, evidently sure she wouldn't allow the situation to continue. They didn't want her as much as I did!

Before I went entirely insane, Hilda and Conner came in. Once they understood the situation, they stood at the entrance door and told everyone the problem, so only half the seniors came to see me.

At 9:45, the lights went on briefly. I ran out to turn on the heat, and see if Hilda would make coffee, but the lights went out before I got to the kitchen. I wondered if anyone would mind if I sat on the floor and cried. Hilda came over and patted my shoulder. Conner said he was going to call Phil. I wasn't sure the maintenance men would like that, but figured that would be their problem.

I noticed most of the seniors were staying, not going home. They were going to freeze. I wished I had brought my boots. Hell, my fuel company hadn't called yet.

I realized I had to face the kitchen help problem and decided to ignore the phone while I took Hilda and the flashlight to the kitchen. I told her about Mary and the late food.

"Anne, what can we do?" she asked.

To my horror, she was really shaken. I realized I'd sort of expected her to completely take over and probably do something magical. Well, this was my job, what I'd been hired for. Thank God the phone had quit ringing for a while. It gave me a chance to think. "It will be O.K., Hilda. Get the tables set up. Even if the food doesn't come until 11:00, we'll be able to get it done. I'll get you extra help."

Now Phil and Emma had arrived. He went out back to where the men were clustered behind the piano. Emma said,

"Phil thinks the electrical problem is on the roof again. He said it might take about an hour to fix." That was cutting it too close. "Now, Anne, Hilda and I'll get Rose and some of the other ladies to help here. You go see if you can find some way to get the food cooked."

I obeyed and after showing them the refrigerator, I went back to the office, vaguely thinking about a big fire. The whole place maybe. Gordy was at the telephone. He was the reason the phone hadn't been ringing continuously. He smiled at me.

"Now, Anne, here are your messages. You want me to stay and keep answering the phone for you?"

"Please, Gordy, if you can."

The lights flickered three times and I caught sight of the list. The cake. I had a faint feeling it might be the only part of the birthday party I'd manage. "First though, Gordy, will you ask Conner or anyone who drives if they'll go over to Safeway at 11:00 and pick up the cake for this afternoon?" I went to the fish envelope and gave him the whole thing. "Pay for it out of this and ask whoever goes to get a receipt."

I picked up the phone.

Emma stuck her head in. "There's no milk yet." I nodded, smiled, and made a gesture, which I hoped she'd take to mean I'd see to it. I certainly would. I was going to kill the driver.

Well, food first. I called McCloud's. I had a hard time getting his receptionist to call him to the phone, but finally convinced her I had to talk to him. "Anne Farley here. We still don't have power." Suddenly I had a fantastic brainstorm. "Can you possible heat it over there for us?"

"Anne, I don't think so. I'm short-handed as it is."

"Please, it wouldn't take too much to heat the food. I guess I don't care if it is overcooked or anything. Just shove everything in it 'till it boils and bring it over."

"That's it. I can heat it, but by now I've no idea how I'll deliver that close to 12:00. It's a madhouse over here. I've got the dishwasher making cookies for the machines."

I didn't have the faintest idea what he was talking about. What cookies? What machines? "If I get a couple of people from here with cars to pick the food up, say at 11:45, will you heat it?"

"If you'll pick up, I'll even heat the rolls."

"You are a darling, a wonderful man. There will be dozen roses on your desk tomorrow or a batch of homemade cookies. Whichever you prefer."

I could hear phones ringing and people shouting on his end. "I'd accept the bribe, but for God's sake, not cookies, and I'd really prefer a bottle of strong cheap wine."

Wishing I'd glommed onto one of Janet's bottles of Scotch and could send it over to him about 3:00, I agreed and hung up. Cars. Who could drive? Even better, who had a van? Time to delegate.

I went out to Brenda who was already taking money. The blind faith of humans! Not as many seniors as usual and everyone bundled to the teeth. Three card tables were ready with two candles and a flashlight.

A glance at the dining area showed Emma or someone rigged candles at the lunch tables too. "Brenda, could you possibly find someone with a van or station wagon or a couple of cars and get them to go over to the caterer' and pick up the food? They'd have to be there at a quarter to twelve."

A touch on my shoulder stopped me. One of our TV regulars. I'd never spoken to him, only seen him eating a sandwich by the set.

"The TV doesn't work."

"I know. The power's off. Phil thinks it will be back on in about, oh, 45 minutes."

"I'm missing my program."

"I'm sorry, but until the power comes on, well, you know..." I'd swear tears were gathering in his eyes.

"It's 'Hospital Ship,' and the little boy is dying unless Nurse Shirley can get to the village."

Now what could I say? "That's a shame. Maybe you'll find out what happened tomorrow." Oh God, a tear was really rolling down his cheek. I looked at Brenda, but she looked as much at a loss as I was. "I know. When I can, I'll call my mother and see if she can find out what happened for you." *I'll even call the damn TV station.* He cheered up a bit, but still stood there, looking forlorn.

Suddenly Bill called out in a high, shrill voice, "Come on over, Don. Sit with me until they get the machine going. You can have lunch at my table. Get that young lady to sell you a ticket."

Young lady? Me or Brenda? Well, Bill was probably a father when Brenda was born and a grandfather when I arrived, and, yes, the seniors were beginning to eat in certain groups at the same table each day. Was that good or bad? And how had Bill heard what was going on? He was stone deaf. *Nuts... Jonah.*

I gave the rest of the instructions to Brenda. She promised to get the cars to pick up the food, and I went back to the office to call and deal with the milk. I told the woman at Jonah's we hadn't gotten our milk. She said the driver had left on time and not called in about any problems. When she didn't come up with any plan for finding our milk, I insisted on talking to Tim. She gave in. Boy, I was really getting brave.

Tim came on the phone, sounding not very pleased. "Good morning, Anne, what can I do for you?"

The coward, she hadn't told him. "Good morning, Tim. Sorry to bother you, but ... no milk."

"That's impossible." A long pause during which Brenda stuck her head in and indicated we had drivers.

"Have you looked out back?"

"Yes, and out front. No milk."

"Oh, God. All this mess over your chintzy account"

"Our chintzy account is part of the City's account, remember."

"I know, Anne, I know. Don't get mad. I know it's not your fault. I may kill the driver."

"If I don't first. How in God's name does he hold a job?"

"Really, he's a good worker. Fast, and the housewives love him. They've stayed with him for years. He doesn't have the highest IQ I've ever known, I must admit. O.K., I'll get the milk to you some way."

"Tim, look, we don't have any power over here, and if we can't have milk by noon, I'd just as soon not have it today. So if I don't get it, OK, but damn it, I'm not letting that driver off the hook." I got a faint chuckle over that and we hung up.

I looked at the clock. 11:30 already and I was giving a birthday party that afternoon. Even so, while leafing through the party folder, I called Mom. "Quick, did you watch 'Hospital Ship'? What happened to Nurse Shirley today?"

"For heaven's sake, Anne, what do you want to know for? I thought you hated soaps."

"I do, passionately. I'll tell you all about it tonight. I'm in a tizzy here."

"Mmm. Let's see. She is trying to reach a village with a sick little boy. She's walking and there's a terrible storm. It's raining..."

"Not details. Just what happened. Did she save the boy?"

"She isn't there yet, Anne. She's fighting her way up this little trail, and well, you said no details. At the end of the show she came upon this big snake..."

Wonder if they introduced themselves.

"...and she can't get by it."

"You're an angel. Talk to you tonight." Bet it will take

Shirley at least a week to get to that village, and she'll be attacked once by a wild animal, nearly drown, and meet a fabulous man—and the kid will be patiently suffering the whole time.

With increasing unease, I went through the party folder. It was well organized. Outlines and every birthday party Royal had put on, costs of cake and punch, that sort of thing. The records told of past themes, but no real plan for today's party. Well, that wasn't true. I bet Royal knew exactly what to do, but it's hopeless for me.

The timetable said songs, 1:00-1:15. Games, 1:15-2:00. What it didn't say was what games or songs they'd already used. Royal would know, and I didn't. Optimistically, I leafed through the books. Nope. Lots of checks on some pages, but no dates.

I felt sick. I couldn't give a party. I had to get books out of the library to plan a birthday party for a six-year old, and even then, it wasn't the winning social event of the year. I'd have to call John. Oh sure. He'd love that. Auditors there in his office, and me wanting help with the birthday party.

A glimmer. Help. I needed a professional. *If only she's home!* Hurriedly I dialed Fay, and the luck was with me. "Fay, dear, it's Anne. I need some help. How would you like to give a birthday party? For my seniors." As I'd known she would, she said she'd love to give a party. She adored parties and always gave the best in town, probably in the country.

"When"

"In an hour and ten minutes."

"Anne, you're out of your mind."

"Unfortunately, I'm not." I went on and told her what had happened. After she quit laughing, I coaxed, "I've got the cake, and I can make punch. I've got the room, the people, all I need is your genius. Truly, Fay. It would save my day and with this mess here, I've no way to even make a stab at it. And fair's fair. You give this party for me, and I'll make chicken breasts cordon bleu for your next dinner party."

She kept protesting she couldn't give a really decent party in an hour, but I didn't care if it was a decent party or not, just a party. With that much agreement, we hung up.

I went out and checked. Gordy was back with the cake. Emma and her gang had everything ready to eat, minus the food. From the sounds of it, Phil and the maintenance crew were on the roof. Bill had shepherded Don to "his" table, Brenda reported we had 42 in for lunch, and I felt like I'd been going for a million years.

The front door opened and a whole troop of people walked in. Tim Jonah and his driver, Janet and Butch with the food, and Agnes, of all people. She headed for the office without saying a word.

I waved Conner's troop to the kitchen and greeted Tim. "What happened this time?"

The driver pulled his hat off. "Ma'am, I'm really sorry, ma'am. I was here. Right at ten."

I snorted.

"I really was, but I looked in, and it was dark, and I couldn't see anybody or anything. So I sort of figured you weren't open, I mean for business. So seeing as how we'd had all that other trouble, I didn't want to leave the milk. I'm surely sorry ma'am."

Tim started to speak but I beat him to it. "You, young man are an idiot. Didn't you come in and check? Shouldn't you have at least called Mr. Jonah, if not the police? This is a City building. It should not be open and empty."

He mumbled, "Yes, Ma'am," and twirled his cap."

Tim said, "We'll bring in the milk, and I'll finish killing him for you."

I restrained myself from sticking out my tongue and went into the office. That driver may have all the housewives fooled, but not me. He was a smooth-talking con man.

Plato was not reading, but she had brought each of us a huge mug of coffee and was taking aspirin with hers. She looked just fine, but somehow my head hurt just looking at her. "I'm sure glad to see you. You've heard about the whole mess?"

She said the news was all over town. "You probably better get to the kitchen, or do you have things to do for the party? I'll answer the phone and I'll call the track pretty soon."

"Thanks, Agnes. With luck, the party is taken care of. A Mrs. Johanson, Fay, is coming to do it. We may be expecting the auditors. Call me if they stick a foot in, please."

She leaned over, moving carefully so as not to jar her head, and removed the slush fund envelope from my drawer. I'd forgotten it, though I don't suppose even the auditors would boggle at the six cents in it. I bowed and went to the kitchen.

The room looked nicer than usual. Candles made a nice touch. The line was forming for lunch. Everyone was so bundled up they looked like a line of Eskimos. Tim and the driver had evidently been persuaded to stay, as they were in line and the driver was carefully not looking at me. Our milk had been supplemented with cartons of orange drink. Tim was never going to clear a profit on us.

Emma was looking tired so I persuaded her to eat and took her place dishing up the spaghetti. To my surprise, they'd gotten Tiny to help. He was giving everyone who wanted cheese a spoonful of Parmesan. I told myself, *now look, Anne, you aren't going to mix it up with him again. The Bastard.* However, he seemed very intent on his job and didn't even give me a grumble. The seniors seemed surprised to see me behind the counter.

About every third man in the line said, "See they finally got you some work to do."

Hah Hah!

I smiled and nodded, so my mind wasn't really on Tiny when he poked me in the ribs and said, "Here comes Zeke, give him a special big serving."

Being dumb, I didn't nod and say yes, and give him the same as everyone else. I had to say it, "He gets as much as everyone else."

"He needs it. Heap it up."

"Don't spill the cheese."

"You dumb broad. Give it to him."

"I certainly shall."

He shut up and I carefully put two spoonfuls on Zeke's plate. Tiny glared at me but evidently figured I'd given in. We finished serving in silence.

There was lots of food left over. I took some of the spaghetti and salad and Tiny gave me one spoonful of Parmesan after I'd helped him to the spaghetti. Dead silence. Hell, this was stupid, so I stopped him. "Tiny, what's wrong with Zeke? Is he hungry?"

His round fat face got redder. "You leave him alone. We take care of him. He don't want no do-gooder lady interfering."

My own face felt like it was getting redder too. "If I understood, I might not give you such a bad time."

"Ha, no broad gives me a bad time."

I know. You give them a bad time. "To spell it out, if he's hungry, it isn't a good idea to overload him with food at one time. Do you want to take some of the lunch home with you for his dinner?" I saw Fay come in, loaded with packages. "If you do, package it up and keep it in the refrigerator..." Oh hell, no refrigerator. "Well, not today. Take it home and put it in the refrigerator for him."

I got my plate and went over to Fay, who was looking in awe at the rug. I took her into the office.

The blessed woman was ready to give a party. She had

prizes, flowers, a fancy tablecloth, napkins, funny hats, and what looked like a zillion sheets of paper and pens.

"I don't believe that rug, Anne. It glows. However, this place looks like it needs it. I know you said you were out of power, but it feels like the morgue."

As if the Center resented her comments, the lights went on, and I could hear the furnace go on, the TV blare, and the seniors cheering.

By the time we got out to the dining room, Phil had come in. "What was it, Phil?"

Emma smiled at him with delight. "Phil was right. It was the lead-in wire on the roof. It was hard to fix this time."

"I'm certainly glad it's fixed. Is it permanently fixed or just temporarily?"

Emma said, "It's fixed, but the maintenance men have to put some of the roofing back on and clean up. They'll be down in about an hour. This the way you want it set up for the party, Anne?"

I introduced Fay to her and Emma promised to help if Fay needed it and she went back to the kitchen. Phil took some tools to the storeroom.

Fay said, "Can he talk?"

"What?"

"That man, Phil, can he talk, or does she always do it for him?"

I mentally reviewed the conversation and thought about our previous interchanges. "Honestly, I don't know. I hadn't thought about it. Wait. Yes, I heard him say 'eight ball' one day."

Fay looked at me and then started setting up her party. I'd sort of imagined I'd go back to the office and try and get some work done, but she kept snapping orders at me, so I ran around, got vases, wrapped presents, found more candles, and acted as her general gofer. I did take a few minutes to run in and ask Agnes to call Lillian and tell her we had power. Agnes even nodded her head. Brenda and Janet were at my desk counting money.

Back at the party, we had a ball. Fay made magic. She played the piano and got everyone singing. She led them in a series of dizzy games that had everyone howling with laughter. They were so noisy, one table of card players came in and joined us, and the kitchen crew abandoned the dishes and played with the rest. Fay had thrown some additions into our blah, pink punch. It tasted so good, and the seniors kept coming back for more until it was all gone. I was suspicious she'd spiked it.

I was standing there with a glass of the pink punch in my hand, a purple foil hat on my head, frosting on my face, and laughing 'til tears came to my eyes at Bill and Rose doing a charade about the Sheik of Araby, when John and two men, who could only be auditors, came in the back door. I added John to my kill list, since there was nothing else I could do for the evil grin on his face when he saw me—not being able to levitate back to my desk.

So, I went over and was introduced. I offered them cake, and when they accepted, I managed to tell Emma to go warn Agnes they were here. I got the men their cake and whispered to Fay I had to go play like I worked here and for her to in no way ask me for money. I'd call her tonight and explain. The coffee finally perked, so I got the auditors some coffee too. Shame the punch had run out.

We chatted about the weather while they had their cake. John stared at my head until I remembered to take the hat off. I felt better when the auditors began to chuckle and then really laugh when Butch and Barbara were Tarzan and Jane.

When they calmed down and the party began to break up, we went into the office. Agnes sat beside the phone, Brenda and Janet were gone, the lunch money was in a neat manila envelope, and the day's records were added to my sheet. John introduced Agnes and she took the phone outside.

At John's direction, I opened the files. They looked at Royal's records and looked through the cash box. I identified the trip money—somehow they didn't look very interested.

To my horror, they did ask for my records, and I showed them my sheets. I told them I'd not received any bills yet and acknowledged that yes, I had receipts for the appliances and dishes. I produced them from the bottom file drawer that Royal had given me. John looked relieved.

While one man added up my sheets, the other looked at the grant.

John whispered, "Where's the fish money?"

What in the hell had I done with the fish money? It seemed like ages before I remembered. "I gave it to Gordy to pay for the cake."

"Smart work."

Well maybe. If I'd done it on purpose.

The gray haired auditor noted, "Mrs. Farley, 9 and 6 is 15, not 16. That is the reason your cash did not balance today."

I thanked him and they left. I sat down at Royal's desk wishing I could curl up on it. Agnes brought the phone back, said my friend had left, and that she was going home. I babbled on, thanking her over and over again.

She said, "Be quiet, Anne," and left.

After the front door slammed, I sat listening to the noises inside the building. I looked out, and all the seniors had gone home and the kitchen crew had left the kitchen spotless as usual. The party was over. Only a neat pile of hats was left on the table.

❧ CHAPTER THIRTEEN ❧

It was ten after 4:00. I tried calling Mr. Finester, but his receptionist said he was out. I asked to have him call me back by 9:00 the next morning.

I called Mom and as I'd suspected, no repairman. I had quite a struggle convincing her I really should come home and not spend the night with her. Finally I confessed I was exhausted and that going home to bed with a hot water bottle was easier than packing a bag. Even so, I took time to tell her about Don and his worry about Nurse Shirley.

As soon as she hung up I called the Fuel Company. I was really too tired to tell them what I thought of them. Besides, the man I'd talked to before wasn't there. His secretary knew nothing about me, but was reasonable, and said she's have the repairman to my house at 1:00 tomorrow if I could have someone there to open it for him. I promised I would, called Mom back, and arranged for her to do it.

When I hung up, the silence of the Center struck hard, especially when I thought I heard a door open quietly. *Jerk, get out there and check*, I ordered myself.

I finally made myself go look. Sure enough, the dance lights were flashing and Helen was staring at them, sitting in a chair this time. Lord, I didn't need her. I went through the closing process, but left the dance lights on. Finally, I switched the dance lights off and went over to her. "Closing time, Helen.

Time to go home."

"Go, snow."

"Yes, go. Goodbye."

She didn't move, just sat. I took her hand and let her out. Blessedly, she went quietly. I locked the door after her and dashed for the front door to get it locked in case she came around. Before I got there, Tiny bustled in. "Locking up early when the boss isn't here?"

I did not kick him. "Helen was just here. I can't deal with her here when I close. Can I help you?" Not that I wanted to.

He was evidently nervous about Helen too, because he dashed over to the pool table, grabbed a package, and started out. "Forgot Zeke's food."

"You didn't refrigerate it?"

"Pick, pick, nag, nag."

"That food is probably spoiled by now..."

"Shove it, lady."

With that he left, slamming the door. Arms akimbo, I said every swear word I knew, including Sacre bleu and bloody hell. After I locked the door, still fuming, I called Lillian. "This place is now deserted, I'm exhausted, and I just got rid of Helen, so I'm going home. Tell His Honor the place is secured and both of you are to pray for Royal's recovery."

She promised, and I went home, deciding stew was probably easier than stopping for a hamburger. A lot cheaper anyway. While the stew heated, I turned on the oven, stood in front of it, still in my coat, and called Fay and explained about the auditors. Then I took the mug of stew and went to bed with a magazine and the hot water bottles.

The phone rang around 10:00, and for the first time in a life of compulsive phone answering, I let it ring. I paid for my dissipation of course. I woke at 2:00 am, again at 3:00, and really woke at 3:33 and was beginning to have lousy dreams. At 4:00 I got out of bed.

The bedroom was icy, so I put Terry's robe on over mine and finally put my ratty old muskrat coat on top. Then I started the coffeepot and built a fire in the study. I got out a length of wool tweed, spread it on the floor, and laid out a skirt pattern. I took a couple of measurements. Jeez, I was down to a size eight.

I jumped a foot when the phone rang. All of a sudden, the house was as quiet and disturbing as the Center had been earlier. I picked it up. "Hello," I said.

"Anne, are you all right? Why are you up now?"

"Jo? You scared me to death. What are you doing up?"

"I can't sleep. I tried to call you about ten when I got back. Anne, I put Greg in the hospital last evening and I'm going nuts. I can't get to sleep, the whole house is creaking, and I keep thinking I hear someone out front. Then I saw your lights."

"What's wrong with Greg?" I stopped. "No, look. Come on over. I've got coffee on and a fire. Bundle up well, I have no heat. I'll turn the backyard lights on and wait on the porch for you."

She agreed without argument. Knowing I was being a scaredy cat over nothing, I took my shears with me. It was only three minutes before Jo came through the fence.

I looked at the gorgeous night—a three-quarter moon, no breeze. The moonlight made the yard look like a pen and ink drawing.

The sky wasn't black though. Instead it was a real midnight blue. I don't think I'd ever seen it that color before. It was cold out for March, nearly April. My God, Terry had been dead for exactly six months.

I poured us coffee and took the brandy bottle, a loaf of bread, butter, and the toaster into the study. While I made toast and gave her the jazzed up coffee, Jo told me about Greg.

To my surprise, there were no tears. Well, at least on her part. Mine kept spilling down. I'd remembered what day it was. And why was it I hadn't remembered before?

Greg had had a business meeting in L.A. He hadn't come back Saturday, as I knew, but he'd called her from San Francisco, scared to death and awfully drunk. He didn't know why he was in 'Frisco and couldn't remember if he'd even gone to L.A. He promised to stay in his room. She'd called the hotel, and told them to get him a doctor and had taken off.

"The doctor had him in the hospital by the time I arrived, Anne. He was unconscious, and I couldn't talk to him. The doctor said he was killing himself. A couple more drinks might have done it."

I poured more coffee.

"They let me bring him back this afternoon when he agreed to go directly into the hospital. They had him so doped up, he slept the whole trip. Oh, God, Anne. I had to have an ambulance meet us.

"I don't know what Greg is going to do, but I committed him. Well, not really, I guess that can't be done anymore, but I signed the papers and the hospital can make it hard for him to leave unless I agree. Greg is going to be furious."

"Let him."

"You don't like him much, do you, Anne?"

"I used to, Jo. But, the last couple of years, it's like he's someone different, most of the time."

"I know."

"What are you going to do?" I poured more brandy into her cup."

"I haven't told you before, but I've been going to Al-Anon for several months. Since that time Greg went to AA a couple of times. Anyway, I've made up my mind. If Greg will stay in the hospital until they say he can leave, go to a counselor or

AA, or church, or whatever he chooses and stay sober, I'll stay with him and do anything we think necessary to work out our problems. If he starts to drink again, I'm through.

"Oh, Jo, I'm so proud of you. I hope Greg makes it, for both of you, but I'm here and anything I can do—well, you know."

She cried then, and I bundled her up on the couch.

She went right to sleep after she said, "What on earth are you wearing your old fur coat for?"

I realized I was hot. I threw the coat out into the living room and got my skirt cut out and marked by 6:30 am. I made my bed, showered and dressed, left Jo a note, and headed out for breakfast. She needed more sleep.

I went to Denny's and was nearly through my eggs and the front section of the paper, when John slid in across the booth from me. He was going to think I was chasing him in restaurants.

"Good morning, sir. Can't you cook, or do you campaign this way?" Hell. That sounded bitchy.

"I'm a good cook, but I get tired of it. My range is somewhat limited. Come to dinner, and I'll show you."

I smiled, wide-eyed, and murmured an unintelligible sound.

"Same to you. Don't you cook?"

"Like you, I'm a good cook, but I got tired of my own cooking about a hundred years ago. Seriously, I had a guest, but she was still sleeping, and I didn't want to wake her."

"She?"

I stared at him. "You know, I think I feel bitchy this morning. Yes, she. A neighbor with a husband in the hospital and creaking porches.

"Hey, Anne, I was trying to be funny. I'm sorry. I didn't mean to be nosy. Is it serious? Your neighbor's husband?"

He probably knew Greg. "I'm not sure. He's pretty sick, but I don't think it's dangerous."

"Do your porches creak too, Anne?"

"Sometimes. But Terry was gone a lot. I'm used to it."

"Funny, even though I'm a man, after Elly died, I heard noises when I was alone until I swore we were having a crime influx. Do you have a dog? A big one is a real protection."

Oh, bloody blue hell, I was crying again. John looked aghast. I was going to have to get my tear ducts tied. I scrubbed with the napkin, ruining my mascara. I choked on my coffee. Nothing helped. The damned tears streamed.

In desperation I hid in the paper. I was finally able to say, "I'm sorry. Dumb of me. We had a dog, a Samoyed. He was getting old and died a couple of weeks after Terry. I found out he had cancer *too*."

John poured me more coffee and gave me a piece of toast. I'd dripped coffee all over the table."

"You had a busy day yesterday," he said. "Royal will probably be back tomorrow, but things should be easier today, no lunch."

I nodded. He probably wished he'd hired someone else, someone who didn't drip. I said, "It has to be easier, unless you have some more surprises, like auditors."

"Not for you. Us, we get them all week."

I groaned for him, finished his toast, and dashed off.

Thank God it was a quiet morning. Maybe the news had spread about the lack of heat. The seniors stayed away in droves. I got all the previous day's tasks done, had some of yesterday's casserole for lunch, and shared it with Fred, Tiny, Zeke, and several others.

In the afternoon I got out all my records and started the report for John. I even ran out of work by 4:00 and had a lovely boring time catching up on the filing.

At 5:00, I went out to close up. There was one table of card players still at it, Gordy, and three others. I unplugged the coffee, cleaned the pot, gathered up coffee cups, locked the back door, and turned out the dining room lights. The men played on. I closed the files, put my coat on, locked the office, and drifted around the table. They just ignored me.

"Hey, guys, it's 5:00—after five actually. Time to go."

"You go on, Anne, we'll lock up."

I looked at them. I couldn't just give them my key and leave them, could I? "Sorry, time to go." *What would Royal do?*

"We'll just finish the game."

"OK." I putzed around some more, throwing out some old magazines.

Finally I realized I'd been snookered. The kids had done it to me all the time. "Game" did not mean "hand." God only knew how many points were needed for this game. I didn't dare sit down. 4:00 am was too long ago, and I was definitely getting sleepy. As I was about to get firm, they finally broke up.

"Come and have a beer with us."

Me? They meant me. I needed to go home and get to bed, but if I did, I'd be up at 4:00 again. "Where are you going?"

"Just to the Wagon Wheel. Come on and relax before you go home?"

Should I? I knew Gordy fairly well. The other three I'd only seen around. Well, part of my job seemed to be to get to know new people. Anyway, I'd never been to the Wagon Wheel. "Thanks, I'd like to. I've time for just one."

We went through the parking lot and into the old tavern. I was sort of disappointed. It didn't have much atmosphere. The guys headed toward a corner table. Theirs? Gordy pulled out a chair for me. The bartender brought each of them a glass of tap beer. I nodded my agreement and he brought me one too. The tables were old and not especially clean.

The men more or less ignored me. Their conversation was evidently a carryover from the card game.

Joe said, "We really worked back then. One winter in thirty-three I cut wood. Only work I could find. We had the farm, and I'd always worked winters. I got a dollar a cord, and that included the splitting and stalking. The missus and I got up at 5:00 every morning. She had breakfast ready for the kids and me by the time I'd done chores. Then I walked three miles to the wood lot. I worked steady, none of these coffee breaks. I carried a lunch. Took sandwiches made of the wife's homemade bread, and some fresh milk. We couldn't waste money on coffee, though we usually managed to have it at breakfast.

"I walked home again at 5:00 and did chores. I don't know, the work didn't seem to hurt us. We had good times just sitting around the fire. The missus would set out a bowl of apples or pop some corn. Sometimes she and the kids made taffy. The kids would do their homework, and we'd talk about the day. I don't think kids nowadays have as good a time with all their TVs, stereos, computers, and riding around in cars."

They all nodded. I nursed my beer. I couldn't see any wagon wheel.

Gordy took up the story. "I was working for the railroad. On the extra list. Lordy, I'd go a couple of months without a day's work. We had a big garden, and my wife canned all summer long. Still there were times I didn't see how we'd get through the winter. Bill, my oldest kid, got a paper route. He turned every penny over to me. Made him real proud and it just about saved us. Sure nothing like the grandkids thinking they've got to have an allowance."

Alan put in, "I didn't have any problems at all. I wasn't married and was in the Navy. Sent most of my pay home to my folks. It doesn't sound like much now, but it kept them off relief. Still, always had a few coins to clink and really had myself a time. Saw the world, just like the posters promised—

Hawaii, the Philippines, China, Burma. Saw all the sights and, Lord, the babes..."

The four of them looked at me, and I decided my beer was finished, though I thought Alan's stories might be a little more interesting than cutting wood and eating apples. Gordy insisted on walking me to my car, lifted his cap, and stood until I'd driven out of the parking lot. The Center had had one definite affect on me—I felt younger every day.

When I got home I found my stew frozen in neat little packets and a stuffed pork chop hot in the oven. A rack of brownies was on the counter. Heaven. *Thanks, Mom.*

I called Jo when I saw lights on in her kitchen. Greg was better, but feeling hellish.

She'd called his boss. "I told him Greg would need a leave of absence and told him why." She paused. "I promised myself I'd never cover up for him again. The only way people won't know about his drinking will be if he doesn't drink. His boss knew, of course. He said he'd been thinking of sending Greg to the company doctor. He is going to have the doctor call the hospital. You know, Anne, I didn't even know the company had an alcoholism program. Greg could always out-talk me. If they'd only done something a year ago!"

She said she wouldn't share my chop. Her son was flying in and she was going to the airport to pick him up. So, I ate my chop in front of the TV while I listened to the news. I took a plate of cookies to the sewing machine and finished the skirt, except for the hem. I was pleased. It fit and the bulky wool made me look a little less skinny. I'd have to wait on the hem 'til Jo or Mom could mark it for me.

I gave the skirt a final pressing and put all my sewing away. I knew I was trying to waste time, but I hated going to bed.

I finally climbed in about midnight and lay there. Anniversaries of the death of a spouse are supposed to be hard. Maybe this was a self-fulfilling prophecy, but I didn't really feel bad, or cry, or anything. I just lay there and couldn't get to sleep.

My hot water bottle had been nice, so I got up, filled it, and curled up with it against my back. Still I just lay there, wide-awake.

At 3:00 I heated some milk. I looked up at Joe's. It was dark. I drank my milk and went back to bed. I began to mentally plan a memo for Royal about the Church's Sunday program. Gradually, I relaxed and fell asleep. Thank God for my job.

❧ CHAPTER FOURTEEN ❦

Royal was back on Wednesday, looking pale, but she said she'd decided to live, and work was a lot less boring than home. Amen to that. She stayed close to her desk, and I did the running around for her—over to City Hall for the mail, to Safeway to restock the coffee, things like that. It made a nice change.

By Friday, Royal was herself again and mad that she'd already gained back two of the five pounds her stomach flu had removed. The flu seemed to be going around. Several seniors were down, and both Emma and Conner had it too.

I hated to see Friday come. Next week I'd be in only three days. Of course, there were all sorts of things to do at home, and Mom was anxious for me to have more free time with her. But work was more fun.

About noon, Royal said, "As soon as the food is served, let's get out of here. I think it's about time we treated ourselves to lunch. Suppose I call Lil and see if she needs a break too."

I mentally reviewed my money and agreed.

I went out and asked Agnes if she'd mind the office for us, told Mary what we planned, and was assured they could do without me. That I knew.

Suddenly I realized things looked different. All the ladies had on matching aprons made of a beautiful blue-green print, and the splash area behind the sink and stove was covered in the same print. Wonderingly I went over and touched it. The print was neatly sealed behind clear vinyl. "Mary, when did all this happen?"

She watched me, evidently pleased with my double take.

"We've been making the aprons at home. Willie and I picked out the material, and Willie, she made several, and I made some, and a couple more ladies each made one. Phil did the measuring and bought the vinyl, and Emma and I put up the material. We used the regular wallpaper paste. Then Phil and Butch stuck the vinyl on this morning as you went in the office. We wanted to surprise you."

"A surprise? It's like magic. Like the elves—you know."

"Elves?"

"Oh, the old fairy story, *The Elves and the Shoemaker.* The shoemaker would wake up in the morning to find all his shoes finished."

She looked a little puzzled.

"It's just like that here at the Center. When there's a problem, or even trouble Royal and I don't know about, bang, all of you fix it. Just like the elves."

She finally smiled, but I could see she suspected me of being a little nuts.

Terry had always accused me of making mental connections no one else understood.

"We made you an apron too, Anne. Here."

My apron was really beautiful—more like a jacket.

Mary said, "Willie made yours and I made Royal's. Willie sews real good."

Indeed she did. Every seam was finished, and it fit. I usually got swallowed up in most aprons.

I admired the kitchen and aprons some more, delighted at how they brightened the drab room—though it made the pink walls and fuchsia rug even gaudier.

Then, followed by the kitchen crew, Mary took Royal's apron to her. I found out Royal hadn't known about the improvements either. She looked cute in hers. It was made like a mama-san apron and opened in the back. Agnes came in and we all went back to the kitchen and admired the new look.

Mary said reflectively, "I think I'll get some more of the material and make mats for the tables. Just small ones for the centers. We could put vases with flowers on them."

Royal cautiously asked, "Mary, the aprons and the backboards are very nice, but how were they paid for?"

"We had a raffle."

"Here?"

"Oh, no. We know we can't have raffles on City property. We did it at the bridge club and the grandmother's club. Places like that.

Royal said, "I wish you had told me."

Mary looked unhappy.

"As much as I like them, and I know everyone will, I should know about any plan that affects the Center. This doesn't make any difference. I would have approved— though perhaps we might have worked out a way to reflect the Center's color scheme.

My god, I bet Royal picked out the rug and wall colors!

Mary nodded. I swear I could read her face. That was what they hadn't wanted.

"There are some funny City regulations, and sometimes I have to talk to John and the City Attorney If I don't know about the plans, we could get into trouble."

"We wanted it to be a surprise, Royal."

'I know, and it was. It was a good surprise. But next time, talk to me first."

Everyone smiled, and Royal and I left.

"We'll meet Lila at Las Enchiladas. Is Mexican okay with you? They have American dishes too."

"Love it. I feel sort of guilty. Like I should have known

what was going on in the kitchen. It's part of my job."

"Don't." They do it all the time. I keep reminding them. They keep doing exactly what they want. They are sort of uncanny. They never do anything that's really against regulations—though I keep expecting to come back after a vacation and find the building down and a new Center nearly finished. They've been agitating for a new one ever since this one opened."

"We sure need one. This one is..." I coughed, just catching myself before mentioning the colors, "... is very inadequate."

During lunch I finally got time to tell Royal about the Church's idea for Sundays. I promised to put it all in writing. To my surprise, she wasn't wildly enthusiastic.

"Other groups have come up with the same idea, Anne, and it works for a while, then people get tired of giving up their Sundays, but are furious when I won't keep the Center open by myself."

I promised I'd field complaints if that happened, but said I didn't think Mrs. Grand would let it flop. Royal said she'd have to think about it.

Lil told us the auditors were still at City Hall and seemed to be reasonably happy—for auditors anyway.

We had a nice lunch. The food was good—spicy but not too hot—and the sopapillas and honey were scrumptious.

As we walked back to the Center, luxuriating in the spring-like sun, Royal said, "Anne, do you think you'd be able to do the arboretum trip and play next month? It's on a Thursday. With your art class, it would mean coming in five days."

"You mean going on the trip with them?"

She nodded. "Sounds like fun. Sure you don't want to go?"

"It is fun, in a way, but hard work, keeping everyone together and making sure they all get back on the bus. I'd rather start catching up on my work. Maybe get a head start on May's calendar."

Tiny met us at the entrance when we came in, held the door for us, and left chuckling. It was good to see him in a decent mood

Everything at the Center was going as usual. The tie-dying class had put up their tables, and the teacher was already setting up.

I was almost through the report when the phone rang. It was John for Royal. Pretty soon I couldn't help listening to their conversation.

"For heaven's sake, John, you know better than to pay attention to Tiny. Anne was with Lil and me, we went out to lunch just like we do every month or so. No, the office wasn't empty. Agnes was handling the phone, and we didn't leave until after the food was served." There was a long pause. "I think you are crazy to even let him talk to you. The meal was served on time, we had adequate help during lunch, and there were no problems while we were gone." Another pause. "How on earth could he make up a story like that? No, there was no fire, no fire department, and we were not at a bar. Las Enchiladas doesn't even have a liquor license."

I was frothing, and Royal looked mad, though she was beginning to laugh.

"John, I've had it with that man. He has hated every person we've had helping here. This time he can't come back until he's talked to you and you've set him straight. If he weren't so good to Zeke, I'd say he's not human."

When she hung up, I was shaking, I was so mad. "Royal, how could John believe him? What makes Tiny tick? He's not senile." I rubbed my ear furiously.

"Sit down, Anne, and stop that, you are going to make your ear raw."

"But Royal..."

"I know, I know. It's infuriating, but John didn't believe him, he just had to check. Something could have happened that he hadn't heard of yet, and you and I could have been mopping up the place after some sort of fire. I really mean it this time, Tiny does not come back until he talks with John."

"Ha!"

"If you think that's bad, Anne, you should hear the stories Tiny thought up about Bertram. Even at my age, I get embarrassed just thinking about it."

That distracted me. I finally sat down. "Tell me."

"I'll give you all the gory details later. Major theme is that he was calling on all the ladies and trading food stamps for, oh well, their sexual favors."

"But, I understood Bertram was a college student."

"He was."

Then she evidently understood my bewilderment.

"Why, Anne, I do believe you think no one could even make up a story about these nice old ladies and sex."

"Well, you've got to admit, it's quite an age difference."

"*Harold and Maude.*"

"En mass?"

"Oh, of course. You know, that may have been the origin of his tale. I think that was about the time *Harold and Maude* played here."

"What do food stamps have to do with it?"

"That's the only true part of the story. One of the things Bertram did was to visit seniors who were eligible for food stamps and help them fill out their paperwork. I imagine he easily ate five-thousand cookies, drank a thousand cups of tea, and probably downed fifty beers during his visits."

"Beer?"

"He visited some of the men, too." Royal added, "Tiny's not senile."

I snorted. "But he's a perfect example of a mean man who has more time to practice his meanness now that he's retired. I may poison his rolls. He manages to get at least three every meal. Maybe I can find a poison that won't hurt anyone who eats one, but will nail Tiny."

Still mad, I got all my records together and took them over to John. I was embarrassed after Tiny's story and glad John was in a hurry. It was the auditors' last day. It ended with my leaving him copies to study later.

Royal and I left at 5:00 exactly, with no more excitement.

I spent most of the weekend with Jo. We gardened. We cooked dinner together Saturday, and went to a movie Sunday afternoon. I felt rested again by Monday morning.

Around 9:00 on Monday, Mary called me. "I'll be late, Anne, and I'll need two other helpers. Emma will stay with Hilda."

"Is Hilda worse? Should she be in the hospital?"

There was a long pause. Then I realized she was almost crying.

"You haven't heard? Conner died last night."

"Oh, God, Mary. I'd not heard. I just barely knew he was sick. Is Hilda all right?"

"She's almost over the flu. She had seemed worse than he did, but they both were apparently better yesterday. My brother and I went over for a while in the afternoon. I took them some soup. Then, last night, Conner died in his sleep."

"Is there anything we can do?"

"Nothing, Anne. Just tell people, and get me some help in the kitchen."

I told Royal, and she said she'd go over for a while. As she left she said, "I wonder who will be next."

"What do you mean?"

"It seems we never get one death. They come in groups— almost as if one person's going breaks whatever holds them all here."

"Oh, Royal..."

"I know, it sounds superstitious, but it happens."

She left and I went out to the kitchen. Nothing had been started, and no one was around. I'd have to wait a while to get help, so I started setting tables. I'd gotten the plates on when Rose came in. When she saw me, she came into the dining room.

"Why are you setting tables, Anne?"

"Conner died last night, Rose. Emma and Mary are with Hilda."

"My, that's a shame. But I knew. I told Hilda."

I looked at her.

"I know things like that. It was like a big, dark cloud around him, so I knew. I had to warn Hilda, I didn't want her to be unprepared. I've always been glad I knew before Turner died. I had time to prepare."

Without my saying anything, she put on an apron and began helping set tables. "I had a good black dress ready, and I had his best suit cleaned. Then I ordered a gravestone."

I stared at her. Could she be for real?

"We had our lots. It pays to be ready. I hope you were ready, Anne. I hear you are a widow too."

I nodded.

"It's hard isn't it?" She went back for more napkins. "Still, once you know how it is, you can adjust. Much as I loved Turner, I've had a good life since he died. I go to the movies every week. Turner didn't like the movies. And I watch the TV shows I like best. Turner always fancied those sports things. Me, I like a good game show. I heard you like 'Hospital Ship'. I was so glad when Nurse Shirley saved that little boy's life."

So she'd done it, had she, and hadn't even taken a week to get there. Good for her.

The food came, and I checked it in. The milk arrived right behind the food. The driver sort of avoided me, and I kept busy finishing up the tables. He put the milk in the refrigerator, took the cookie Rose produced, poured himself some coffee, and went over to chat with the men playing cards. Tim was right—

he was friendly, and the men seemed glad to see him.

I put the food on to heat while Rose filled the pitchers with salad dressing. Willie came in at 10:30 and Rose recruited her. We dished up dessert and put the rolls in the roaster, ready for heating.

Rose said, "Really, the nicest thing about being a widow is not having to cook if I don't want to. I eat here at noon and just have a sandwich at night with my TV show." She began washing lettuce.

I said to Willie, "It's a good thing we all seem to find some things we like about being widows."

"Ya, but she does too good a job of it."

I didn't know Willie very well, but she'd never struck me as the catty type. "I don't know, it's important to be cheerful."

"Then she ought to wait 'til he's dead."

"Dead? 'Till he's dead? Of course he's dead, that's what makes her a widow. What do you mean?"

"You don't know?"

I shook my head. The soft Germanic voice went on.

"She decided he was dying. Year ago. Nothing he said, nothing the doctor said could make her give it up. She came one day and said he was dead, and she is still saying it now."

"You mean he's not dead?"

"No. He is a living dead man, alive as can be." She put the gravy on to heat.

I leaned over the counter. "How do they manage? I mean, did he move out?"

"No, the house, it's all paid for. He made himself an apartment in the basement, bought himself a little black and white TV while she's got the color set, and he does work in the workshop and keeps a garden."

"It sounds scary."

"Yes, in a way, but he is used to it, and as you see, she is a good widow."

Yes, easy. She must have been good and tired of cooking meals and watching sports programs. Still, it was a little extreme to have him die off, so to speak, but simple, easier than a divorce. "You know, Willie, it's hard to believe. Doesn't she know he's around? What if she sees him in the garden?"

"She calls him 'that man.' Even brings us fresh vegetables from 'that man.'"

I wanted to know more, but Mary came and we all crowded around her. She had nothing new to tell us. Hilda was in bed. The doctor didn't want her to strain her heart, what with the shock on top of the flu.

Emma and Phil were going to stay with her until her sister arrived from Phoenix. Mary didn't seem to want to talk much about it, so I filled her in on the kitchen progress and went back to the office. God, that nice man would never come in again. How was Hilda going to stand it?

"Royal, do people here know about the Widow's Counseling Group?"

"Oh, yes, Anne. Sometimes we persuade someone to call them."

"Do you think it would be a good idea for Hilda? I sometimes think they nearly saved me. My sanity anyway."

"We'll have to see, Anne. Usually the other ladies are all the help needed."

"I'm sure, but maybe something a little more professional..."

"You watch, Anne. They'll help her keep busy, and they'll let her talk about it as much as she wants. She'll always have several people she can count on."

It had been so hard for me. My friends and family wouldn't let me talk about Terry. They kept telling me I mustn't upset myself.

If it hadn't been for the women at the WICs, it would have seemed like Terry was only a dream, one I was forbidden to try and remember. How could you start anew without a past to grow out of?

Royal knew about Rose. She asked me to keep an eye on her any time she was helping if Mary or one of the other regulars weren't in the kitchen.

"She gets some funny ideas at times. Her husband used to come here and play pool, but it made him and everyone else so uncomfortable, seeing her look right through him, that he almost never comes in anymore."

Both Royal and Mary left as soon as they had eaten lunch, so I went in and helped clean the kitchen. Putting all those dishes through a home style dishwasher was a chore, but Willie was dynamite and had the pots and pans scrubbed and put away before the first load of dishes was finished. I tried to persuade her to leave and let me finish, but she kept scrubbing tables and polishing while I unloaded and reloaded the machine. God, too bad we couldn't have a commercial machine. The thirty minutes a load was a drag.

Willie told me Conner's funeral would be Wednesday. They'd set it for 3:30 so everyone at the Center would be free to go. "Royal said she'll have that lady in the mayor's office come and answer our phone so we can all go."

I nodded. I never wanted to go to another funeral, but I would have to.

"Hilda is going to come eat at the potluck Thursday, and she said she'd help serve Friday but probably not help clean up. The flu hit her pretty hard."

"My God, she shouldn't try and come and work so soon."

"Now, Anne, you know that's silly. What else is she going to do? They've been coming down here every day for years. She likes to keep busy. Why would she start taking it easy now that she's going to be so lonely?"

"You're right, of course, but she must be careful after having been sick." Yes, even without Conner, she could come here and keep her days filled, though she'd still have the nights and weekends to survive."

The kitchen was sparkling by the time Willie was through. She'd even washed and scoured the garbage cans. She left, saying she was going to find a card for people to sign for Hilda.

Royal came back at 4:00 and we picked up, tidied, and locked. I killed the remaining time by filing. My "to be filed" folder had more stuff in it than anything else. Handy though, everything I needed was usually there.

Our nice weather disappeared Tuesday, and it was too wet outside even for me. I spent the morning doing housework and making a grocery list. I shopped around lunchtime and stopped at the Center to ask Royal about flowers for Conner. Some seniors were taking up a collection so I donated to that and signed the card.

Royal needed to go to City Hall, and Agnes wasn't in, so I phone-sat for an hour for her. I was home by 2:00.

I talked to Mom on the phone for a long time. As we talked, I pushed the scraps of tweed from my skirt around, and by using a piece of ultra-suede I had from a suit I'd made Liz, I was able to get a vest cut out to go with the skirt. I spent the rest of the afternoon sewing.

I put my machine where I could watch the TV and did the basic work during an old John Wayne movie. I liked him a lot better when he was older. He looked insipid in this one.

I pressed the skirt while one of my packages of stew heated and started the hard work with the news. I'd have liked to have worn it on Wednesday, but I didn't have the right buttons.

I'd saved every button that came my way during the years I'd been married, but I swear, I always had to buy new ones for everything I made.

I spent a half-hour pouring over the button box. I found four beautiful ones that looked perfect and were the right size, but I needed five. The buttons had been on a brown plaid jacket I'd made Terry for our tenth anniversary. There were six buttons off a coat Mom had given Carla when she was in high school, but somehow they looked purple against the tweed. I gave up, piled them away, and put a scrap of tweed in my purse to match buttons with.

❧ CHAPTER FIFTEEN ❦

The Tuesday of my first art class came. I'd worked hard planning the lesson. I'd talked to seniors who'd taken the previous classes and decided to begin each session with a brief lecture and demonstration of one technique. I'd start the first lesson with some brushwork, and then I'd leave a short period for them to paint what they wanted while I circulated and helped. I also planned to set up a still life display they could work from if they wanted, one from which the new techniques could be easily utilized.

I got to the Center an hour before class to set up. I thought I'd put the tables in a squared U-shape with my still life at the open end, next to my easel and junk.

Two of the men who'd signed up for the class came in to help. I'd not seen them before—they said they were Tom and Dick. I resisted asking about Harry. When I told them the way I wanted the tables, they said how about the way they'd had them before? It would catch the light better and they didn't want to get in each other's way. They proceeded to put a table under each light across the end of the room. They ignored me when I talked about wanting to be able to hear them and their being able to see what I was doing. Damn! Why wouldn't anyone pay attention?

I set up my table and rearranged my fruit on the piece of dull brown velveteen I'd brought. I put up my easel and mixed the paints I wanted.

Several other members of the class wandered in. Each one spread several layers of newspaper over the tabletop. I noticed most of them had partially completed paintings, so I wandered around and looked at their work. I found most of them were copying a colored print. Well, it was one way to learn. As I approached Rose, she covered her work and said, "Don't look. Don't peak."

"Oh, hi, Rose. I'm the teacher, can't I have a look?"

"No, no. I don't like anyone to look until I'm done."

Oh, fine. Great help I was going to be. "All right, if you don't want me to. Did you bring the practice canvas I had on my list and a number 6 brush?"

"I didn't have one, Anne, and I'm anxious to get my picture done. I'm going to give it to my daughter for her birthday."

I had more than a suspicion this wasn't going to go my way at all. At 10:00 I called the class to attention, introduced myself to the seniors I didn't know, and told them about the format I'd planned for the class.

As I talked I watched them uneasily. Most of them were already starting on their previous work. Rose and her neighbor were talking. Only Phil had a blank piece of canvas up and was waiting for me to go on. I hadn't noticed his name on the class list.

I finally rapped on the table and said, "Excuse me, we haven't a long time together. I will talk only a short while, so please give me your attention."

Those nearest to me looked up. Most kept painting, and Rose kept talking. Feeling desperate, I launched into my lesson.

With Phil as my only audience, I talked and demonstrated. In the face of the lack of enthusiasm, I kept rushing and skipping parts. My fifteen-minute lecture took six minutes. When I finished everyone looked up and I received a polite patter of applause.

Wishing I could disappear, I painted out my still life and put my notes away. The class went back to their painting. Rose's neighbor talked, and Rose was smoothing a pale purple paint onto her mystery picture. Purple cows?

Phil had put out a relatively large canvas. He was doing a lovely piece of work, a head of a black and white collie, and he was not copying a picture.

"Nice, Phil."

He smiled at me.

"From memory?"

He nodded and pointed to some pale sketch lines. *How come Anne the student is about a thousand times better than Anne the teacher?*

To my amazement, he spoke to me. "I don't like the background."

I nodded. "Have you thought about some scenery, maybe just an impression of branches?" I was aghast when he immediately began squeezing some green on his pallet. "I mean, think about it. Your picture is very good, you're the best judge of what you need."

He mixed a little black and a fleck of crimson into his green and hummed softly.

The next woman, another Mary, was painting white and yellow daisies against a pink tablecloth and a blue sky. She made it clear she didn't want any changes. I kept my hands off and said it was pretty, and maybe she might want to gray the white a little on the flowers in the background. She looked offended, but I persisted and pointed to the flowers in the print she was copying.

She studied it a while, looking doubtful, so I moved on.

I took care to stay on the backside of Rose's picture and looked at that of her friend's. More daisies. She was doing a competent job. I asked her if she wanted any help. She didn't, but talked about her problems with outlining. On my sample canvas I showed her how I would do it.

All the while I was trying to get a look at Rose's picture. Damned if I could tell what she was doing. It had to be surrealistic, with all the thick piled-on color. I didn't dare take a closer look, but I sort of liked it.

I was moving on to Selma's picture when I finally got a good glimpse of the print Rose was copying. Pansies! I liked her version better than the original. Thank God I didn't have to talk to her about it.

I got to everyone at least once. Rose's partner called me over twice by raising her hand and calling out "Teacher." Mostly she wanted to know if I still liked her daisies.

Time passed slowly, but at last it was 12:00. I took one last look at Phil's collie. He'd added a tiny image of my still like, almost hidden in the grass at the lower left. Oh boy, oh boy.

Phil nodded to me and I think I heard him say, "Good morning."

Everyone packed up. I cleared off the tables and Tom and Dick put them away. When I was finished, I took the still life into the front room, left it to dry, staggered into the office, and flopped into my chair.

Royal looked up, "How was it?"

"Awful. A failure."

"A failure? Rose and Laura came in and said it was the best class they'd ever had. They were impressed with your lecture, and Mary told me she'd learned a lot."

"Honestly, Royal? Rose and Laura, if that's Rose's seat mate's name, never listened to a word of my lecture, and Mary acted as if I'd offended her. They don't need a teacher. They're just having fun painting. If it weren't for Phil, I'd go to Europe, too. Golly, I'm no expert, but that guy is good. I suspect he could sell. But he doesn't need me as a teacher, he probably should be teaching the class."

"Are you really upset, Anne, or just talking?"

"Oh, Royal, I don't know. But truly, they didn't pay any attention. If they came in and said they liked it, they were just being polite."

"Not that bunch. Anne, I've gone through three teachers already."

"That's encouraging."

"Anne! They'd have let you know if they didn't like the class. Of course, you're right, most of them are just having fun, but why else are we here?"

I looked at her. How come she was such a scatterbrain at times and at others seemed to know so much? Maybe I wanted to believe her.

"I looked in a couple of times."

"I didn't see you."

"I could tell it was going just fine. You keep on and you'll find out the best way to handle the classes. You can't expect it to be just like a Girl Scout troop."

"I'd brain Girl Scouts who acted like that." Through the office door I could see Phil showing Emma his painting, so I went out to them.

Emma said, "Isn't it pretty, Anne? When he finishes it, I'm going to put it up over the fireplace."

"It's more than pretty. While I'm not an expert, I think it's a very fine piece of work. What more are you planning to do? It looks finished to me."

"Oh, Phil always keeps going after the picture is done," Emma replied. "I can't see he adds anything, but he keeps putting a tiny bit here and there 'til he feels it's right, then he frames it and lets me hang it."

I had heard him talk, so he really could.

"I'd love to see more of your pictures," I said, speaking directly to Phil.

Emma intercepted. "Maybe you'll have dinner with us and look at his pictures and his frames."

"I'd like that."

"How about Sunday? Say three o'clock. We still keep to the old way and have dinner early."

"If it's not too much trouble."

"Course not. We live in those apartments, south of town. The Royal Arms, D 102. You park along the fence—or would you come by bus?"

"I'll drive. Thanks for asking me. Could I bring something?"

"No, just yourself?"

Feeling pleased about my dinner date, I went back to the office, retrieved my coat, and said goodbye to Royal. I wondered if the seniors had ever had an art show. I'd have to ask Royal. Maybe we could work something out. If I lasted as teacher, that is.

I backed out of the parking lot and pulled out to the street, all clear. All clear, except for a parked car.

Luckily reflexes took over next. I hit the gas pedal, spun the wheel hard to the left, my right arm flying to the right to hold my absent, now grown daughter in the non-existent car seat, and then I stomped on the brakes as I brushed by the no-longer parked brown car.

As I sat, absolutely shaken, the brown car jerked down the road and turned right at the corner. Butch was driving and looked as if he'd not seen me. Janet Nemmers was with him and looked back, showing some concern.

A blast on a horn behind me got me going. Still shaking, I pulled over to the curb.

I was the one who'd picked him to drive errands. Maybe he was blind. Hell, Janet was crazy to be in the car with him.

Praise the Lord I was a good driver. I even had a cup for third place in the women's point-to-point at the district meet. That had been during the period Terry had been enamored with racing.

I'd started competing too when I'd gotten so damned

bored sitting around the tracks every weekend. It seemed like I'd kept some of the old skills. I hadn't minded at all when he'd lost interest and eventually sold his Jaguar. Even though his disinterest stemmed from the time I'd begun to win.

Come on, Anne, face it. What are you going to do about driving? I didn't mind driving around town, but the freeways...I sat. I hadn't talked to anyone about it.

It had started during those days of seemingly endless trips driving Terry to the doctors, the hospital, and the clinic while he choked and coughed his life away beside me. The traffic on the freeways always delayed us in getting him help—and I loathed them.

Well, what was I going to do about it? I just proved I could still drive. Was I going to stay stuck in town and on back roads the rest of my life or until the world's gas ran out?

I came to a sudden decision, and not giving myself time to come up with excuses, I headed for Atherton and the community college, via the freeway. That damned road was *just* that—a road.

I found an empty visitor's parking place right in front of the administration building. The registration hall was filled with a mass of kids who all looked about eleven to me. I finally worked my way up to the desk. The guy in front of me was asking about an engineering class. Now how come an eleven year old was going to school on the GI Bill?

The pretty little girl behind the desk gave me a catalog and a blank form and directed me to a counter around the edge of the room. Standing next to the would-be engineer, I began my search for the grant writing class in the booklet.

I'd taken several art and sewing classes here, but damned if I could find what department the dumb class was in. Business Administration, no. Political science, no. Where else would it be? There wasn't a separate Grant Writing section in the catalog either.

Resisting the impulse to look under Creative Writing, I turned to the engineer in despair. "Please, have you any idea where to find Grant Writing in this mystery book?"

He flipped the catalog open to the English Department section. I should have known. There it was under 'Writing, Special.'

"Thank you," I said.

He didn't even grunt a reply, just kept efficiently filling in his form with a weird-looking combination of letters and numbers. How come young guys like him could make a middle-aged woman feel invisible?

Grant Writing, T-Th; 7-1-; His B, 307, Tabor, 2. As best I could tell, all that meant Grant Writing met on Tuesday and Thursdays, from 7:00 to 10:00, in a room somewhere on campus, for two credits. Maybe someone named Tabor taught it.

When I saw the engineer looking at a campus map, I looked too and saw that "His B" was the History building, wing B. I also found out it was located at the south end of the campus near parking lot K3. 307 must be the room number.

Feeling like I'd worked the crossword puzzle successfully, I turned to my form. First, I had to look up my social security number. The engineer had filled his in without looking. I remembered Carla and Elizabeth could rattle theirs off too.

I searched everywhere, but couldn't figure out what the section number for the class was, and somewhere in the thirty plus years I'd been out of school, my high school grade point had escaped me. Also, why was I taking the course? My choices were for a two-year degree, or to fulfill requirements for a four-year degree.

The engineer had already finished his form and was in line talking with deep pleasure to a girl in jeans and hip-length hair. I glanced at my neat skirt and pumps. I couldn't have been more out of place.

When I made it to the front of the line, the clerk wrote in

section II in red, put an x through all of the choices for taking the class, and sent me off to the treasurer. There I blew five weeks worth of wages from teaching the art class. I'd be broke the last week of the month again.

Using knowledge from my art classes, I found the bookstore and gave them a copy of my registration. In return for it and ten dollars, I got a paperback book about the size of an IRS pamphlet.

The bookstore was next to the cafeteria, but even without lunch, I wasn't tempted to go in. A loudspeaker system vibrated with hard rock, and the room was crowded with infants all trying to shout above the music.

Instead, I walked over to the Art building and wandered the halls for an hour looking at the displays. There was some lovely pottery and a lot of good paintings. Nothing as direct and simple as Phil's collie, but nothing as good either, at least I thought so.

I stood for a while in front of three still lifes. Some class must have been using pallet knives only. I wondered if Rose would like it.

Figuring I had better go grocery shopping while I still had money, I went back to the car. Hell, I'd need a parking permit. I dashed back, filled out another form, and gave them another ten dollars. It was 4:00 before I got back to Danville and Safeway.

I went over to Jo's after I'd put my loot away. I was distressed to find Greg home. She hadn't said anything about his getting out.

I declined dinner but took some coffee. Greg and I sat in the breakfast nook and watched her cook. As usual, Jo somehow managed to get as many dishes dirty as if thirty were coming. I thought she looked better, a little less strained.

Greg looked like he'd lost twenty pounds, but he sure looked better than he had the last time I saw him. *Well, Anne, say something. The silence is getting loud.*

"You're looking better, Greg."

"I feel better. I'd give my eye teeth for a drink though."

Jo stopped and stood stiff. Obviously, I was going to be in the middle. "Hard going?"

"Hell."

Jo began tossing her salad again and the silence got long again.

"What are you going to do?"

"Stay sober if I can."

Jo was salting the salad with tears.

"Greg, Terry and I loved you and Jo. It's nice to have you back." Why was it so hard to say what I meant? "It's been like it wasn't you here, but a stranger?"

Jo put the salad down in front of us and sat down, obviously crying now. Suddenly Greg reached over and took her hand. God, I felt better. I took her other hand and fished out a Kleenex for her and then one for Greg and for myself.

"Have you two talked? I mean, really talked?"

Jo shook her head. "I'm so scared."

We both nodded.

"I'd better go and let you two get to it." Oh, that sounded encouraging. "I mean, well, you'll want to talk."

Jo looked at me imploringly and Greg said, "Stay a while, Anne. I think Jo's had enough to take for now. She needs you. Just stay a little while."

"Of course, but I don't know what to say. I sort of seem to say such dumb stuff."

A shadow of Greg's old grin showed. "You'll blurt it out, just like you always do, Annie. Maybe we'll talk at last."

Yep, right in the middle. "What are you going to do? You're not going back to work right away, are you?"

"Not yet." He looked at Jo. "I'm going to AA tonight. I've got to. Maybe I can get through tonight without a drink, and maybe tomorrow. But not for long."

Jo jerked her hand from his, gripping mine until it ached and said, "And I'll sit here, alone, and wonder where you really are, AA or a bar."

I looked at her, horrified. "Jo!" That was no way to handle it.

"You can come with me, Jo," Greg offered.

"I'm not the drunk, Greg. You are."

"Yes...you've never said anything like that before, Jo."

"Jo, you can see he's trying," I added. "You've got to help. This is the time to be giving him support, not a hard time."

He shook his head. "You're wrong, Anne. At least she's being honest. A guy from AA is going to pick me up, Jo. I think you know his wife. She goes to Alanon. You could go there tonight. I know you've been going. I already went to AA once, from the hospital, escorted by an aide like a kid, who can't be depended on to go to school by himself."

"I didn't think you paid any attention when I told you I was going to Alanon."

"Somehow I did. I remembered, Jo. Of all the things I can't remember this last year, I remembered that. Look, I don't want to drink anymore. I'm scared to. Scared to death. But I need a drink so badly. They tell me I'll have to go to a meeting every day, maybe for months—and maybe I'll have to go every week the rest of my life. When I go back to work, I'll be gone even more than I've been for a long time. If I can make it, I hope you'll stick it out with me."

"I'm really mad at you, Greg."

He nodded.

Suddenly she shrieked, jumped up from the table, and ran into the kitchen.

I rubbed my hand under the cover of the table.

She pulled a desiccated meatloaf out of the oven. "I can't even cook a meal anymore."

I stood up. "Lots of catsup, Jo. I'm going now. Keep me

informed. I really love both of you and I hope it's going to be OK." I started out. "Oh, Greg, we've got a woman at the Center, a really marvelous person. Maybe you can help her. Maybe you could get her to go to AA. I'll give you her..."

"Anne, you're nuts. I'm a drunk who hasn't had a drink for a couple of weeks only because I've been in the hospital, and you want me to start helping some old lady?"

"Oh, Greg. Not now. Later." Jo kissed me and I ran down the stairs.

I put beans on to soak, made a bowl of soup, and sat dunking buttered bread into it while I tried to read my new textbook. If I'd thought our nutrition grant was unintelligible, it paled in comparison to my course book. It looked as though it was put together by the Aztecs.

I was thrilled when the phone rang. It was John.

"Anne, sorry to disturb you, and this is dumb, but how much detergent do I need? I read everything on the box and I'm more confused than ever."

I tried not to laugh into the phone. "What kind of washing machine do you have—front or top load?"

"Just a minute, I'll look."

My god, he didn't know.

"Top load."

"Is it a big machine, small or what?"

"God, you're as bad as the box. I don't know. It's a washing machine."

"John, you're impossible. What kind of detergent do you have?" I heard the phone being put down."

"ALL."

"OK. You can't go too far wrong. Use half a cup. Half a measuring cup."

"Is that all?"

"That's it until you find out what size machine you have. If it is a small one, it may be too much. Look at it after it's been

177

working a few minutes. If you have a lot of suds, use less next time. No suds, more."

"I sort of think it's a big machine. My wife bought this one because she said she was tired of washing every day of her life."

"I entirely understand."

"Thank you, Anne. Maybe I could also cook you dinner and you could take a look at it."

I wanted to avoid that. "I'll bet you need to be told to look at the freezer compartment of your refrigerator, too."

"No, that I know. It's frost free."

"Good luck with your washing."

"Thanks again. See you."

I hung up. Men were as helpless as women when alone— in different ways. In fact, more so in a lot of ways.

I looked around the house. I'd done pretty well.

The phone rang again. It was Howard this time. He wanted to know if I'd signed up for the class. I was glad I could tell him yes after all the effort he'd put in. "But the book is impossible, Howard. The teacher will have to be a genius to make it clear."

"Now, Anne, don't try to read it on your own. It will become clear as you go along."

I bet.

"And I'll be glad to help you any time I can. You will probably have to try writing a grant."

A la Bertram.

"You can use some samples from our files if you want."

"That's nice of you. Though I imagine I'd better work on something from my job if we do."

He didn't sound as if that thrilled him. Hard to play white knight that way, probably. "How's Lala?"

"Fine, I just talked to her. She's still at Laura's."

"Oh." That sure sounded flat. I fumbled. "I hope Laura's all right. She or her kids aren't sick, are they?"

"No, no, just a visit."

"Oh." Stupid.

"The weather has been lovely there."

"In Nebraska?

"She said it was very nice. Spring is after their winter too. Say, Anne, let's have lunch, Sunday. Bring your textbook and let me have a look at it."

"I'm sorry, Howard. I'm going to a friend's. Tell you what, when Lala gets home, call me, and both of you can come out. I'll make your favorite Irish stew." There, that should be plain enough.

"Sounds wonderful." He sounded annoyed. "Anyone I know, that you're having dinner with?"

"No, a couple from work. He's in my painting class."

"You're teaching painting? I thought you had something to do with meals."

"Oh yes, but this is extra. They lost their teacher, so I'm substituting. You know how I've always fooled around with painting. Lala and I took a class together a couple of years ago, at the barn."

"Yes, well, I imagine it's nice for you."

"Well, maybe nice isn't the word, but it's interesting." I seemed to have reestablished my fluffy image for him."

He said, "Tell you what, I'll drop by Sunday evening, and take a look at the book for you. I've found a new wine, you'll like it. Say about 7:00?"

He managed to hang up before I came up with another excuse. Hell and damnation. My soup was icy. I dumped it and poured coffee. I sat dunking my bread in it.

Was I or was I not imagining things? Some of the women at the WICs said a lot of the guys were on the prowl and figured a widow was an easy mark. Other women said they might as well be living in a man-less world. Howard could be feeling sorry for me, or just plain lonely. Probably by playing dumb and obtuse enough, I could keep it that way. Anyway, I could bring it up with Jo and have her drop by. John was something else. I couldn't read him, and he seemed more the wary bachelor type. Still he was pretty social. He was probably just being friendly.

Well, they said the desire for sex would rear its ugly head at some point. It seemed to have reared. I was damn lonely.

❧ CHAPTER SIXTEEN ❦

I was trying to make the lunch money balance with the amount we should have taken in. God, just once, even by accident, it should agree. How the hell could I have eighty-three cents too much when each lunch cost a dollar and a quarter? An even amount—thirty cents, sixty-five cents perhaps. Never, never eighty-*three*. The place bred money.

"Anne?" I looked up. "Is Royal there?"

"She's over at City Hall, Sylvia. Can I help?"

"Well, I don't know, Anne. It's about my check."

If it was about the money, I was the last person she ought to talk to. Trying to be helpful in some way, I pulled out Royal's chair for her, but she stayed in the doorway. She was a pretty woman with shimmering silver hair, but the most god-awful makeup. Gobs and bogs of it. "Your check?"

"Yes, it didn't come this month."

"Your social security check?"

She nodded and came down the step into the office.

I felt better, not craning up at her. "Let's see. It's the sixth. I haven't heard of any other checks being late except for one lady's whose forms were missing. Still, it's pretty early in the month. Have you called the office?"

She fluttered back smeared eyelashes. "I wanted Royal to call for me. They listen so nicely to her. She called Medicare for me, too, and they paid attention to her and paid the doctor right away. I've got palpitations, you know."

Feeling like a broken record, I went into my spiel. "Are you on blood pressure medication, Sylvia?"

"Oh, no, Anne. It's just my nerves." She finally edged over to Royal's chair and sank into it. She was as graceful as a model. Over sixty-five and legs like Marlena Dietrich. Damn, I should look so good.

"Well, I guess I could call Social Security for you, if you want, or you could wait for Royal."

"Maybe I'd better not. Tom and I are going into the Seattle Center to dance, and we want to catch the 2:30 bus, but I'd so hoped I'd have my check.'

I grabbed the clipboard and copied Social Security's number.

Jeez, her legs were covered with bruises. Huge ones, black, blue, and green. Who was Tom? I was just about to ask her if she was getting any vitamin C in her diet when I shut my mouth. *Time to mind my own business.* These people were adults, and there was no reason to take my nutrition title so seriously. *Lunch Lady it is, remember?* Still I couldn't resist a quick look at her hands. She had on long sleeves, but the left thumb was faintly bruised. "Could I have your Social Security card number and your address, Sylvia? I imagine they'll need them."

She began fumbling in her purse, but she was distressed and kept looking out the door. What was up? Then I caught a whiff of it too. My God, it was awful. We stared at each other. My impulse was to call the fire department, but I made myself go look. Smoke! Billows and layers of it. Pretty in a way. Blue, turning lavender as the pink dance lights revolved. Hell and damnation, the lights. Helen must be back, and Royal wasn't in. I'd have to do something.

Oh, damn, move it, Anne, fire comes first. That reek! I was going to be sick.

Tiny was at a card table right in front of the office door. It was obvious he was the center of the smog. That man! I hoped he was on fire. Why had John let him come back? I marched around the table and leaned over it. He had a huge black pipe caked with old tobacco and drippings, chipped, scarred, and never cleaned. In it Tiny was smoking a green wet cigar butt. He beamed through the smoke, little eyes gleaming with pleasure.

I stepped back in time to avoid a pinch, and demanded, "Put it out. Now!" and stalked back to the office. It would be hours before I could take a bath. I wanted to bet John would pick this afternoon to drop in and see how we were doing. "Just fine," I'd say, "running an eatery and bedlam all by ourselves."

Sylvia was still in Royal's chair, a handkerchief over her nose. I slammed the door. Of course the damned office didn't have a window, but no use letting any more smoke in.

Oh, hell, when would I learn to think? I went back into the recreation room, shoved open the outside door, jammed the doorstep under it, and went back to the office. Tiny had disposed of his smoke bomb and was cackling over his game of solitaire. He must have realized I was really mad, because he didn't try and pat me as I went by.

I told Sylvia what the smell was, and she handed me her wallet and a blank check with her address on it. I fished out her Social Security card and called them. Having heard Royal do this a few times, I had a good act ready.

"This is Mrs. Farley at the Danville Senior Center. I'm calling for a client, Sylvia Bettman, who has not received her check this month." I listened to the woman rattle off phrases about it being early and why not wait until after Monday's mail. "I think it would be better if you instituted a search today and then called me back. Mrs. Bettman is in difficulty." To my great pleasure, she agreed.

That had really worked. I gave her all the information, hung up, and turned to Sylvia to give her back her card. Somehow I missed and she dropped it. We both bent over and cracked heads. Oh, God, it hurt. Tears poured down my face.

"Sylvia, are you all right?" She was crying too, and hunting for her handkerchief. I took it off the desk and put it in her hand.

While she mopped up, I wiped my face on her blouse hem. I put "tissues" on the list.

"Sylvia, I don't know when she'll call back. Do you want me to call you, say, tomorrow?"

"Thank you, Anne. Please do. Now Tom and I can go dancing and I don't have to worry." She stood up, went to the door, and put her coat on.

Like me, she tripped on the step. I heard her gasp as she went past Tiny, and I decided she'd gotten patted, not pinched, since she hadn't shrieked. I went back to my money. No way would it balance, so I finally took the eighty-three cents and put it in my envelope.

Royal got back. "What's Tiny been doing now?"

"How did you know he'd been doing anything?"

"He's sitting out there, laughing to himself, doing nothing, while the pool table is free. He's been up to something."

"You're right. That evil old man was smoking a cigar butt in the most villainous pipe I've ever seen. The smell was indescribable. And then, he's put the card table right where he can grab someone every time anyone goes in or out of the office. He got Sylvia. The way she bruises, it will be a miracle if she can sit down. I'd like to throw him out. Did he ever talk to John?"

She nodded at me, but didn't suggest we get rid of him or talk about Sylvia. Helpful. "Helen is back, Royal."

"I saw the lights on." She paused. "Are you afraid of her, Anne?"

"I guess I am. I feel sorry for her, but it's eerie. The way she talks and stares at the lights. She doesn't eat with us, Royal, and she's so thin. If we cover her while she's on that icy floor, she cries and shoves the cover off. She's best with Hilda, but Hilda hasn't been in today. Can't you have Helen sent to a hospital or something?"

"I've tried everything I can, Anne, since the St. Vincent de Paul people asked if she could come in the Center. There's not an agency in a ten-mile radius that hasn't tried to help. But there is no way we can have her committed."

"What about her family?"

"They gave up long ago. You've never seen Helen during one of her good times, have you?"

I shook my head.

"Really a nice woman. When she starts watching television, we know she's getting better for a time."

The phone rang. It was Social Security for me. When I hung up, I was thoroughly bewildered. Social Security reported that Mrs. Bettman's check had been sent to the bank and the bank reported it had been received. Sylvia hadn't said anything about the bank not having her check. She'd said she hadn't gotten it.

Royal didn't know anything about it but said Sylvia hadn't seemed especially forgetful and that Tom was a nice guy and long time boyfriend. Then, she settled down on the phone to plan the trips for the next month.

That kept the phone from ringing, so I was able to finish up my meal records and start the monthly report. We both left at 5:15. Helen had slipped out some time earlier, so I turned off the dance lights before locking up. The lights reminded me of the old Trianon Ballroom's dance lights. Terry and I had danced there in our teens. It had been at least ten years since we'd danced, and of course, there was no way to go dancing anymore. How I'd loved it—and missed it.

The next morning I tried to call Sylvia around 9:00, before any of the potluck seniors arrived. No answer. By 10:00 I was madly trying to help Hilda and Emma make Swedish Meatballs for fifty. It had sounded like a good idea when Royal and I had decided what to do with some donated hamburger.

Like a lot of my ideas, it wasn't as simple as it had sounded. Hilda wanted to make big ones and get it over with. Emma was making one-inchers so the meat would go further. Mine were all sizes and some of them kept falling apart. That obviously worried Hilda. She kept picking up the pieces and redoing them. We still had a good five pounds left to shape when Sylvia came in. There I was, hands covered with meat and not wanting to talk with her in front of Hilda and Emma. "Sylvia, good morning. Are you coming to the potluck?"

She beamed. "Good morning. We thought we would. Tom is bringing rolls for us and I put in some of my blackberry jelly. Anne, did you hear anything?"

"Yes. I tried to call you but must have missed you this morning. I'll be in the office as soon as we've finished the meatballs."

Hilda gave me a nudge. "You go and fix Sylvia up, Anne. Me and Emma will finish. Willie's coming in. We'll start browning these here ones, and we'll be done in jig time." She untied my apron and handed me the soap, giving me the distinct impression they would get on better without me.

Sylvia was standing hesitantly in the office door. She insisted I go in first. We finally got settled, and feeling completely out of my depth, I said, "Sylvia, I'm a little confused. Social Security said your check was in your bank."

"In my bank? But..." She hesitated. "My check always comes to my apartment."

"A lot of people have them sent to the bank. It is safer. Are you sure you didn't ask to have it sent to your bank?"

She looked at me and then away into the doorway. I could swear she looked scared. Now why scared? Embarrassed, mad, annoyed, dumb. But scared? So far I'd guessed she was deaf, senile, malnourished, and beaten. It was about time I stopped guessing and did something to help her. Think. What was it Beth told me that worked on the kids who were acting up in school?

Get them to tell you what the problem was, not what the teacher thought it was. Oh, God, that sounded good, but how? "Uh, Sylvia, what could have happened?"

"I don't know, Anne. I know lots of people have their checks sent to the bank. Tom does. But I always get mine, usually on the third. And then Tom and I take it to the bank."

Again that flutter, and I'd swear a faint blush. Tom, always Tom. But Royal thought he was an OK guy. Could he be ripping her off? Still the check was in the bank. "Something happened, Sylvia. What could have happened?"

"Oh, Anne, everything is in such a muddle. I don't know."

To my horror, tears were slowly running down her cheek, washing mascara in blue-black streaks. This wasn't just a lost check. I pulled a Kleenex out of my new box and put it in her hand. "What's a muddle, Sylvia?"

"Everything. Everything is a mess. It's so hard."

"So hard?"

"All those papers, all that small print. And even the Center is kept so dark."

Oh, God. "Small print?"

"I'm so dumb, Anne. All those Medicare papers and Social Security papers and rent reviews. I can't seem to handle it anymore. I don't seem to be able to take care of myself. If I didn't have Tom, I think I'd die."

"I'm glad you have Tom, Sylvia. But you aren't dumb. There is something else the matter." I gave her another Kleenex. Someone opened the office door and then closed it again quietly.

Sylvia didn't even look. "But why can't I do things anymore?"

"What kind of things? Your housework?"

"No, housework is easy. I love it. I help Tom do his too. It's those papers and money."

"And anything else?"

"Anne, it's almost everything. And I'm so tired, and I'm

always hurting myself. I didn't used to be so clumsy."

"You don't look clumsy, Sylvia. You move like a dancer, and you've got the prettiest legs I've ever seen."

That got a slight smile and she lowered the Kleenex. "I don't think I see very well, Anne."

"It's your eyesight?"

"How do you tell, Anne? I can dance and not bump into people, and I keep my apartment and myself with no trouble. But all those papers mix me up. I'm just stupid."

"No, really. I don't think so. You know, Sylvia, sometimes when people are having vision problems, it is mainly with small print and in changes of light and dark." Hell, I hoped that was right. "If Tom helped you with your papers, maybe he had your Social Security check sent directly to the bank. Uh, did you talk to him about your check being missing?"

"Oh, dear, no. I try not to bother him. Men get so fussed, you know."

That I did.

"He likes to take care of things, but he does get upset when I get things messed up. And I don't remember saying the check was to go to the bank. I'd have to sign it, wouldn't I?"

"Yes, I suppose so. But Tom wanted you to send your check to the bank. Does he sign papers for you?"

"No, he gets them all ready, so neat and efficient, and then I sign."

"Does he explain?" I had visions of Terry lining papers up for me, explaining, shuffling them before I'd figured out which was what. I'd get completely lost and plan menus while I nodded and uh-huh'd.

"Well, yes."

"Do you understand?"

We grinned at each other. "No."

"Could that be how it happened?"

"Oh, Anne, probably. He must have told me again all about

how it was safer and everything, and I sat there and tried to remember the words to *Deep Purple*."

"Boy, do I know, Sylvia. Do you suppose they plan hunting trips while we explain all about the latest book we've read?"

She giggled. "You're married, aren't you, Anne? It shows."

I struggled to keep a smile going. "I was for a long time. He's dead." She didn't blink or look sorry for me. It was rather comforting.

"It sure happens. I hope you find someone as nice as Tom. We have a lot of fun."

"Thank you. I hope so, too." Now, how do I get us back on the subject?

"So you probably signed the request to have your Social Security checks sent to the bank, 'cause you really can't see the print?"

"Anne, can people be going blind and not know it?"

"You're getting out of my depth, Sylvia. But I think you're jumping to conclusions, thinking about being blind. It really looks like you're having trouble with your eyes, but maybe you only need new glasses."

"I've never had glasses. No one in our family has."

"Have you seen a doctor?"

"No."

This wasn't going so well. Should I offer to make an appointment? What had Beth said to do next? Jeez. "What do you think you should do?"

"I'd hate having glasses, Anne. 'Men never make passes at lasses with glasses,' goes the saying."

Wow, I didn't think I'd heard that one since I'd read my father-in-law's autograph album. "Glasses are pretty now. Glamorous."

"But, Anne, Tom likes my eyes. He says the nicest things. He wouldn't like glasses."

I was beginning to wonder about Tom's eyesight, or his

amazing tact. "Which is more important, eyesight or being pretty?"

"I know I'm vain."

"God, who isn't? But, Sylvia, your makeup..." I almost said it was a mess... "isn't done the way I think you'd want it."

She gasped and started to stand up. "What do you mean? It's not fair. I thought my makeup was all right, I've done it so long. And Tom never said anything."

"I imagine he'd love you any way you look. But what will keep happening if you don't see well?"

"Do I look like a clown, Anne?"

"Of course not, it's just your makeup is too heavy. You have such white skin, and you look so fragile. It's too much."

"Oh, dear."

"If you need glasses, you could get ones that would make your eyes even prettier."

"What if I don't need glasses? What if I have something terrible? I couldn't stand not being able to do things or go places."

She was crying again. Why the hell didn't Royal get back? She would know what to do. "Sylvia, what is going to happen if you continue to neglect your eyes?"

She continued to cry and didn't even try to talk. I got another Kleenex and finally patted her hand.

"What should I do, Anne?"

"That's up to you, Sylvia."

"If I went to a doctor, could Tom go with me?"

"Of course."

"But I don't know any eye doctors and we can only go places by bus. Tom doesn't have a car."

"We are having vision screening next week. You could sign up for it, and they will refer you if you have a problem. Maybe the doctor's office will be on a bus line."

"I can pay my way, I don't need something free."

"Vision screening is free to anyone, but I think you have to pay any of the doctors they send you to."

"I pay my way."

"That's good."

"Tom and I don't approve of all these free things. That's charity."

"Gee, I don't know, Sylvia. We've all paid taxes for years, and some of the people who come in here haven't a cent left over after rent and food. But, if you want to pay, you can make a donation to the Vision Service or help out that day." Woops, she certainly couldn't take names. "We'd need someone to answer the phone or call people into the nurse."

"I used to be a secretary. I could answer the phone."

"Shall I put you down for vision screening and tell Royal you'll answer phones for us on Wednesday?"

She still looked nervous, but agreed and left the office, carefully giving her eyes time to adjust before she took the big step out. I sat back, feeling shocked, stupid, and like a busybody. I wrote a note for Royal. What the hell was I to do if she didn't come in Wednesday? Something really bad could be wrong. In fact, she maybe could go to a doctor right away.

I finally decided to wait and talk to Royal and went back to the dining room. The women had the tables set, and meatballs baking. I'd never get used to how efficient they were. I fluttered around for a while, mainly making myself feel like I was doing my job.

Lunch over and six women doing dishes, I went back to the office. Agnes was handling the phone. She was reading *War and Peace* this time.

It was a hard afternoon for me. Royal had gotten a small orchestra and the seniors were having a dance. I sat at the desk and listened to the dance music. The beat was definite and the tunes were old and familiar. God, how I wanted to dance, but of course, I was working. That was my life now.

❧ CHAPTER SEVENTEEN ❦

On Sunday I went to Phil and Emma's for lunch after church, as I planned. I'd done some more thinking about my budget, so I left the car at home, walked a mile, and took the bus. I'd forgotten it was only seventy cents. I couldn't run the car three miles for that anymore.

Mary and her brother were there, too. I'd not met him before—a tall man, heavy, though not as heavy as Mary, and he looked quite a bit younger. I didn't catch his name, but they called him Buster.

Before we sat down to dinner, Phil showed me the apartment and Emma called a running commentary from the kitchen. I gathered they'd bought the apartment five years before and Phil had worked steadily on it. They had paneled the living room in a soft, golden brown walnut and he had framed most of his pictures in slightly darker wooden frames. The wall opposite the window looking over the river was covered with his paintings. It was a lovely room.

While I looked at the pictures, Phil went out and brought in a tray of martinis. That I hadn't expected. Why not? They were adults. I settled on the couch and Buster joined me. The cocktails were strong, with exclamation marks! I sipped mine, cautiously. Breakfast was seven hours behind me, so I began on the chips and dip.

Mary and I were deep in a discussion about next week's

meals when Buster said, "Now, ladies, no shop talk." He meant us.

What fun. I bet I'd said that a hundred times, always aimed at the men. But he was right of course. Still, it was hard to make conversation. All we knew about each other occurred at the Center. Luckily, Emma soon called us to the table.

It was a good meal. Pot roast and vegetables, and a particularly superb apple pie. I ate 'til I thought I might pop. Buster and I should have earned gold stars for our efforts, but he topped me by managing a second piece of pie that Emma covered with about a pint of ice cream. We all had more coffee to keep him company.

Mary said, "It's good to see you eat something, Anne. You just pick at lunch."

"You know how it is. I get busy and hate to stop."

She interjected, "Can't say that has ever bothered me. The more I'm around food, the more I enjoy it."

We laughed. "Anyway, Emma, this is the best meal I've had in ages. I think you're a better cook even than my mom."

"Does your mother live around here?"

"Uh-huh, the other side of town. She has an apartment not too far from me."

"You should bring her over to the Center."

"I'd like to, but so far she hasn't been interested. She keeps pretty busy."

"You take her the calendar, and someday she'll find a trip she wants to go on."

"That would be nice." Did I want Mom down there? She'd try and help, and pretty soon she'd work me out of my job!

Phil got out the cards, and he, Emma, and Mary played Pinochle. Buster and I refused, so Emma got us out the Scrabble set after we discovered that we were both addicts.

I beat him by several hundred points. I killed him with my collection of two-letter words memorized from the chart Terry had made of all the two-letter words he'd found in our four dictionaries. When I put SQUAMA on a double word square with the Q on a triple, he nearly quit. He recovered his temper when he played HISTORY and got his fifty-point bonus. It was fun.

I decided to head home at 5:00. When they discovered I'd taken the bus, they insisted I let Buster drive me home, and I couldn't talk them out of it. He drove an immaculate old Studebaker. It ran perfectly. I found out he was a mechanic and still worked several days a week whenever the shop he'd once owned needed help.

I started to get out when we got to my house, but he leaned over and held the door. "Uh, Anne, would you like to go to a movie some night this week?"

"Why, Buster," I began. What a name. "How nice. Would a weekend be all right? I still get pretty tired during the week."

"I'm sorry, I'm not free most weekends. Maybe I could pick you up at work. We could grab a hamburger and still make the six-thirty feature."

He let go of the door, so I opened it. "Fine, you call me."

"How about Wednesday? The Grand is showing *Casablanca*. I'll call you about the time?"

"Oh, that would be fun. OK." Before I could get out, he leaned over and brushed a kiss on my cheek. I know I blushed, and ran for the house. His mustache had tickled.

Howard stood on the porch, arms akimbo.

"Hi, have you waited long?" I asked.

"Just got here. Who's the beau?"

"That was Buster. He's the brother of one of the women who helps me a lot in the kitchen at the Center." Why was I explaining? I let him in.

Damn, I'd forgotten to call Jo, and Howard certainly didn't seem to be in a very good humor. I took him into the study. "You light the fire, and I'll make us some coffee."

I shot off before he could mention the wine under his arm.

I put the coffee together and got some of Mom's cookies out of the freezer. I put my Kutani cups on the tray and went back to Howard, picking up my textbook on the way. He had the fire going, but still looked cross. I decided attack was the best defense.

"When is Lala coming back? It's been a long trip this time."

He ignored me. "God, what a name, Buster. Can't you do better than that? And his coach wasn't exactly princely."

"Look, Howard. What I do is my own business, but what you saw was misleading. Buster is the brother of a friend. He is a nice, friendly man I'd never met before today and who brought me home at my hostess' suggestion to save me a bus ride. The kiss was probably a lonely man's attempt to thank me for saying I'd go to a movie with him. I can assure you it was not the preliminary to a rape, and I can handle it."

"Hey, Anne, calm down. I didn't mean to pick on you. But Terry was my friend, and it shook me to think you were dating already, and with such a character."

I sat down and poured coffee. "I understand, but lay off. I've got to make a balanced life for myself, and I'll go out if I meet men I like, and there are places I want to go."

"I don't know, Anne. You're damned naïve, and I was shook. That guy, his car, and mustache, and you being kissed."

"I'm not naïve. I may act it, but for God's sake I'm forty-five and was married for twenty-three years. And that kiss was a lot friendlier and easier to take than Graham's."

He laughed at that. "Still, I don't think you know much about what life is like. Terry kept you in cotton wool."

"Don't fuss, Howard. It's all very innocent. A movie date, mid-week, and coming home early is not going to get me in trouble. Have a cookie."

He took two and sipped his coffee. "Do you want to re-marry?" he asked, looking at the fire.

"I don't know. Right now I can say no. I still feel married.

Maybe someday I will want to. How can I tell? Anyway, I suspect the world is not exactly crawling with interesting, handsome, wealthy, eligible, men who'd take an interest in me."

"We could have you over to dinner and introduce you to some guys. There's this fellow I play golf with. He's divorced and says it's really hard to meet a nice, decent woman."

"Oh, God, Howard, no. It sounds so, so arranged. It's nice of you, and maybe someday I'd feel OK about it. You know, I bet that is what happened today. I bet they asked Buster to come over for me. Still, it sounded as if he and Mary do a lot together."

Howard was justifiably confused. "Mary?"

He'd evidently decided we'd worn the subject out and picked up the text and started leafing through it. "Anne, put the wine on to chill, would you? Do you have any brie or camembert? These cookies won't go with it."

"Not a speck of anything but cheddar. Besides, the two of us can't drink a whole bottle, and you need to drive home safely. You'd better save it for a dinner. Unless—yes, I'll ask Jo and Greg over to try it out. Oh, God, no. I'm nuts. You just save it."

"Why not call them? You're not mad at Jo, are you?"

"Oh, of course not. I just remembered they aren't free."

"We don't have to drink it all. In spite of the purists, I'll take it home for dinner tomorrow."

So I got out two glasses and my cheddar. It was a nice wine, not that I knew much about wine.

Howard turned the pages of the book slowly, frowning. I suspected his mind wasn't on Grant Writing. "Have you heard from Lala, Anne?" he asked.

"Gee, Howard, no. She's never called when she's gone. We're friends, but not that close."

"I know. I guess I was just hoping."

"You two had a real fight?"

"That's putting it mildly." He poked the fire.

Should I ask him why he's here? Did he want to talk about

Lala? We sat some more. It seemed up to me.

"Bad one?"

"Yeah. Haven't heard from her."

"What about the spring weather you told me about?"

"I've talked to Laura. She relays messages."

"I'd like to help, but honestly, I don't know much about your situation, and Lala and I never talked about our marriages." *And I don't want to get mixed up in it.*

"What gets into women? Did you ever leave Terry?"

"No. Well, not really. I got so mad one night, I stormed out. I decided to really give me something to worry about. So I went to a motel. I thought he would wonder where I was for a change and have to manage to get the kids to bed, then get their breakfast and send them off to school without help." That had been a bad year.

I was startled when Howard took my hand and asked, "What happened?"

I took my hand back and reached for the cheese. "Nothing. I was bored at the motel. I hadn't brought anything to read, and there was nothing but junk on TV. Anyway, I had a long, lovely bath. No interruptions, and I didn't have to worry about running out of hot water. After the bath, I crawled into bed and went right to sleep." *After crying buckets.* "When I woke up it was dark, but it was winter, and I felt rested. It was then I found out my watch had stopped and there was no clock in the room. The telephone was connected to the office switchboard, but I didn't have enough nerve to wake them. There wasn't a light on in the place."

He reached over and patted my knee. "You're crazy, you know. What did you do?"

"I got worried about the kids. I was afraid they'd be upset if I wasn't home when they got up. So, I got dressed and went home. Big deal. Like I said, nothing. Terry was sound asleep. It was all of eleven-thirty, so I went to bed." *Yeah, and the next morning they all asked me how the movie was. Big rebellion.*

"What were you mad about?"

Why go into it? Why didn't he go home? "Oh, the usual. Terry was working late a lot, and there always seemed to be some big deal on weekends—golf with you, a client to show around. We never did anything together, and I was doing nothing but taking care of kids."

"Yeah. Lala gets mad too, but the job is like that. There are times when it takes a hell of a lot of time and effort."

"Is that what you and Lala are fighting about?"

He nodded.

"Look at it from her side. How many more years is she going to have to wait around for you to schedule her some time? It's been thirty or more already. Sure the job is important, but isn't she equally important? What's wrong with you scheduling time for her?"

"Now, look, Anne. I don't schedule a rush on purpose."

"Of course not, but you do schedule a golf game after a week of working nights."

"Crap, I've got to have some relaxation."

"Oh, shit, Howard." He looked aghast. "You're married. Plan some relaxation and exercise with Lala. Wives don't want all of your time. Just some evidence that you know we're alive and want to be with us." I was steaming as all my old gripes came out.

"You've got the energy to take your secretary out for a big dinner of thanks for special effort. How come you can't make the Club Scout dinner?"

"Come off it, Anne, Dennis hasn't been a Cub Scout for years."

"That's beside the point. When did you last take Lala out to a nice dinner that wasn't for the company, just you two? Any flowers? Did you get her a Valentine? Do you talk to her, or are you so tired when you get home that you watch TV after you finish the paper and then head off to bed?"

"Wow, are you mad at me for Lala's sake, or are you mad at Terry?" I looked at him. "Both I suppose."

"I sort of thought you and Terry got along pretty well."

"We did, but things weren't perfect or always good even."

"He loved you, Anne. I don't like to think of you two fighting."

"We didn't fight, hardly ever. He didn't like to, and I'm as inefficient at fighting as at everything else." Why did he look so surprised? "So mostly we muddled along. I'd be worried sick, and he never knew, or maybe ignored it. Now I'll never know."

"Know what?"

Did I really want to know? "All that evening work. Was it really work, or was it a woman, or maybe women?"

"For Christ's sakes, we work our asses off, and you think we're involved somewhere else just because we aren't always hot to romp in the sack and make like Romeo?"

Oops. "Now I'll ask. Are you mad at me or at Lala?"

"Obvious, isn't it? Both of you. I'd better go."

"Yes."

"Yes? Great little hostess, aren't you. I come over to help you, and you do nothing but pick a fight and try and hurry me off."

Now what? How the hell did you ever straighten out messes like this? And why bother? *Maybe, Annie, because this is awfully familiar.*

"Sit down, Howard, and listen. Listen to what I'm trying to say, even if I am muddled. First, why did you come here tonight? And why is Lala mad at you? Does she think there's another woman? Is there another woman? And was Terry playing around? I really want to know, so I can put it aside. Things weren't perfect, but I loved him a lot, and I finally realized it again, this last year."

He poured more wine in his glass. I shook my head, and he

put his hand over mine. "Sorry I blew up," he said. "Mostly I'm mad at myself. Yeah, Lala's mad about another woman. Another woman. I've been feeling sort of self-righteous because nothing had come of it, and the night she blew up, I really was working. But, hell, I'd been trying to make time with her, and Lala seemed to know." He stopped, seemed to be brooding.

"Why?"

"Why, what?"

"Why would a guy like you want to 'make time' when you've got a good wife like Lala? Pretty, smart, nice, a good mother, a great housekeeper, gardener, and cook." I was getting mad again. "What in God's name does a woman have to be to keep a husband interested in her, or at least get equal attention with his other interests?"

"I don't know. I don't think it's that. I think it's more us. Me, anyway." Another long pause.

"You?"

"Yeah. I want to be more, well, you know—Galahad, John Wayne, the President—and I'm just me, and I want more."

"But Howard, you're, you're..." I stared at him. Did Terry feel like this too? "You're successful, handsome, you're even President of your own company, and..."

"Brave, helpful, courteous. Nuts. I'm just a man."

"Well, aren't we all? I mean... you know, just people?"

He shrugged.

"I mean, talk to Lala about it." *Oh, yeah, me and Ann Landers—full of great advice.*

"Oh, sure, talk to my wife about all the reasons I'm unfaithful."

I jumped up and threw a log on the fire, hard. "Why not? If you don't like it, and she doesn't like it, why not talk? If you don't know why, and she doesn't know why, try and find out. And I can promise you one thing, she'll be glad to know it isn't all because of her. She probably thinks you think she's dull, that she's lost her looks, and not sexy—a failure as a wife. Go home, Howard."

"I didn't answer your other questions."

"I can't remember what they were. Go home. You are Lala's problem, not mine, and I don't need to get so upset. So go home."

He filled my glass. "No, Terry wasn't after any woman. We used to kid him, called him 'Straight Arrow.' But, yes, he was working all those evenings, as far as I know, and I was working most of the evenings he was."

"Then why...?"

"Why were you sitting home alone and lonesome, like Lala?"

I nodded.

"That I don't know. I do think Terry was faithful, at least as far as I knew. I envied him."

I nodded again. No need to talk to him about Marny. No, Howard wouldn't have known about her. That was early in our marriage, and then again, later. Why did those times matter? What good did it to drag it all out for the millionth time? So Terry had been faithful for all those middle years.

I drained my glass. I was still mad. I didn't know which one of us he'd been faithful to, or at with what kind of struggle. I'd said I wanted to know so I could put it aside. Aside, under, buried, but over—finally over.

Oh, hell, I'd told him we couldn't drink the whole bottle, and we had, and I shouldn't have. I stood up, carefully. "I'll make you some coffee or a sandwich if you want, Howard, then you must go. I'm half looped and tired, and I want to go to bed."

He followed me to the kitchen.

Softly, he asked, "With me?"

"Huh?"

"Bed. We're both lonely. I'll make you happy."

"No."

"Why not?"

"Don't be stupid, Howard. You sound like a teenager. *Why?* And such a romantic approach. Women don't have to say why. We're liberated now. We can just say no."

"I've always had a yen for you, Anne."

"This is ridiculous. Drink your coffee and go. Drive carefully, and don't come again alone."

"You asked?"

"I'm dumb."

"Look, why not? Don't tell me you're not lonely. We can have fun together."

"Go home."

"You're caught in Victorian morality. Sex is wonderful. What's wrong with wanting each other?"

The wine had definitely caught up with me. I started to laugh. *Boy, just like a bad novel.* "Here I am, wringing my soul out, thinking I'm helping you get it all straight." *Little Miss Nobility.* "I had visions of you flying after Lala and you two talking the whole thing out, and you realizing you'd loved only her, and you'd be faithful the rest of your life. The two of you, happy, going into the sunset together."

"Stop it, Sweet. You're upset." He came around the counter.

I picked up the coffeepot.

"OK. I'll go home. I'm curious though. Did that little, curly headed guy you were with last week have any more luck than me?"

I waved the coffeepot and some of the coffee sloshed toward him. He picked up his coat and left pretty fast.

Had he been that nasty with Terry? Maybe that's why Terry worked so damned hard. If he hadn't, would Howard have been so vindictive? I looked at the sandwich I'd begun to make. Ugh. I couldn't eat it—but it would freeze.

Maybe it was just a macho thing. He couldn't take "no"

from a woman without his ego being battered.

I yelped and jumped when the back door opened. It was Howard. I grabbed the coffeepot.

"No, don't, Annie. Scalding me won't help. Besides, you don't need to. I've come to apologize. What I said was unforgivable—but please, forgive me?"

I set the pot down, but kept my hand on it. "All right... now go."

"I really am lonely, and I let that persuade me you'd be receptive. I'm sorry, especially because talking to you seemed to start to clear some things up for me."

I nodded and opened the door for him.

Eying the coffee pot, he left.

❧ CHAPTER EIGHTEEN ❧

I was glad to go back to work on Monday. Work problems seemed to have solutions. I got my records started, checked the day out with Mary, and helped set up tables until Royal called me into the office.

"If you can spare the time, Anne, I'd like to go over some ideas I have."

"Sure." I grabbed a pad and pen and slid my chair over to her desk.

"I have a day honoring the seniors each May. Before, it's been sort of a tea, with the mayor and some of the councilmen making speeches, and maybe some entertainment. Now that you're here, and John says you can have some extra hours for it, how about a luncheon?"

"From McCloud's, or something fancier?"

"Fancier. Could you come up with a menu? Something we could cook here?"

"Wow, with that kitchen it could be sort of hairy. How many are you planning for?"

"Last year we had 80. With a lunch, maybe 100 to 125."

"That's a lot of seniors."

"I'd like you to do all the planning and supervising of the lunch part, the decorations, and arranging for help. I'll do the program, speakers and timing, that sort of thing. Of course, we'll work together, and share ideas. Do you think we could have a meeting first thing Friday morning and we'll see how it's coming along? We'll set a firm date then, and get it on the May calendar."

"What sort of budget is there?"

"Don't laugh, but the official budget says $40.00."

"Royal, I can't feed 100 people with $40.00."

"Nor forty for your part Anne, forty over all."

Magic, that's what we'll need. "You mean we charge for the lunch? The seniors are being honored, they do all the work, and they'll also have to pay?"

"You get an A."

"It doesn't seem right."

"I know, but that's how the budget reads."

"What idiot came up with that figure?"

"John and I did."

Yep—foot in mouth disease—terminal case. "I'm sorry, Royal, but it seems so, so inadequate."

"Yes. But Danville isn't a rich town, and John does keep income and out-go balanced. I hate budget time. You rob Peter to pay Paul. Anyway, the meal will have to pay for itself. Now I do have some, let us say, surplus, money. If you go a few dollars over, I can absorb it. Though honestly, Anne, a very few. I'll give you ten of the forty for decorations and such. Don't splurge, darling."

I made a face and went back to my desk. I got out a file and labeled it, "May Luncheon," and started in. One oven, four burners, a roaster, and a medium refrigerator. Fun. Let's see. Menu, table decorations, table placement, serving, kitchen help before and after.

So, Annie, menu first. Everything else will depend on it.

I sat and brooded, answered the phone, and occasionally drifted out to the kitchen. It would be fun to have something really different. Like stroganoff maybe, or real steak, or... "Royal. That's really less, counting our subsidy, than we pay McCloud's for each of his meals."

"Uh huh, but we've got free help."

"Thank God." Back to work.

Stuffed pork chops. Now that might work. Brown and stuff them the afternoon before. Could I cook 100 in the oven? Maybe. But hell, how'd I refrigerate them overnight with all the salad, cream, and butter? Nuts. I made another list: -*milk? -coffee? -cream? -sugar?* We'd see.

I called McCloud's and even got through to him without a struggle. "Hi. Anne Farley here. We're planning a big luncheon in May and I wondered if I could get our entrée and maybe a cake through you? What would it cost?"

"Depends, Anne. Say you want ham. That would be 65 cents a serving. Cake, plain, 25 cents; decorated, 30 cents each."

"Oh, boy. That answers that. I can't afford it."

"How much do you have to work with?"

"A dollar per person."

"Oh, come off it, Anne. You can't do it. I could give you meat loaf and pudding and stretch a point for you for, say, 70 cents."

"Thanks, really, but we want it to be special. I'll have to come up with something we can cook here."

"I shouldn't, but I've a couple of ideas for you. The Egyptian would probably cook the meat for you. They have in the past for some of the service organizations. Then there's the high school. They've got a 'Cooking for Profit' class. They serve a public lunch every Thursday and do some catering, mostly for the school, and it's all at cost."

"Hey, thanks, you're a doll. That gives me some hope." We hung up, and I got another brainstorm and went out to see Mary in the kitchen. She was having coffee, so I poured her a cup and joined her. I told her what Royal and McCloud had said.

She agreed that stuffed pork chops would be nice. "Or stuffed meat loaf, Anne."

"Stuffed meat loaf? How?"

"You roll your meat loaf out like a pie crust, put a bread dressing on it, and roll it up like a jelly roll."

"Sounds good. Is it easy to roll? And how does it slice?"

"Well, it rolls OK. You use wax paper or plastic, but it can be a problem to put it in the pan, and then sometimes it is a little hard to get out."

"Maybe we'd better put that idea aside unless we get into real money problems."

"Do you have to decide today?"

"No, Royal wants it pretty definite by Friday, but I'd like to get my menu first so I can figure out the other things."

"I've got an idea, Anne, but I've got to check on it. Suppose you figure out a menu for the stuffed pork chops or meat loaf, and then if I can't work my idea out, maybe we can decide which we want."

"Great. But there are problems with the chops too. Refrigeration."

"Let's see. Sabrina lives just down the block, and I think she's got a big refrigerator in her apartment. She'd let us keep them there overnight. Or maybe, if we get the restaurant or school to cook them, they'd store them for us."

"Mary, you're wonderful. That should work. Are you coming in tomorrow?" She nodded. "Can I meet with you, say at 9:30, before the painting class?"

That set up, I went back to the office.

The week whizzed by. I didn't hear from Howard, thank God, but neither did I hear from Buster. That surprised me. I guess I thought he really meant it. I was almost tempted to call someone and go see *Casablanca* anyway.

Mary's idea was that we serve salmon. Her brother-in-law's brother was a hot shot in a salmon packing company. On Tuesday she told me she could get us enough free salmon for a dinner. By Wednesday she had it all arranged. Phil would pick the salmon up by the day before the dinner and the company would have them thawed for us.

I was the one to have the next brainstorm. First, I checked the grant contact, and as far as I could tell, it didn't matter who cooked the food, just so long as there were three meals a week served at the Center. There was even a provision that days could be skipped because of holidays and such, and made up later. So I asked Royal why it wouldn't be all right for us to get the subsidy and use the money to provide a really neat meal. She thought it sounded OK, but said I'd better talk to John. I made an appointment to see him Thursday afternoon.

On the assumption I'd have some more money to play with, and having a free entrée, Mary and I came up with two menus. One for the extra money, and one to live with the $1.00 per person budget.

I called Fay, and having been given enough warning, she said she'd love to help. We talked a long time on the phone, she bubbling all over about plans for a spring garden. Understandably, she didn't believe me when I said she could have ten dollars for expenses. "Honestly, Fay, my share of the budget for the luncheon is ten bucks. No, I can't ask for any more, there isn't any more. Look, come over next week on Tuesday, right after painting class. We can go out for lunch and then we can look through the storeroom so you can see what we've got. We'll make definite plans and get you a committee."

"It's a good thing you offer such a challenge, Anne. I must be a nut to be willing to help."

"Admittedly, being nuts helps. But honestly, wasn't the birthday party fun?""

Thinking of Tiny, I crossed my fingers. She promised to meet me Tuesday at noon and said she hadn't forgotten the chicken cordon bleu that I'd promised to make for her.

On Thursday I slept until 7:00 and spent the morning doing housework.

At 11:00 I made a big green salad, took it over to the

Center, added it to the potluck, and ate at a table with Janet, Butch, Tom, and Sylvia. Sylvia sported new glasses—lovely, large modern frames. Her makeup was perfect. Well, she wore more than I'd ever consider wearing, but it looked good. Tom was beaming. "Sylvia, is your check all straightened out?" She nodded. "Janet, is your check mix-up OK?"

"Afraid not."

"But Janet, I thought Mrs. McCaully said it would be cleared up right away. I'm sorry. I should have asked sooner. The day that man called, my heat was out, or I might have realized something was wrong. Can I do anything?"

"I don't think so. I can't figure out what happened. I filled everything out again. Then, when nothing came, I called Mrs. McCaully. She never called back, but finally that man called, a Mr. Romera. He said he'd check into it."

"How dumb. Maybe you should call Olympia."

"What good would that do?"

"Gosh, I don't know. Maybe shake them up. Call your Congressman." I didn't dare ask how she was managing without money, not in front of everyone. Maybe Butch was the answer. "Seriously, if you come in tomorrow morning, let's get Royal to call."

"Thank you. I'll do that. It's crazy, no one seems to know anything about it. I'm beginning to feel like I don't exist."

With an eye on the clock, I ate and listened to the four of them plan to go to Seattle for a Friday night dance. My God, Butch wasn't going to drive, was he? Nope, they were going to take the Metro.

Sylvia told them, "We'll meet you at five by the drug store and catch the 5:05. That'll get us into town by six. We'll take the monorail and be out at the Seattle Center in time for dinner. That'll give us plenty of time and we can be ready to dance by seven-thirty. Tom checked the buses, and if we leave at 9:30, we can catch the 9:58 home. That's not too late, is it?"

Janet cut in. "Tell you what, Syl, you and I can sit together on the way home and let the guys sleep." Butch made a face.

Sylvia asked, "What are you going to wear?"

I picked up my dishes and left them debating the merits of Sylvia's blue pleated dress or the yellow print. Then I went around and picked up deserted coffee cups until it was time to go see John. I was going out the door when Buster came in.

He beamed. "Anne, I was afraid you wouldn't be here. Come play Scrabble."

"Sorry, Buster, I'm due at a meeting. See you later, huh?" I started out the door. He followed.

"Anne, wait. I'm sorry I didn't call earlier, but my wife was pretty bad, so I've been going over there every day and staying kind of late in the evenings."

"Your wife?" That really stopped me. I hadn't flipped. He asked me out, but he was married. I knew the shock showed.

He looked worried. "You knew my wife was in the nursing home, didn't you?"

"No. I didn't know you were married." *Jeez, Anne, get off your high horse.* "I'm sorry she's sick. Is she getting better?"

"Not really, though the emergency's over. Would you...?"

"Buster, I'm sorry, I have to get over to City Hall. I'm late already." I started off again, and Buster followed.

"Could you go to the movie tonight?"

"Oh, Buster, I'm sorry, my class starts tonight."

"Anne, are you upset because I'm married? I thought everybody at the Center knew. She's been in a nursing home for three years now. It's multiple sclerosis, really bad. She can't walk and doesn't know us most of the time."

"That's awful. It must be hard for you." I headed for John's office, then stopped. "Honest, Buster, I've got to get to my meeting. I guess I was surprised you're married, but I'm not upset." I slipped into John's office and shut the door in Buster's face. Cripes. Being single had some unexpected problems.

Lil waved me in. John was munching on a hamburger, his desk and guest chair piled high. I stood and explained about the luncheon and that I wanted to use the supplement even though we planned to charge $1.00 for the lunch.

He just looked at me.

"Royal and I can't tell for sure from the grant paperwork whether it's legal."

He sighed. I had the distinct impression he didn't want to be bothered by my problem.

"Do you have a copy of the grant with you?"

"Yes."

He picked up the phone and dialed. "Jed, if you're free, I'm sending over a Mrs. Farley from the Senior Center. She'll tell you her problem." He hung up. "OK?"

"Thank you." I scuttled out. I asked Lillian where and who Jed was.

"He's the City Attorney, room 133. Did John bite?"

"You mean it isn't just me?"

"Nope, it seems to be the whole world."

"Well, don't freeze. If the chill is still on tomorrow, come eat with us."

I found 133. "J.D. Butler" was on the door.

"Mr. Butler? I'm Mrs. Farley." He gave me a chair, and I explained again about the lunch.

He leafed through the grant and sighed. "I sometimes wonder who first set up the model for grants. They tell you everything you don't need and never what you're looking for. Tell you what. Have your meal, send your records in like you always do, but don't send the City the money. Give Lil a memo requesting payment of the supplement to the Center, not to the caterer. I think that should cover it."

"Thank you. I appreciate that." John's mood made me cautious. "Would you initial the memo?"

He nodded.

"Great. Come eat lunch with us someday. We always like guests." He nodded again, and I escaped.

Buster was waiting at the entrance. "Come have coffee, Anne. I'm embarrassed and would like to explain."

"Honest, Buster," I began. What was his real name? "It's OK. I've got to go back to the office and get a memo out. No, that can wait until tomorrow. Tell you what, I'm having an attack of terminal sweet tooth. Why don't we go to the ice cream shop? I want a gooey sundae. You can have coffee if you want."

We walked over to Main Street and down to the shop. I read the menu and finally selected a Trinity—three flavors of ice cream, three sauces, whipped cream, and marshmallow topping. He picked butterscotch malt. While we waited for our order, he started talking.

"There's no hope of my wife ever getting out of the nursing home, so I've tried making a life for myself. Our kids are grown. We sold our house when Nan started getting bad, so I've just got the apartment. I work all the hours I can get, but I've still got a lot of empty time. It's hard to find friends, especially a woman, who's free to go out occasionally."

"I see." And I did, of course, but what should I do? "Do you come into the Center much? There are a lot of women, people, who like to go places." And why was it all right for them if not for me?

"I go over with Mary sometimes, but God, Anne, it's embarrassing. Those women act, well, so eager. They...they push!"

Our ice cream arrived.

"Mmm, well not all of them," I responded. "There are some awfully nice women, and men too, down there."

"Sure, I know, and I promised Mary I'd come in more often and give myself a chance to meet people. I think I'll take that driftwood class, unless I get called on a job."

"Good. It takes awhile, you know."

"Of course. Now, how about you, Anne? Just a movie."

"Fine, I'd like to. You do understand, don't you, Buster? I've not been a window very long, and I guess I didn't stop to think about anyone else's problems. I see why you need to go places and don't want to be alone all the time, but..." I stopped dead. How could I say it? "The kiss on the cheek was OK, but nothing else. I, well, I'm just not up to it, yet."

"Sure, just an occasional date, someone to talk to. I've never tried to be a sheik."

Now, I'd never heard of anyone say that before. "Great, call me. I'd better rush. Like I said, I've got this class, Tuesdays and Thursdays. I've got to get ready."

We squabbled briefly over the check. I gave up and let him pay for it, rushed back to the Center, got my car, and went home. After the sundae I didn't want dinner, but made myself eat a salad. I had time for an hour in the garden before I had to change for class. Clothes were a dilemma. I wasn't going to go in jeans and a shirt and flip-flops like all the kids I'd seen wear, but my suit was too much, even though there'd probably be more adults at night. I finally compromised by wearing slacks, a checkered shirt, and my old penny-loafers.

I found the parking lot and building with no trouble, which made me early, and the classroom was dark. There was no place to wait, so I got brave, went in, and turned on the lights. I took a desk in the middle of the room and set out my notebook, pen, and text. The next person in was a fat kid in jeans and a sweatshirt.

He sat on top of a desk in the front row, looked doubtfully at me, and said, "This is the Grant Writing class."

"Yes, I know." *Oh, hell, he wasn't asking, he's telling. He doesn't think I'm the type to be taking Grant Writing. And that fat kid is the instructor?* Before I could think of anything else to say, five more students came in. Yep, all in jeans. Gradually, a total of fifteen showed up. One woman was, say, in her early thirties.

The rest were young.

Mt. Tabor opened class by calling roll. Then he told us that he believed in learning by doing, and that each of us would be expected to write a grant as the quarter's project. He then went down his attendance list and asked each of us what project we would work on. Everyone but me had an answer.

Most of them wanted funding for some special study. The thirtyish blonde wanted to get money to finance a study on the needs of women in the catchment area served by the college.

When my turn came, I still hadn't dreamed up anything. "I'm sorry, I haven't a definite idea yet." He then proceeded to lecture for an hour. I took notes like mad. He told us he had put references for our reading requirements in the library.

One cagey student had a tape recorder. Thank God, it seemed I hadn't lost my ability to take notes, though I'd have to type them up. No one else could have read them.

He dismissed class a bit early, so I dashed to the library, hoping to get there before the ten o'clock closing. I grabbed the reserve list and looked under Tabor. Nothing, so I took it over to the clerk. "Mr. Tabor is supposed to have three bulletins in reserve. I can't seem to locate them. Is there some other arrangement?"

She took the book and checked. "No, he doesn't seem to have anything saved yet. It's pretty early in the quarter."

"This is for Tuesday."

"Sorry."

The bastard. I was putting the reference list away when the blonde came in. "We're too early," I said. "He doesn't have them on reserve yet."

"Typical."

"Have you had a class from him before?"

"Yes, 'Government by Initiative'. He can teach, but he's a monster."

Amen.

"Come on, maybe we can dig them out."

She obviously knew her way around the library. Finally we found two of the booklets, so we each took one and checked it out. This was going to be fun. We talked out to the parking lot together. She said she worked at the Multi Service Center.

As she got in her car she added, "If you can meet me in front of City Hall at a quarter to eight tomorrow morning, we could trade pamphlets, though I'm tempted to keep these out the three days, we're allowed. But that would only mess it up for the others. I'll return mine tomorrow night."

I'll have to read thirty pages and take notes tonight! I agreed to meet her, dashed home, climbed into bed, and read the pamphlet. Then I read it again. No go. At midnight I gave up, and using the old 'the first sentence of a paragraph is usually the key sentence', I copied the main facts from each key phrase—I hoped. I was done by 1:00 am.

I crawled out of bed at 7:00, feeling bleary-eyed. I showered, had cornflakes and coffee for breakfast, and was at City Hall by 7:45. We exchanged pamphlets as agreed, and I went to the Center and opened the building. It took me a hell of a long time to get going and start to work. How long did housewifely conditioning last? Why was I disorganized just because I'd left an unmade bed and undone dishes at home?

I finally got the memo done and showed it to Royal, who initialed it and put it in the in-house mail to go to J. D. Butler and then to John.

Royal seemed to be in one of her distracted moods and put off our talk about the Recognition Day program, saying she'd be out most of the day. I told her about Janet, but she just looked gloomy. Luckily Janet didn't show. I worked on plans for the luncheon until I ran out of information, and then made an outline for Tuesday's painting class. No one besides Phil cared two whoops what I taught, so I went out and coaxed him from the poolroom, and asked what he was interested in. I couldn't pry a thing out of him.

"Anything you want, Anne, is just fine," he said repeatedly.

"But surely you're interested in something special. I know you know more than I do, but maybe you'd like to review something or see if I've got an angle you'd like to explore."

"Oh, no, Anne. I just like to paint. I'll like anything you want to do."

I stared at him in exasperation. "Should I continue with some more on brush strokes?" He nodded, and I gave up. I went back to my notes and decided to bring my pewter pitcher and my red velvet pillow.

Around eleven Mary came in. "You'd better come in and look at the lunch, Anne."

"Anything wrong?"

"I don't know. It just doesn't look very good. I mean, it tastes all right. I tried it, but, well, you come see."

I checked the menu; fillet of Sole, parsley potatoes, miracle salad, green peas, rolls, and chocolate cake. Sounded OK. Fish was never the most popular lunch. It didn't re-heat well, but it made a change.

In the kitchen, Mary opened the oven. She was heating the fish. It had a white sauce that would keep it from drying out. Selma uncovered the pan of salad. Miracle salad seemed to be a Jell-O mix, probably lemon, whipped with, I bet, Miracle Whip salad dressing, and a few shreds of vegetables. It looked blah, but I knew from experience it tasted fine and the seniors loved it. The usual green salad was hard on a lot of those with false teeth. I took the lid off the peas. *Oh.* Instead of peas it was frozen cauliflower.

With a feeling of precognition, I checked the tables. The rolls were white bread and the cake was yellow with white frosting. They'd sent us a white meal. Yep, the parsley potatoes had nary a flake of parsley. "It's all white." The women looked at me and started to laugh.

Mary said, "Why so it is. I just knew it didn't seem right, but I couldn't see what was wrong."

"Haven't you ever done it? I did it to company once. We consumed trout coated in cornmeal, baked potatoes, carrots, and orange Jell-O salad with vegetables. Dessert was Baked Alaska. To make it even worse, I had a beige tablecloth, sort of on the gold side. OK, how do we rescue this? Did they send some parsley?"

Mary shook her head. "The delivery man said they'd run out."

"Lovely. I'll go to the store and get some for the potatoes. And how about if we add some peas and carrots to the white sauce on the fish? Then I'll get lettuce for under the salad. Wish we had brown rolls, but I guess that'd cost too much. I'll be back in half an hour. That'll give us enough time to fix it up."

Selma called as I dashed out, "Get some of those colored sprinkles for the cake."

"Great idea."

I was back in twenty minutes, having hit a quiet time at Safeway. Mary took the lettuce, Selma the peas and carrots, and Sarah the parsley. I started shaking the sprinkles on the cake, but Phyllis took over, so I went back to the office. Oh damn, John was sitting at Royal's desk talking on the phone. I'd forgotten to get someone to cover that.

As I came in, he put his hand over the mouthpiece. "What's the lesson in the painting class?"

"Broad brushstrokes."

"She says that was last week."

"More this week. Want me to talk to her?"

He shook his head and hung up in a few seconds. He was shaking his head. "Who's painting a secret masterpiece? I just promised not to peak."

He sounded in a better temper. "That's Rose. She seems shy about sharing what she's doing until it's finished."

"How can you help her if you can't see the picture?"

"I can't. She talks all during my lesson, too, so maybe it sinks in my osmosis."

He snorted. "All of them are incredible. Anyway, you should tell them what the next lesson is. Maybe someone will want to do some advance studying. At least it would cut down on the phone calls."

"Ha. That painting class could be run with a store dummy up front. However, I had the dumb idea of giving the first class and then deciding what the needs are and planning the term. No way!"

"Didn't work out?"

"That's putting it mildly. Only one man paid the least attention to me. Less than half wanted any help, and as you know, one wouldn't even show me her painting."

"Watch it, Anne, you'll talk yourself out of a job."

I sat down. "I don't know. Royal seemed to think it went OK and that they liked the class. It shook me, though. I've cut the lecture time and will work on areas of greatest weakness and on stuff I like." Anyway, it looked like the phone issue was sidetracked.

"Don't panic. Trust Royal. She knows what they want. By the way, where is she?"

Who knows? "She had a whole list of things to do. She said she'd be at City Hall some of the time. Anything I can do?"

"No, I was just making like a supervisor. I wondered about the wing-ding honoring the seniors—whether she expected me to make a speech again, or what. Your part working out OK?"

I glanced at him. I had a faint suspicion I was being apologized to. "Everything is going fine. The menu is planned. We've been given a donation of salmon, so we are going to have a good dinner, non-catered. We have help on the decorations, and I happen to know you are the first speaker."

"Got your entertainment lined up?"

"I don't know the status of that."

He wrote in a pocket notebook. "It's almost lunch time. If you're not over-booked, I'll stay."

"I'll go see." I went out to Brenda. Luckily we were full. "You're fourth on the waiting list. Want to wait and eat with the latecomers? It will probably be canned roast beef and better than today's meal." As soon as I said it I realized I had big-mouth-itis.

He sat up and looked all business. "What's wrong with the meal?"

"It's white."

"White? Anne, talking to you is sometimes almost like talking to Royal."

It's this place. It's catching. "McCloud's sent us a white meal. White fish, potatoes, white vegetable, white bread, salad, and cake. The works. We're rescuing it somewhat, but it will never make the gourmet Meal of the Week. And that reminds me..." I wrote 'Call McCloud's' on the top of my list.

John watched me. "I can't resist. I'm staying, only you shuffle something so I get a regular meal, and then I want to hear you call McCloud's. I'm curious."

And you also don't trust me. I went in to Mary, told her the mayor wanted a white meal, and she offered with pleasure to give him hers. As I'd suspected, she was already heating roast beef.

Back in the office I called McCloud's. He was out in the kitchen and the secretary promised he'd call back. I told John, "Better go get a seat. Do you want to say anything?"

"No. Come eat with me."

"I'm smart. I'm eating leftovers. Seriously, I can't eat yet."

"I'll save you a seat. You shouldn't skip meals."

"I don't, but I've got to get the money out of sight and make announcements."

"Sure, go along, but come and eat soon." He went on in to

the dining room.

I took the money from Brenda and hid it in the files. Plato wasn't around, so the phone would be uncovered. I went out to make announcements. I'd finally gotten used to it and the microphone usually behaved. I reminded them of events they needed to sign up for, that today was the last day to pay for the Arboretum trip, and that today was Greg's eighty-fifth birthday. Everyone clapped. Greg stood up and we all sang "Happy Birthday."

When we were through singing, Mary called out, "And today is also Pet and Antonia's anniversary."

"Wonderful," I said. "Happy Anniversary to you both. How many years?"

"Eighteen."

Everyone shouted Happy Anniversary. *Must be a second marriage.* Mary got the serving line going. I took the card room coffeepot to the kitchen, poured the dregs into the luncheon coffee, and made a fresh pot. I finally went over and joined John. He ate his lunch with apparent enjoyment. Our doctoring really had improved the looks of the meal. When everyone was served, Mary brought me a plate and joined us. She'd somehow found time to make us a green salad. With the beef and gravy on bread and a couple of Selma's cookies instead of the cake, we did very well. John took my empty plate, and I got back to the office in time to catch McCloud's call. I'd explained my objections when John came in. Didn't he have anything to do at City Hall?

McCloud said, "Look, Anne, I'm sorry. I'll send over a jar of parsley tomorrow to make up for today."

"But what happened? Just parsley wouldn't have improved it much."

"The peas were off-color so we substituted, and unfortunately it was cauliflower we had enough of. The bakery had problems and sent bread instead of whole-wheat rolls. I'm still trying to find out why they made white cake instead of chocolate. You're not the first person to call in."

"OK, I understand, but I looked through the month's menus, and on the 28th, you've got a yellow meal."

"Oh, hell. OK, I'll rethink it. I swear every cycle I've double checked everything, and we either foul up the color or serve three casseroles in a row."

I hung up and told John the story. I was thrilled when he didn't seem to think I should have demanded McCloud's make up for the sprinkles and lettuce.

Finally John got up and started to leave. At the door he paused, "I promised I'd show you I could cook. I'm giving a party a week from Saturday. I'm inviting some of the City people like Lil and her husband, Royal, and a few others. I hope you can come."

"Why, thanks. That would be nice. Can I bring anything?"

"No, I'm the cook. Come about 7:00."

I started counting money. Neat. A party with my co-workers.

❧ CHAPTER NINETEEN ❧

Royal put in a brief appearance about 2:00, promised to be in for Janet on Monday, asked me to close, then disappeared for the rest of the day. The seniors cleared out early, so I locked up at 4:30 and rushed over to the library. The pamphlets were now listed in the reserve file, but of course all three were out. I went over and searched the shelves again, and nothing. Hell! I sat in a carrel, read the blonde's pamphlet, and took notes. Hers made a little more sense than mine had, but not a lot. I returned that pamphlet.

I got home at seven, stuck a Stouffer's dinner in the oven, and typed up my notes. I called Jo while I ate. We caught each other up on what had been happening. I told her about Buster. Surprisingly, she was very disapproving.

"Truly, Anne, you can't go out with a married man, an old man at that."

"But why not? It's just to see a movie with someone. It's nothing serious."

"Think of appearances. You know Terry wouldn't want you going out with someone who is already married."

"Honestly, Jo, I thought you'd think it was funny. Me and this improbable man, even though he's very nice."

"Nice, maybe, but the phrase 'Dirty Old Man' has a reason."

"Well, maybe. Anyway, he'll probably never get around to really asking me out. How's Greg?"

"Fine so far. He's at an AA meeting."

"Are you going to Alanon?"

"Once a week."

"Great."

"Anne, let's not talk about it. I'm beginning to think I'll never have anything to think about but alcoholism. I'm fed up."

"I bet. Want to come to work and help at our dinner?" I told her about our salmon feed, but she was doubtful.

"I just don't know. I don't think I should commit myself. If there's something I can do at home, give me a call." I thanked her, and we said goodbye.

I ran the dishes through the dishwasher even though I didn't have a full load. I put the clothes in the washer, puttered a bit straightening things, and went to bed early.

I went back to the library Saturday morning. No article. The librarian could offer no help, but she said Mr. Tabor had put the next week's reading on reserve, so I read two of next week's pamphlets. I took notes before I went to meet Mom to take her to the airport. She was going to Chicago to her sister's. I spent the weekend grubbing.

On Monday when I arrived at the Center, Janet was already in with Royal, who was calling Social Security.

"When will Mrs. McCaully be in? Oh, you've no idea when she'll be in? Then who can I talk to about Mrs. Nemmers' Social Security Supplement payments? This is Mrs. Paige of the Danville Senior Center. I believe a Mr. Romero also was looking into her missing check. Yes, she applied at your division, *twice.* No, now listen. It is too late in the month for this to be just a late check. This woman is destitute, and another tracer is not enough. I'm sorry, I will not wait for Mrs. McCaully or Mr. Romero to call back. Something must be done now. Let me speak to another caseworker. No? This is ridiculous. Give me your supervisor."

Royal rolled her eyes. Janet and I sat and listened. It was

like a radio play. Royal repeated the whole story. I listened with awe.

"Mrs. Lewis, Mrs. Nemmers has been in, let's see, three times. I have no idea how many calls have been made. Somehow, something has to be done, today. Yes, I understand a tracer will be placed, but that has already been done before, and we get no information. If I do not hear from you or someone down there, preferably your supervisor, by 2:00 this afternoon, I will call Olympia. Yes, thank you, goodbye."

Royal assured us she would make good her threat. Janet swore she wasn't starving, so we figured it was pretty clear Butch was coming to her rescue.

After Janet left, Royal and I went over the Recognition Banquet briefly. I made myself a copy of the program from her verbal outline and she showed me how to make a proportioned sketch of the dining room and table placement for the meal.

I was getting ready to go to the storeroom for the tape measure when Mary came into the office. She sighed and lowered herself onto the corner of my desk.

"Anne, can you come out to the kitchen and help?"

"Sure, what's up?" I got up, but Mary sat there.

"I don't know how I can be so dumb, but it's not really all my fault. Still, I just can't manage."

I stared in amazement. This was Mary, who ran that kitchen with real efficiency and no effort.

"What has happened, and what did you do?"

"You remember that Polish woman who came in Thursday? No, that's right, you'd gone. Well this lady came in, and she went over to the corner and just sat there. I think Emma introduced herself and asked her to play cards, but she just shook her head and sat there, doing nothing.

"After a while, I noticed she was sort of crying, she had tears running down her cheek and she kept dabbing at her face with a Kleenex. So I went over and asked her if she was all right.

Was she sick or hungry or anything? She kept on shaking her head and was still crying, so I kept trying to find out what was wrong."

"Finally she must have realized I wasn't going to go away, or maybe she figured she had to tell someone, so she started jabbering away at me. I guess it was Polish, I did made out she's from Poland. She knows a few American words. Something about her son, maybe she's come out here to live with him. I couldn't figure out much more. She said 'New York' several times. Anyway, I called Willie on the phone. I figured maybe she could use some extra help. I told her the lady's name was something like Marianska, and that she was so lonely she wanted to die—so I asked her to come in and help in the kitchen today."

"How'd you do that?"

"I took her to the kitchen and showed her around and the food left from the meal. I showed her the menu and pointed to the food. Then I showed her today's menu, the calendar, and the clock."

"Wow, ingenious."

"Well, I got through to her, because she's here today. Are you having trouble getting her to understand what's to be done?"

"Sort of, but that's not all Anne. You remember Beulah Ashford? Her son married a Japanese girl during the Viet Nam War, and now his mother-in-law has come to live with them. Beulah says Tomiko, that's the daughter-in-law, is going nuts with her mother around all the time, so Beulah brought Mrs. Suzuki down today to help. Seems she thought it would be real nice to come help out, but Anne, she doesn't speak any English either.

"Both ladies are in there, and they keep talking away at me. I have to show them how to do everything I want done. Then they do it so fast, I have to show them some more—and I can't get anything done myself."

I couldn't help laughing.

"That's not all, Anne. Rose is the other helper today, and she's off her rocker again, as balmy as she can be."

"Oops, and they're alone in there now. Come on."

We rushed out to the kitchen. Marianska and Mrs. Suzuki were standing by the sink while Rose was talking at a rapid rate to them. They sure looked bewildered. Mary introduced me.

I said hopefully, "Guten morgen." And dredging up my smattering of Japanese from the business trip I'd taken to Niigata with Terry, I added "Konichiwa," and bowed.

That sure as hell was a mistake. Mrs. Suzuki's face lit up and she bowed deeper, so I bowed again. Then she bowed three times, each time deeper than before, and let loose a stream of staccato Japanese. I got two words, which was a miracle. Something about eating, and "Sensei" for teacher.

Caught up in the game, Marianska, Rose, and Mary all dipped their heads in bows, and for a while, I thought we'd never quit. In desperation I pointed to Marianska and said 'Poland'; to Mrs. Suzuki, 'Japan'; and to Rose, Mary, and me, 'America.' Everyone nodded at this sage statement.

"Mary, she says you are the teacher. You concentrate on Mrs. Suzuki and getting the food heated." I looked at the tables. Placemats and napkins were on. "Rose, you do the silverware." That usually kept her busy for ages. "Marianska." Was that her first name? It sounded wrong. "You do the plates, please."

I handed her a plate, repeating the word 'plate.' I pulled the cart out and said, 'seventy.' She looked bewildered. I flipped my fingers up seven times and said 'seventy' again slowly.

She let out a long "Ahhh," and flapped her fingers seven times, then said, "Plates, seventy, put..." With amazing speed, she piled plates on the cart and started setting them around.

Every time Mrs. Suzuki passed me, she'd bow and let out more Japanese. I never understood another word. So, I'd bow and say the word I'd used the most in Japan, "*Wakarimasen*, I don't understand."

She didn't either—my accent was probably so atrocious—but she'd bow again, and I'd run for the dining room with the salt and pepper and sugar—stuff like that.

On my second trip out, Rose stopped me.

"Anne, I think you should know."

I sighed.

"There is a graveyard under the Center."

I stared at her.

"An old graveyard. Indians."

Now what? "Is that so? How interesting?"

"I think it's very dangerous. Just think of all those decaying bodies. Why, we could all be poisoned."

"Oh, no, Rose. If it were an Indian burial ground, the bodies would be all decayed by now." *Oh great, lunch is going to be just delicious.* "There would be no danger. How did you hear about it?"

"My nephew told me. He's a teacher at the college."

"An archeologist?"

"That's it—something like that. Anne, I think we should tell the mayor. Just think of all those decaying bodies, maybe even bones getting into the sewer and coming up the toilet. I'm afraid to even go in there."

You keep this up, and I'll be afraid to use it too. "Now Rose, there is no danger of that, and if there is a graveyard under here, I'm sure the mayor already knows." *Oh, boy, John, you are going to love this one.* "I know, why don't we get your nephew to come and tell us all about it?" I was sure she'd back off, not wanting to be caught in her storytelling. Obviously, I really didn't understand.

"That would be a wonderful idea. You call him and ask. I think this needs to be brought out into the open. It ain't right for the City to put us seniors in such danger. We've paid our taxes.

Now that we're old, they just want to get rid of us."

Did she really believe all this? "You come into the office later, and we'll talk to Royal." I escaped to help dish up salad with Mrs. Suzuki. I'd point to the lettuce and say 'lettuce.' She'd say, "rettuce," and then tell me the Japanese name and giggle over my pronunciation. By 11:30 I was exhausted. Everything was done, so we took a break until it was time to serve. I got a cup of coffee and checked with Brenda.

What a day, sixty-five signed up. That meant extra. I beckoned to Mary. She said a lot of the ladies didn't want two pieces of chicken, so there'd be enough to go around. The salad and vegetables would stretch, and she had plenty of rolls and cookies in the freezer.

Brenda asked, "What's this about there being a lot of bodies under the Center? Rose was telling me."

Hell. "I don't really know. She heard something that made her think there was an old Indian burial ground here."

"Awful. Why would anyone put a building up over a graveyard?"

I added cautiously, "I don't really think it's true. I think Rose got something mixed up."

Mary murmured, "Yeah," and made circles over her temples.

Brenda looked confused, and I hurried on to tell them about my Grant class. I couldn't stand any more talk about bodies and bones.

When we went back to the kitchen, I continued thinking about the class. I'd have to go back to the library again tonight, and I was sick of it already. Dumb stuff—and I still didn't have a project to write a grant for.

We got seventy-seven seniors served, then I snuck out of the kitchen, leaving Mary to cope with Polish, Japanese, and bellows.

Sam Ashford had come to help with the dishes, and he was

nearly as deaf as Bill.

While I stacked and counted money, I asked Royal if she had any ideas on something I could write a grant for. "I don't want to spring any surprises on you. I thought maybe I could do something like, oh, say, a subsidy for milk, coffee, and tea. Something little like that. I'd love to see Tim Jonah's face when he was to cope with getting his money from a grant. I bet we could foul up the whole system."

"Now, Anne, don't be silly. It could be done so there wouldn't be much trouble, but why not do something really worthwhile?"

"I think free milk would be worthwhile, but what about asking for some money we could use for an emergency fund for people like Janet?"

"Mmm. That could be sticky to administer."

"How about a psychiatrist for Rose?"

"What's she up to now?"

"You haven't heard about the Indian graveyard under the Center?"

"You're kidding."

"Nope, and she thinks the City should be ashamed of itself."

"Oh, no. I'll have to call John."

I went on and told her about the nephew and trying to ask him about it. She said we'd never track him down, because Rose would never let herself be trapped that way.

"Anne, I know what would be perfect for a grant. I'll call John and get him to come over. We can brief him on the Indians and get his advice on your grant. You can write one for money for the new Center."

"Not on your life, Royal. I'm willing to write for a few hundred for something for the Center so I can learn how to renew the grant we have, but I'm not going to get involved in asking for thousands or millions."

"Not millions. Anyway, John has been talking about plans for a new Center. This would stir him up."

"I don't want to stir him up. I wouldn't have time anyway. I can barely find time to do my reading for this class."

She ignored me and was on the phone calling John. "John, Anne has had the best idea about a new Center."

Oh, I had, had I?

"All right, neither of us has eaten. We'll join you at 1:00. The Egyptian. Fine, great."

"Royal, honest, we shouldn't bother him. There is no way I could write a grant for a new Center. We shouldn't talk to John. Something like that probably takes a professional, and it would be a full time job."

Her talent for paying no attention to problems she wasn't interested in was remarkable. It was obvious her mind had fled elsewhere. She shuffled papers, muttered about Indians, and said, "Your rinse needs re-doing."

That galvanized me, and I dashed for the restroom. She was right. I knew better. I was overdue, and I combed my hair to hide it as best as possible.

Plato took over the phone. We met John at the Egyptian and ordered.

"What's this about a new Center, Anne?" He looked awfully tired.

"There's a sort of mix-up. I need to write a grant for my class. It's just a beginner's class, and I think it should be something small, not important—but Royal says there is talk of a new Center, and thought this might be an approach—but I don't feel comfortable nor competent."

Royal jumped in. "I don't understand you, Anne. You keep tearing yourself down. Of course you could do it."

John interrupted, "Hold on, Royal. Getting the financing together for a new Center is extremely complicated. And what makes you think we are going to build a new Center? You bugged the hell out of me until we got you the building you have. You've only been there three years. This is the first I've heard of a new building."

Our hamburgers came. By gesture, I got a refill on my coffee.

"No, it isn't, John. You know we're getting a little crowded. The wiring is antique. The plumbing's shaky, and the restrooms are disasters."

"OK. OK. You've been hinting, but I don't think we stand a chance of getting financing."

"That's why it's so timely that Anne has to write a grant. Why can't we use her?"

I interrupted, "Royal, listen to me. I don't know enough to write a grant like that. I haven't got the time. That is probably a full-time job, and would take a year or more."

"Oh, Anne!"

"She's right, Royal, but let's toss it around. First, you have to prove to me that you need a new Center." He held up a hand, stopping Royal, who was looking indignant. "Now, listen, maybe, well, yes, I understand why you want a new Center, but I'd have to prove the need for it to the City Council and probably the County if we decided to try and finance it with bonds."

We'd finished our hamburgers, but John and Royal were talking so intently, the waitress knew we weren't leaving and ignored us. My coffee was gone. She wouldn't acknowledge my gestures, so I slid out and filled my own cup and filched another cream pitcher. When I got back, John was still talking.

"We need some idea where we'd best place a new Center. What would it need? And a million other things." He came up for air and looked around. "Pie?" he said, and the waitress trotted over.

The world was not fair.

Royal took it up again. "Seriously, John, I've been doing some thinking about it, and I've started a file on ideas, pamphlets, and regulations, that sort of thing. Anne would have a start, and if we get a volunteer to do the money and fill in the reports, she would have her afternoons free to work on the grant for a new Center."

Sure, and the Awards dinner, and the potlucks, and the closings I do can be tucked into corners...

"Why not let her try it?"

"Maybe a grant to supply free milk, or a fund so we could give emergency financial help."

He shuddered. "I can see the verification needed for an emergency fund."

I felt defensive. "We certainly need emergency money. We've had a woman coming in who has less than a dollar and no food. Even ten dollars would be a help." Now I was embarrassed. John was going through his pockets. "No, no, it's being taken care of. So, if you don't like emergency funds, what about for free milk?"

"Mmm...so-so. It wouldn't lead to much of a learning experience for you."

He hadn't a clue. Just getting that blasted reading list was enough of a learning experience.

He snapped his fingers and said, "Look, I've got an idea. Do you think we need a new Center?"

"Of course, but with a bigger place and room for more programs, you'd need a larger staff to do everything."

"That would need to be part of it. So how about you writing a grant to get financing for feasibility study and needs assessment for a new Senior Center?"

"That sounds possible, but how on earth could I find an agency to fund such a thing? And I do have to submit it."

"Simple. Ask the City."

Royal and I chorused, "The City?"

John looked smug. "Yes, there are funds in the budget that can be allocated to investigate needed new services, buildings, staffing, and things like that."

"Has anyone ever asked for a grant from the City before?"

"No, but there's no reason it can't be done that way."

"Gosh, I don't know. The City people seem awfully stuffy. Who'd have the say so?"

He grinned a familiar evil grin. "Jed and I."

What could I say but, "Oh."

We paid our bills and went back to work.

About 2:30 Janet came back and we sat again and listened to Royal call Mrs. Lewis.

"No trace of the claim? How could that be? She has filed it twice." There was a long pause. Royal repeated key words softly. "Tracer...Olympia...Emergency funds... Ah, so...so. But why hasn't Mrs. McCaully called us? What? Transferred? When? For God's sake."

I had never, ever heard Royal swear.

"Why wasn't Mrs. Nemmers told? We've called and called. Who has been officially handling her case?" Another long pause. "Mr. Romeo is officially handling the case and he's on vacation? We asked, why couldn't the receptionist have told us that?" She made faces. "Impossible. Well, as I said, I'm calling Olympia. Nonsense, of course it's necessary.

"Now, Mrs. Nemmers will be up tomorrow morning. I'll have her ask for you, and I assume you will have some emergency money for her as you suggested. And of course, I will tell the Olympia office that too." She hung up with a bang. "I swear, I'll never figure that group out. There is a directive preventing anyone being told a worker has been transferred or is on vacation, so we could have been calling McCaully and Romero for a couple of weeks."

"Where is Mrs. McCaully?"

"Transferred to the north-end office three weeks ago. Janet, if it's all right with you, if you'll go up to the office tomorrow, Mrs. Lewis will have a partial payment for you, and

I'll wait to call Olympia until you're back, just in case we've shook something loose."

Royal and I got busy on our routine work. At 5:00, we went out and coaxed about six seniors to leave. My card playing, beer-drinking friends were in one group, but they didn't suggest a tavern hop this time, much to my relief. I wasn't sure how Royal would have taken it.

We locked up, and I made that dumb trip to the library. Hallelujah, the missing pamphlet was in. A short one. I took notes and even understood some of it. At the bottom of the page of my notes I wrote 'Grant Proposal' and 'Needs Assessment and Feasibility Study for a New Senior Center for Danville.' That should settle Fatty down.

↬ CHAPTER TWENTY ↫

I spent the time while I waited for Fay trying to list some needs for the Senior Center for the Grant class. Feasibility was something else again. I'd have to talk to Royal and John about that, but the wording sounded so right, so official—technical, like I knew what I was doing. Fay showed up just as I came to the end of everything I knew about the need for a new Senior Center.

She'd heard about a new restaurant in the old train depot, so we walked over there. The interior reminded me of a movie tavern set, with wobbly tables, a long bar, and the waitress looking like she also danced in a can-can number. However, the room was quiet, not crowded, and the chicken salad was good.

Efficient as usual, Fay had lists, floor plans, a color scheme, and a new punch recipe. We batted ideas around, and I told her which three ladies had agreed to work with her. We were through our work by the time the "Coal Car Devil's Food Cake" arrived.

"Anne, I know you know Lala Pierce. Her husband was in Terry's firm, wasn't he?" Fay asked.

"Terry's boss. Why?"

"She's back. She was gone for nearly a month, and...and she says Howard had an affair with you while she was away."

"Me? Why on earth would she say that? Did she tell you, or someone else? Why, I've only seen Howard once, no twice since

Terry died. Ugh, I Feel sick." I pushed my cake away. Howard, that bastard! I bet he got reconciliation by confessing—about me. He's the only one who could even dream this up."

"I knew this would upset you, Anne, and I told her I couldn't imagine you even being interested in a married man."

Oh, god, Buster!

"But I think you should call her, because I wasn't the only one there, and several women knew you, so they'll all be talking."

Oh, boy, me and Elizabeth Taylor. Now what? "Where was this?"

"At the tennis club. We were planning the spring dance. Are you coming?"

I shook my head. I'd dropped the tennis club after my first look at my new budget. "What a mess! Fay, please, there is no truth to it. As I said, I've seen Howard only twice since Terry died. I ran into him by accident at a political thing down town. I asked for his advice about a Grant Writing class and danced once with him. He called me back about a class and later to make sure I'd gotten in. When I complained about the textbook, he came over, oh, a couple of Sundays ago. I fed him coffee and cookies." Was it a lie not to mention the wine and cheese? "That's it." How I wanted to tell her all of it. Howard, you monster!

"Well, somehow, she has you cast as a home wrecker. You'd better set her straight."

"Do you suppose she'd believe me? It makes me shaky to think of calling her. Maybe it would be better to ignore the whole thing."

"That's up to you, but Mrs. McIntosh, the pastor's wife, was at the meeting."

A mental image of a scarlet A on my chest and being thrown bodily out of church flashed through my mind. "Oh boy, I could do without all this. Come on, I'll take you back to the

Center and get you together with your committee. Then I'm going home and decide what to do."

I got a basket, my weeding spade, and set to work on the flowerbeds. Should I call Lala or shouldn't I?

All I could say was that Howard was lying. That sure wouldn't make her feel better, but dam it, I was working now and couldn't take the chance of gossip labeling me immoral. I could just imagine what some of the seniors would do if they thought I was promiscuous, and with a married man no less.

Reluctantly I went in and dialed Lala's number. My usual luck was with me. She answered after only two rings. "Lala, this is Anne Farley."

There was a long pause with no response.

"I think we need t talk."

Silence.

"I did not have an affair with Howard. In fact, I've only seen him twice since Terry died."

"I can't imagine how you can be so brazen as to call and lie to me, Anne. I thought you were my friend."

"Lala, please, I'm not lying. I can't imagine where you got such an idea."

"Oh, can't you? Well, Howard finally confessed, and if you had any idea that you'd get something permanent, forget it. He's tired of you already. How could you be so cheap?"

"Lala, it's a lie. I did not have an affair with Howard. I don't know why he would say such a thing, though maybe you can guess form what you know about his past. However, you have no right to gossip about me to our friends."

There was a loud crash as she hung up on me. The whole side of my face felt on fire and my head began to ache.

I started to dial back, but quit. I'd said everything I could, unless I told her everything Howard had said about himself—and she certainly wasn't in any mood to listen to me. I shivered.

I went and put on Terry's robe, got his down comforter,

and curled up on the couch in the study. Surprisingly I napped until time to leave for class.

The blond came in behind me and took the neighboring desk. Turned out her name was Ann, too, no e. Ann Smith. She'd gotten hold of all the reading material, but hadn't finished all of them for next week's assignments.

Tabor was late, so we exchanged notes. I was reading them when the young man behind me poked me.

"Here's a copy of the term's pop quizzes. Take one and pass the rest on."

"What?"

"Hurry up. Jim's keeping Fatty busy so we can get them passed around."

I passed the pile on and repeated the message. Then I turned back to the guy behind me. "Look, this isn't fair, it's cheating. Besides he'll probably change the questions."

"Not Tabor, he's too lazy. These questions are the only things that will get most of us through this class with a passing grade. He's the hardest grader in the school. For every missing comma, he knocks points off."

"But..."

"Lady, you don't have to use them."

"But..." I started again, and then Tabor walked in. Out of the corner of my eye, I could see the pile of papers over in the last row. I closed my notebook over my copy.

Tabor called roll and looked over the class. I could swear he knew what was going on.

"Farley," he called.

My God, why me?

"Got your grant subject ready?"

I sighed with relief. "Yes. A needs assessment and feasibility study for a new Senior Center."

"Where?"

"Oh, in Danville."

"Then put that in your title. You know, but the reader doesn't."

I nodded. He was right of course.

"Now, the rest of you pay attention. I'm going to ask Farley some questions. You'll have to be able to answer some similar ones. Okay, Farley, who the hell are you going to send a grant like that to? You do remember you have to really submit it?"

I resisted saying, 'Yes sir. I remember.' "I will submit the grant to the mayor of Danville."

He thrust his head forward. I could see a 'gotcha' look on his face. "I have never heard of a small city like Danville accepting grants."

"Danville has a small amount in their budge to be used for studies of needed services, buildings, employees, things like that."

The whole class wrote that down. Was John going to be sorry!

"What makes you think there is any interest in your subject?"

"My boss, the director of the Senior Center, is interested in a new Center. She approached the mayor, who is her boss, and suggested I write a grant for a new Center."

Tabor shuddered.

"I agree—I insisted that I am not the person to write such a grant. We finally decided that a more logical and needed step would be for me to work on the reasons for a new Center."

"Why would you need any money for that?"

I stared at him. I hadn't thought of that—though I'd be damned if I'd tell that to Fatty.

"It's so early yet that I'm not sure. However, there would be compensation for the time involved, expenses for paperwork, things like that."

"Have you discussed whether it would be legal for you to be paid while you are already employed by the City?"

"No, not specifically, but I'm only working part time, and there have already been arrangements made for me to be paid for extra hours."

"That's working on an assumption, which is stupid. Check it out."

I nodded. *Now to go find someone else's to work over.*

"Have you been keeping track of the time you've spent on this?"

"Yes."

"How?"

"I have a folder I'm keeping my work in. I've been writing my time in it."

"Date each entry and what the work was regarding, and bring your folder on Thursday. I'll check it. What are you working on first?"

"Needs."

He nodded. "What next?"

"I don't know. I need to talk to my boss, and the mayor, and I think the City Attorney."

"OK. We'll consider it more on Thursday. Now, there was a complaint about my plans to have the class reading available. Any trouble/"

Oh, go pick on someone else. "Yes, the reading material was not on reserve last Thursday night. I've had to drive over here to the library every day to check for it."

He just nodded. "OK. Get a piece of paper out for a quiz. You'll have ten minutes."

He wrote ten questions on the board, and the whole class wrote furiously. I had glimmers on seven of them, but certainly not answers. Once we passed our papers in, Tabor lectured.

At 8:30 we got a ten-minute break. Ann and I dashed for the Coke machine.

"What are you going to do with the pop quiz questions that guy handed out before class?"

"Use them. You saw the questions tonight. There is no way to answer them unless we can study for them ahead of time. The questions are nitpicky with no real relevance," Ann confided.

We drank our Coke and drifted back to class. Tabor was grading the quizzes. We sat silently until he finished and passed them back. I couldn't believe it. I had a big fat 0 at the top of mine. Scrawled in red was, "State question in answers." Ten questions in ten minutes, and we were supposed to write the question out?!

Fatty rapped for attention. "That was a disgusting exhibition. There were only two decent papers. Keep up the good work, Jima and Berny."

Uh huh, he was pointing to the guy behind me and the student who'd delayed Fatty in the hall. Then he went through the questions and gave answers. Damn him anyway, I'd have gotten about 80% except for his grade school mentality.

We spent the last hour on the text. Much as I hated to admit it, he was a good lecturer. At ten we were dismissed. Ann said, "Let's get a real drink. Meet me at the Blue Bonnet?"

The Blue Bonnet seemed to be the school hangout. Nearly half the class was there. We spent a lovely hour cursing Fatty. I wasn't the only one with a zero.

Ann was apologetic. "I should have told you he always insists the questions be restated in the answer." She rapped on her glass. "Listen everyone, Tabor follows the college's Guide for Formal Papers. Use the format from it on margins, headings, footnotes, everything. He marks off on all that, and misspellings too. And, if you don't use the correct form, he won't read it and you flunk."

Comforted by my sweet drink, I got home at 11:30 pm.

Wednesday was the day of the trip I'd so innocently promised to go on. I got to work by a quarter to eight feeling that another four hours of sleep would be about right.

When I unlocked the door, ten trippers were already

waiting out front. As I turned on the lights, Beulah and Sam Ashford headed for the coffeepot. She plugged it in and he got a tray of cups from the kitchen.

I opened the office, took the sign-up list, and checked off the ones already present. Buster's name was first on the waiting list and there was one cancellation. He'd be going.

By eight-thirty the entire group, including Buster, stood around the door, ready to go. Eight thirty-five came, and no bus.

Beulah grumbled. "Late. Why can't anything go right? You'd better call them up, Anne, maybe they got the time wrong. Why once they came the next day, and one time they took us to Wenatchee instead of Yakima, and I had wanted to visit my cousin."

I escaped into my office. Not a very smart move. Three seniors were already in complaining to Royal. Sally glared at me as if I was somehow keeping the bus from coming.

Royal grimaced at me and called Finisterre. "Bob, this is Royal, Danville Senior Center. Your bus isn't here yet. Any problem?" There was a long pause. "OK. I'll give it another fifteen minutes." She hung up.

"Everything is all right. The bus is on its way. It should be here any minute now. I'll go out and talk to everyone. Anne, you call Atherton and tell them we'll be a little late."

I got a Peg at the Atherton Senior Center. "Peg, it's Anne at Danville. We are going to be a little late picking your group up. The bus seems to be delayed, but..."

"What do you mean, Anne? Our group already left, oh, fifteen minutes ago."

"You mean they picked your group up first? That's out of the way?"

"I know, but I didn't know your group wasn't on the bus. I just figured the driver was a few minutes ahead of schedule, and since everyone on our list was here, I didn't check."

"Lordy, I hope they're headed here and haven't forgotten

us." A horn sounded. "Nope, they're here. Talk to you later. Pray for us, I'm beginning to think this day may be totally snafu."

I grabbed my coat and rushed out. There was a knot of seniors on the steps of the bus and in the doorway. It sounded like everyone was shouting. Royal was bouncing up and down trying to get on the bus. She grabbed my arm and started shoving me through the crowd. She yelled in my ear, "You've got to sit up front so you can use the mike."

I pushed and shoved. Amy's big purse stopped me completely. What in hell was holding us up? "Amy, let me through, please."

She glanced at me, and then went back to trying to push her way on.

From behind me, Buster bellowed, "Stand back, and let Anne through. We can't go 'til she gets on first."

The jam eased a little. I was able to shove Amy's purse aside, slip through, and make it to the steps. Puffing and wiggling, I got on board.

The driver had his hands over his head and was yelling, "Now wait a minute, now wait a minute."

Beulah and Sally both screamed in my ear, which was itching furiously. "They took the front seats, and it's our turn to sit up front first."

A woman in a front seat bellowed, "We got on the bus first so we get the front seats."

Someone behind me hollered, "We were supposed to be on first, so the seats are ours."

The noise grew. There were shouts of "No!" and some of "Yes!"

Pandemonium. I spotted the mike hanging behind the driver's seat. I could just reach it. Hoping it was on, I cried, "Good Morning!" The bus practically shook from the noise I made, but everyone shut up, from shock evidently. However, they recovered rapidly and several began their complaints again. I raised the mike again. "If we don't leave right away, we are going to be late for the Arboretum tour. Now, Danville seniors, get in and move back. Hurry up. Come on, hurry."

I put the mike down by my side and looked at the woman in the seat behind the driver. "You'll have to move back. I need to be behind the driver. I kept waving our seniors on."

The lady in the single front seat said, "No, I got here first."

Evidently the driver had had it. He'd finally gotten behind the wheel again, but he whirled around and scowled at both of us. "Mathilda, move or I won't move the bus."

She made one more try. "I get carsick in back." But she moved.

Every third senior boarding said, "It's our turn to sit up front, Anne."

Sally said, "I'm going to tell Royal."

It was like herding a class of whiney first graders off on a field trip, but finally, with everyone on, the bus jerked out of our parking lot. Royal waved, and we were on our way. The level of noise was still high and I could hear a few remarks of, "Selfish...inconsiderate...rude." It sounded like a riot was brewing.

I picked up the mike and tried, "Good Morning," again. "I'm sorry things have been so hectic, but I'm sure we'll have no more trouble."

A chorus of, "Our seats..." drowned me out.

"My name is Anne Farley. I'm your travel guide for today." No one smiled. "I'm sorry..." *Why am I saying I'm sorry again?* "...you aren't happy about the seating arrangement, but it would have delayed us to make the change at Danville."

More, "Our seats..." sounded.

"On the way back, Danville gets the front seats and Atherton the back. It's our turn this time," a Danville senior yelled.

I went on. "When we get back, Peg, Royal, and I will work

something out so no one will be cheated out of the front section in the future."

Babble from the troops.

"Now, everyone has a seatmate. Remember who he or she is and learn their name, because if anyone is missing when we start again, you can tell me who it is. And please, try to know where your partner is. It will save time if we don't all get back on time. We don't want to lose anyone."

From the glares, it looked like each group would like to lose the other permanently. I sighed and began to try and count the seniors. There were two empty seats. That made forty-eight. *Now, back to the mike.* "At the Arboretum, a guide will join us and show us the main areas. Then we will tour the Tea Garden. At noon, we are going to be served lunch at a restaurant called the Isle de Paris."

Sally shouted, "There's a good Chinese place on the Avenue. Why can't we go there?"

"You may eat anywhere you like as long as you're back on the bus at 1:00. However, you've already paid for eating at the Isle de Paris."

Sally was waving her hands. "I'll talk to you at the Arboretum, Sally. At 1:00 we go to the Playhouse where we'll see the comedy, 'The Man Who Came to Dinner.' The play is over at 3:00. We will load immediately, heading home by way of the Village. There will only be a forty-five minute stop there. We are expected back at Atherton at 6:00 and Danville at 6:20. If anyone plans to stay behind at any stop, let me know beforehand."

I was jounced into my seat, but I'd had my say, and they all seemed to be distracted from the seating arrangement situation. I settled back into my single seat. We were heading up to the freeway. With luck, I might get in a thirty-minute nap. This "Leave the driving to us," was the greatest.

I had just drifted off into a rather prosaic dream of copying menus on the typewriter when the woman behind me poked my arm. I jerked awake.

"When are you going to start the singing?"

"Singing?"

"Yes. Peg always brings songbooks along and we sing."

"I don't see your songbooks. I'm sorry…" *Again!* "I didn't know you usually sing, so I didn't bring any." I'd never heard Royal say a word about singing.

"Well, start some anyway."

"I can't sing. I don't know any songs. Maybe you'd like to start it. I'll pass you the mike."

"Oh, no. I can't lead a song. You'll need to do that."

"Well, I can't. Not unless they want *The Three Little Kittens* or *Ninety-Nine Bottles of Bear on the Wall.*"

The driver saved me. He tiled his head slightly toward me. "Give me the mike. I'll start them."

In a minute, they were all singing, *It's a Long Way to Tipperary.* By the second verse I was back to my dream typing, though this time I seemed to be working in a place that looked like the White House. It was the closing notes of *Mairsey D'Oats* that woke me. We were going off the freeway and were only five minutes from the Arboretum. The nap had helped—I didn't feel quite so apprehensive about the day. I ran my fingers through my hair and felt wide-awake. Why was my ear itching so?

The bus pulled over at the gates. The driver turned to me, "Where are you going to meet your guide?"

Oh, God. Silence.

"I suppose that means you don't know?" He glared at me. "You people set this up. Didn't you find out when you made the arrangements?"

"I didn't make the arrangements. As I understand it, your office handled the details."

"Oh, God." He said aloud. "Here we go again. Why do they always give me the runs that have everything screwed up?"

There was a little giggle from the woman behind me. I realized we had an audience. "OK, take us over to the building near the herb gardens. You know where I mean?"

He nodded and we took the north road. The building looked deserted, and of course, it was. After pounding on the door and getting no answer, I decided I wasn't going to die, just because it seemed the best thing to do at the moment.

So, I went back to the bus and took the mike. "We are at the Arboretum's famous herb gardens. You may get off the bus here and look at the plants." *Should I say, 'While we look for the guide?' Never.* "I'm going to make some calls and see if I can clear up what happened to our guide."

They unloaded, the driver helping each one down. I checked my purse. No change of course. Buster was hovering close to me. "Buster, please do you have any change?" He gave me a handful and I called the Center. Plato answered. "Agnes, we have a problem. Would you ask Royal where we were to meet our guide?"

"Anne, she's gone shopping for prizes for the fishing derby."

"Oh, no. Well, will you call Finisterre's and see what they know? This pay phone's number is 555-4839. Could you call me back right away?"

I stood in the pay phone doorway and watched our group wandering around the beds, most of them looking bored. Luckily it wasn't a long wait. As I'd expected, Finisterre hadn't heard anything about a guide.

With my ear on fire and feeling sick to my stomach, I went back to the bus. The driver tooted his horn and the seniors began to straggle back. I counted as they loaded. Forty-seven. No, God be gracious. I counted seats. Three empties. I went back to my missing passenger's seat partner. "Please, who's missing?"

"It's Irma."

"Do you know where she is?"

"No, she was walking with me, but she went off somewhere."

Sure she did. "Has anyone seen Irma?"

Buster answered, "A lady went in the restroom."

I got off the bus. A sign to the restrooms pointed behind the empty building. I went into Women's. In front of the mirror, a gray haired woman was touching up her makeup.

"Irma?"

She smiled. "Yes, you're our guide, aren't you?"

"We're all waiting you," Anne explained.

"Oh, my, I'll be right along." She got out a comb and began straightening her part.

"Irma. Could you hurry, please? Everyone else is on the bus."

"Certainly." She put her comb away, got a blue scarf out, and tied it carefully over her curls.

I was going to out-wait her. I was not going back without her, though it was tempting.

Then I noticed a box beside the door. *Map and Guide of the Arboretum.* Glory be. I picked up several. Yes! There we were, and just down the road was a Camellia Garden in Section 3: in bloom in April and May.

I grabbed Irma's hand and tugged her back to the bus. I handed the driver a map and took the mike. "Our next stop is the Camellia Garden, Section 3." The driver checked his map and started out. I read from my sheet, "This garden was started in 1936 and now contains over 500 specimens of Camellias. Some bushes have attained the height of twenty feet." I looked at my watch. "We will spend approximately twenty minutes there. The driver will sound the horn after 15 minutes so you can start back to the bus."

As if we'd planned it, we pulled up at Section 3. Again, we unloaded. Nervously I looked around. Yes, there were a lot trees in bloom. Gorgeous in fact. Damn it, the seniors were all hovering around me, but I'd read everything the pamphlet had said.

In desperation I walked toward a tall camellia, a lovely soft pink one. A marker on the ground said, "Camellia, Japonica, Rose Marie." I pointed to the marker and read it aloud. Three women took pictures, and Irma took a picture of me and the tree. I led them to a smaller white-blossomed bush, each star shaped flower showing a soft golden heart. I read its marker to them and quickly started them down the slope to a bed of young bushes. Irma took a picture of Buster holding a fallen bloom.

I'd read at least ten markers when the horn sounded. A quickly check of the map made me decide we could spend fifteen minutes at the Tulip beds, drive through the Rhododendron area, and still have time to go through the Japanese Garden.

At each stop Irma followed me, taking pictures everywhere we paused. When we got off the bus at the Tea House, we all had to wait while Buster helped her put a new roll of film in her camera.

When we finally all got together and went to the gate, it was locked. Automatically I read the sign, "Open week days 1-5, weekends 10-6." During the rising murmurs of discontent, I planned a pleasant scene of Royal and the director of the Tour Company boiling in oil.

I turned to the seniors. *Well, tell them.* "I think this trip is totally jinxed. I have no idea what has happened, but let's get some fun out of this. Look, there's a path that goes up this side. Let's walk up there and look at the Tea House. It's absolutely beautiful and the garden has grown enough so that it is an almost perfect example of a formal Japanese garden."

I led the way as we climbed the gentle sloping path. Luckily there was an excellent view. Drawing on my brief trip and the reading I had done, I told them, "The Japanese Tea ceremony is basically religious, or perhaps a more accurate statement would be an expression of the love of the beautiful in the daily routines of life. The ceremony is usually conducted with five guests. The tea is made from a ground green tea. After the hot water, not boiling water as we use, is added, the tea is beaten to a froth. Actually, it feels rather thick. Many Americans don't like it, but Japanese have learned to like it very much, just as we've learned to love coffee."

"As the tea ceremony, called Chanoyu, developed, a small building began to be used for it. Like this building, they are very beautiful, simple, and uncluttered. As I'm sure you know, the ceremony is conducted at a low table and everyone sits on the floor. The person conducting the ceremony uses very stylized movements. They are lovely to see, and if it is a woman who conducts it, she wears a beautiful kimono. However, the tea master is often a man, and many of the tea ceremony teachers are men."

I had now told them everything I knew.

Amy raised her hand and said, "I bet it's really hard to sit on the floor like that."

The bus horn sounded. Saved!

At the restaurant, I sat at a table with Buster, Irma, and the driver. He had the meal procedure down pat. He had a receipt for the meal and in only a few minutes we were served chicken in a wine sauce. I didn't know if it was any good, I was so tired and nervous. The driver-his name turned out to be Hal-ordered us a bottle of wine. It was the house Chablis, sort of raw, but it revived me.

At 12:45 the driver started everyone back to the bus. Buster, Irma, and I followed behind the crowd. Buster was telling us about having seen Monte Woolley in the movies, when I realized Irma wasn't with us. I waited at the door until everyone was on, Danville up front, Atherton in back. Irma was still a no-show. Sighing, I took the mike, "Did anyone see where Irma went?"

A lot of talk, but no one had seen her slip away. Damn it, we'd be late for the play.

I went back to the restaurant and checked the restroom. No Irma. At the cashier's cage, they hadn't seen her, but suggested I check the gift shop. Thank God, they were right. She was buying a paperweight model of the Space Needle. "Irma, you've got to stay with the group," I told her. "We're on a tight schedule, and you're making us late." I was beginning to suspect she had no sense of time, because she just flashed me a charming smile, slowly counted her change, and calmly walked out to the bus.

We got a faint cheer when we got on. Some shuffling had been done and the empty seat was beside Buster. Maybe I'd lost a beau.

We made the theater with about five minutes to spare. The seats were good and everyone settled down rapidly. In five more minutes they were all laughing heartily and I was free to exercise my one great talent. I went to sleep. I was roused at the end of every scene.

At the end of the second act, I struggled my way through the crowd and got a cup of coffee. Then I managed to stay awake for the third act. It was a funny play, dated maybe, but my crowd obviously loved it. I think they were sorry when it was over.

I tried to get to Irma so she couldn't disappear again, but the crowd was too thick. However, Buster had her hand, and while I would have preferred handcuffs, she got on the bus with everyone else.

Right on time, we made the village. Everyone scattered. If they didn't come back on time I'd have to search the whole place. I found the bookstore, got a new Gothic novel, went to a restaurant, had a bowl of soup, and read. I'd be able to go home and do nothing but study.

Back at the bus forty-five minutes later, there was only half our crowd on board. We waited, and seniors kept straggling in. Buster and Irma were among the last to come. Finally it looked full. I stood up and checked. Hell, an empty seat. It was Sam Ashford's. "Beulah, is Sam missing?" I asked.

She looked at the seat as if she was surprised he wasn't there. "Yes, we went different ways. I haven't seen him since we got off."

"Have you any idea where he might be?"

That got a flat "No."

Now what in the blazes should I do?

The driver leaned over and whispered, "Check the bars. Didn't you keep an eye on him? They always do!"

Oh, hell. I wondered how many bars there were.

Hal and I got out and looked at the locator box. As near as we could tell, there were only two, but there was no indication how many of the restaurants had a liquor license, and there were lots of restaurants. It would take ages.

Hal suggested, "You take that bar and I'll check the other. Take a quick look into the restaurants you pass, and we can each come back along the next street, looking there. That should take about ten minutes. Then we leave if Beulah doesn't raise too much fuss."

We started off. I had three places to look through on the way to the bar. No Sam. However, I hit pay dirt at the bar. There was Sam beneath a deer head.

He saw me and shouted, "Hey, Anne, come on and have a drink." The other five men in the bar all stopped drinking and stared at me. The bartender hurried over. Sam told him, "Another double, and whatever the little lady wants."

"No, no. I mean, no drink please. Sam, the bus is leaving, you've got to come now."

"Nope, I'm going to have my drink."

"Please, Sam, we're going to be late."

HE shook his head. "Hurry, hurry, hurry, don't you ever slow down? Have a drink."

"Not now. " Inspiration. "Let's all have one in Danville." It didn't work.

"Nope. Beulah'd cut my gizzard out before she'd let me go to a bar in Danville."

"The bus really has to leave, Sam. Won't Beulah be mad, or hurt, if you miss it?"

"Sure, so I might as well enjoy myself." The bartender brought him a drink. He took a big swallow, and opened the paper to the sports news.

"Sam, I'm going to have to leave you. How will you get home?"

"Bus." He reached over and patted my fanny.

I left, walking slowly and looking back at him. As I went out the door he gave me a big wink. Feeling like a scene from *The Demon Rum*, I went back to the bus. I told Hal, sotto voce, "He won't leave the bar," and went back to Beulah. Every eye was on us and everyone was straining to hear. "Sam says he's staying here," I whispered. "He says he'll take the bus home."

"Let him," she whispered back. "The old coot. I'll show him."

I sat in my seat. The driver had started the engine when Buster came up front. "Uh, Anne, Irma's not back yet. She said she wanted to get an ice cream cone."

Oh, God, oh God. "I can't believe it."

Buster said, "Now, it'll just take a minute. I'll go get her." He jumped down the stairs.

The driver turned off the motor and several voices said, "That's a good idea," and about ten more got off the bus and headed for the ice cream shop.

"No, no, stay on the bus, we have to leave," I yelled. They ignored him.

Fifteen minutes later they were all back, and we left. We were back in Atherton twenty minutes late. Irma didn't get off. We made up five minutes and were back in Danville only fifteen minutes late. Several sons and daughters were in the parking lot waiting for their parents. Luckily no one complained about the time. I'd had time to compose several squelches, including, "Of course we're late. I'll never go on a trip with seniors again unless we have at least five chaperones along."

I waved them all goodbye and stood out of the way as Beulah tooled a big Mercury out of the lot, taking the corners on two wheels. Boy, I wouldn't want to be in Sam's shoes. When they were all gone, I unlocked the building and wrote a long indignant memo to Royal. Then I made a new list for myself, titled *Questions to Ask About Trips.*

❧ CHAPTER TWENTY-ONE ❦

That night I went straight to bed. No studying, no supper, no shower, no nothing. I stayed home Thursday and studied and worked on the grant.

After a fight with my conscience, I studied from the purloined questions, and that night I got 95 on the quiz. I'd left an 's' out of "assessment." Tabor put me on the grill only briefly. He spent most of the evening torturing a young couple who were working together on a grant for a youth program. He let us out early, and I was able to complete the week's library reading.

On Friday I talked briefly with Royal about the trip. She and Plato had tracked the missing guide down. It was scary. The man had died on his way to work. Just pulled his car over to the curb and quit breathing.

Almost as if to validate Royal's prediction of deaths coming in threes, Tiny came in at 9:30, stood in the doorway, scowled at us, and said, "Zeke died last night." He turned to me. "You announce it at lunch and have a minute of silence for him. I'll have a card for everyone to sign."

He left, still glowering, though I had seen tears in his eyes.

Royal said, "Better not ask for silence, Anne. If Tiny wants to, he can ask. She sighed. "Can we wait to talk about your questions on the trip until later?"

"Of course. You sound tired. Are you OK?"

"I guess I am tired, I don't seem to have much zip. You

know, I'd like a vacation. Somehow, everything seems a lot of work lately, not fun."

"Why don't you take time off now?"

"I can't. Not until after the Recognition Banquet. But I think I'll talk to John about taking a couple of weeks off right after that. Could you work every day?"

"Sure. I imagine Brenda and Janet can do the money for me. With some planning, we can get everything covered." I looked at her. "You know, Royal, you look kind of pale. Are you coming down with something?"

"Do I? You hold the fort, I'll go over and talk to John, and then I think I'll take a sick half-day and go home and have a nap. There's nothing special going on this afternoon except Bridge, and it runs itself. You can call me if anything comes up."

It was a quiet day. I announced Zeke's death. No one asked for a moment of silence. Tiny provided a huge card, and everyone signed it. I noticed when I signed that Milly had written her name on each page of the card.

Bridge did run itself. I watched for a while and discovered two tables were playing auction, one contract. I couldn't imagine how they ever figured who got the prize. Anyway, it was peaceful, and I got a lot done. A good day.

No one went home early. I had to coax them to leave. I didn't get home until 5:30.

I'd been brooding about what to wear to John's dinner party. It would be nice to have something new and fun, so I went to Danville's only department store and browsed. On the sale rack I found a gorgeous pair of deep pink slacks. I was sure my pink sandals would just match. Adding my pink blouse, I'd feel dressed up, but casual enough.

I nearly had the slacks to the counter when I started to think. Fifty-nine dollars—food money. Anyway, who was I trying to impress? Neat, not fancy, that was all that was necessary. My secret delight with the thought of my own first office party diminished, and I went home, without the slacks.

On Saturday I brooded some more about what to wear and what sort of hostess gift you give to a host. I finally called Lil.

"Some kind of slacks so you can sit on the floor, and shoes you can dance in," she advised. "John has a rec room with space to dance."

Odd, I'd always known what to wear to Terry's office doings. This was a different world. Thinking of Terry's office, I had the answer to a gift. I walked over to the new wine and cheese shop and found Howard's wine. Wow, $15.98 a bottle. It was a good thing I hadn't bought the pants.

I finally pulled my pink blouse and sandals out, and the gray slacks I usually wore with them. I called Jo, and she came down and trimmed my bangs. She wouldn't stay and had nothing to say about Greg except that he was "OK." I thought she looked more rested.

Just as she left she said, "I'm going to work a two week trial at Keno's Florists. Kelly Girl, that's me. I was surprised, they liked my botany degree."

"Oh, Jo, that's great. Have a good time. Call me if you can get lunch off. We can have a business woman's lunch."

Promptly at 7:00, I pulled up at John's. Of course, I was the first one there. How come Mom had to instill a time clock in me?

John seemed glad to see me and made no polite disclaimers when I offered to help. I grated Parmesan, made punch, and answered the door for him. It made it easy to fit in at the party.

Thankfully, Lil's advice about clothes was on the mark. Every woman had on some sort of pants, ranging from a Councilwoman in a satin harem outfit to the recreation department's file clerk in white jeans and a crop top. I was comfortably in the middle. Royal came in her fuchsia pants suit. She had a green flower this time. I thought she still looked tired.

I helped John carry his spaghetti out, then accepted a

martini from Jed. I sipped cautiously. Strong, so I ditched it on the mantle and chatted with Lil.

There were about twenty people at the party. Some concentrated on the buffet, a few danced. I danced a while with John. Evidently I'd gotten used to his steps, but his lack of rhythm was still confusing.

When the record finished, he said "You don't have a drink Anne. Let me get you one."

"No, thanks. Here's mine." I grabbed my martini from the mantle. While he fixed himself a scotch, I surreptitiously dumped three-fourths of it and filled the glass with ice. Then I stowed it back on the mantle and danced with Jed. While not fantastic, he knew the beat when he heard it.

It was a nice party. Good food, and no one was grossly abusing the liquor. I took advantage of my status as a helper and replenished ice, spaghetti, rolls, and punch when I ran out of conversation and dancing partners. God it was fun to dance again.

Red, the maintenance man, was about my age, and we did a mean boogie together. Everyone stood back and watched us dance. I was exhausted and happy when the music stopped.

A little later, John put on a conga and Red and I led the line through the house. The younger partiers watched us. Obviously they'd never heard of a conga line, but they soon joined in.

By then I had had it. I still felt eighteen inside, but my body certainly knew it was forty-fie going on forty-six and not used to late nights. So, I joined Red, Royal, and Jed in a penny-ante poke game.

Around 10:00, Royal left, admitting she was still tired. I wondered if she could be having a reoccurrence of the flu.

We coaxed the Councilwoman, Virginia, to take her place in the poker game. She was in an obvious pregnant stage, and claimed "Who Dat," needed to go home. That broke the game up and people started leaving.

I began picking up empty glasses, decided I needed a tray, and went to the kitchen. The Recreation Department girl and Red's assistant were sharing a joint and a glass of my wine punch. I must have looked shocked.

"Hey, Anne, we'll dump it."

"I don't know, only what would John think? Maybe you'd better save it for later. Isn't the Police Chief here?"

"Oh, God, you're right. We'll stash it. Want a drag first?"

"No thanks."

When I came back with the next load, the door was open airing the kitchen, the joint was missing, and they each had a fresh glass of wine. I was putting a load in the dishwasher when John came in with the punch bowl dregs.

"What are you trying to do, freeze?"

The kids shut the door and said, "No, it was, uh, sort of smoky in here, John. Thanks for the neat party. We've got to take off. See you Monday." And they left in a hurry.

John looked at me. "What was that all about?"

I shrugged. "Want me to get this spaghetti for freezing?"

He was fixing himself another scotch. "You look too innocent. Want a drink?"

I shook my head.

"You mix a good punch. Come on, help finish it up and quit making like the maid." He handed me a water glass of the punch.

It was pretty late. I shoved the spaghetti into the refrigerator and followed him. Everyone was gone. "It's been the nicest party I've been to in a long time, John, and you do make wonderful spaghetti."

He'd dropped onto the couch.

"Don't get up. I'm going to get my coat and go, too."

"Come on, Anne. Sit down. Parties are no fun without someone to hash it over. Just until we finish our drinks." He pulled my hand, and I sat down. "I think that's one of the worst things about Elly being gone. No one to talk things over with."

I nodded. "One of them."

He stared at me. "Yeah, one of them."

My ear itched. I wanted to go home.

"What was up in the kitchen?"

"Look, J..."

"I know. You aren't talking...Pot?"

"Well, yes. They hadn't thought too clearly, and got rid of it right away."

"You ever try it?" He reached over and put a leftover bowl of dip and the crumbles of potato chips between us.

I leaned back and scraped up some of the dip. "No. After I preached at the kids, I couldn't give in to temptation. Have you?"

"No. Same reason. Besides, I like my job, and I can just imagine the headlines."

"Mayor Impounded for Popping Pot."

"That's awful. Besides, I don't think you pop it."

"Who knows? Anyway, the smell is enough to discourage me. Still, I wonder what we've missed. I guess I'll never know. Where'd you learn to dance like that?"

"Like what?"

"Boogie?"

"I've got three aunts, not much older than me, I mean, I. I was needed as a partner. Can't really remember when I couldn't dance. I love it. That's another thing I miss. I even want to dance at the Center when that awful orchestra tunes up."

"Don't do it. They'd kill you."

"I know. Royal warned me. Too many women for too few men."

"Want to dance awhile?" He got up and turned the radio on. Dance music flooded out.

"Thank you, no." It was time to go. "I've got to get home." I started to get up.

"Just a minute. I want to ask about Royal. Wait, I'll be right back." He went into the kitchen.

CHAPTER TWENTY-ONE

I got my coat from the closet.

He was back with a bottle of champagne and two glasses. "I saved this one."

"Don't open it, John. I've really got to go, and I'm driving. You'll waste it."

The cork popped. "Royal doesn't look well. Do you know what's wrong?" He handed me the glass.

"I don't know. She said yesterday that she wants to take a vacation as soon as the June calendar is done. She hasn't really seemed herself since that flu. You know, it's hard work at the Center. I hope you pay her well. It may look like fun, but the details take forever and the interruptions take even more time."

Somehow I'd sat down again, and John poured some champagne in my glass.

"I know, and I'm grateful you've taken on some of the load. It's too much for just one person."

"I almost can't figure out what I do, but both of us run all day. The seniors keep taking on more of my work, but there always seems to be more to do."

I put my glass down and got up. I could feel the champagne. It and the music almost made me feel that dancing, even with John, would be lovely. "That's a..."

"One thing more. Watch it with Red."

"Watch it? With Red? I just danced with him. I didn't..."

"Hey, I know. I'm not criticizing. It's because of his wife."

"His wife? I didn't meet any wife. In fact, I thought he was here alone."

"His wife was the gray-haired lady, in the gray pants suit, who sat in the rocker all evening."

"The one knitting?"

"Yep."

"I thought she might be someone's grandmother."

"I think she is, but inside burns Carmen. She thinks every woman is after Red and she has been known to pull hair."

"Wow, thanks for the warning, I guess. Earlier would have been better. Anyway, I'm off. Between the champagne and Red's wife, I can go home and dream I'm a femme fatale."

"Yes."

I stared suspiciously at him, sensing a joke.

He was smiling, and then he stopped. "Don't go Anne."

He reached up and pulled me down beside him. I just missed the dip. And then it wasn't a joke. He kissed me—and it wasn't like high school all over again. It was like it had been years ago with Terry. I knew I should go, but I was holding him as hard as he was holding me.

John murmured, "Mmm," and then his tongue tentatively brushed mine. One hand let me go, reached out, and put the chips and dip on the floor. Gently he turned and pressed me back, and we were lying on the couch together. Being the same height was perfect. We fit everywhere. His left hand cupped my breast.

"I...please John."

"Hush, darling."

Why couldn't the kissing and warmth go on forever? I should go home, now, but in response to his hand I pressed closer. I didn't want to go home. I wanted more and more. He was warm, and hard, and his hair was soft. It curled around my fingers.

My blouse unbuttoned easily for him. I found myself reaching for his buttons, but drew back. He chuckled and put my hand back.

We lay quietly. Such comfort—the warmth. His fingers stroked my back, and then the hook of my bra separated.

No, how could I? This wasn't home. The clothes. It would be so...so messy. Then, the bed. I pushed away.

The long soft stroking started again. The skin behind his ear was smooth and his breathing deepened even more as I traced its folds.

He turned me slightly, his thigh pushing between my legs and his lips brushing my breast. Yes. Yes. The phone shrilled. I jumped.

John swore, ""Hell, no." It rang again. "Anne, lie still. It will stop."

I knew I should have gone home. How could I ever face him at work? I gave up on my bra and fastened my buttons.

John's face looked strained, his mouth hard. The phone rang again and again. I thought I heard him say, "Shit," as he sat up beside me and picked up the receiver.

"John here. Who? Yes of course. Mrs. Paige? What's wrong?" He cupped his hand over the phone. "It's the hospital."

Back on the phone, he listened for what seemed a long time. "Should I come over? You're sure I couldn't see her? All right. Call me if there is any change, I'll be over in the morning. Please reassure her you called me and that I'll tell Mrs. Farley. We'll see that everything goes all right. She's not to worry." He hung up. His beard showed a lot of gray.

What had I done? Terry had ranted about teases.

"Royal has had a heart attack. The hospital said she called the aide car. It must have been almost as soon as she got home. They wouldn't say how bad it is, only that she is in Intensive Care, and they think she is not in any immediate danger. They called me because she is worrying about the Center."

"She mustn't. I can manage. That is, if you want me to, or maybe you should get someone more experienced."

"I think you'll have to. I mean, you'll have to be acting director until Royal is back."

Neither of us said, "If she's back."

"Oh, hell, Anne. We'll work on it tomorrow."

"Of course. Will you call me when you've seen her? I'll go over, too, if they'll let me. Then we can get together and do some planning." I pulled my coat around me and took a step toward the door.

"Don't go, Anne. Please stay." He put his arms around me.

I kissed his cheek. "I can't. Honest, now. I didn't mean to be a tease. I...I wanted you very much, but I've had a chance to think."

"Look, Anne..."

"Honest, it would be awful—later. I don't think I could handle it." I could just imagine. I'd feel possessive, and he'd hate it, so I'd act distant, and he'd feel rejected. He'd fire me. My job was probably ruined anyway. This was why you were never supposed to get involved with people you work with."

"Are you back, Anne?"

"What?"

"Quit thinking so hard. I'll continue to rue Royal's timing. I'll go over to the hospital in the morning about 8:00, call you, and then we'd better have a couple hours to plan. Would you make me breakfast or brunch?"

Knee-jerk syndrome. A man says, "Feed me" and ninety-nine times out of a hundred, women say, "Of course."

"Of course. Eggs Benedict. If I have a lemon, I'll have everything I need." I dodged a final kiss and ran to my car. Poor Royal.

Did John look smug as I left? Well, I could handle it. Acting Director. I closed the car door and drove home.

❧ A FEW MONTHS LATER ❧

It was early in the morning in late July. Anne was working alone in the office, finishing the August calendar. The lights were off since the Center wasn't officially opened for the day yet.

Tap, tap, tap. "Anne, are you busy?"

"Royal! You're back! Come in, come in. It's so good to see you. When did you get back? How were New Mexico and your daughter, Chloe? How are you feeling? You look wonderful!"

"Thanks, Anne. Do you have time for a cup of coffee? I'll answer your questions, and you can fill me in on the Center news."

"All right, but you have to tell me everything first. I'll be right back." Anne ran to the kitchen and returned with two steaming mugs.

"I came back last night from Santa Fe. Anne, you can't imagine how beautiful it is in New Mexico. I loved watching the birds on our patio. The hummingbirds would buzz up to our feeders, flashing green and ruby colors, hanging almost motionless in the air. Then there was our roadrunner. He'd roost on the water tank, then take off running across the desert."

"It sounds fabulous. You'll miss it, I'm sure. But we'll keep you busy here, now that you're back."

"Well, Anne, that's what I came to tell you. I'm not really back. After my stroke, Dr. Nielsen was right when he said I needed a long rest. I feel so much better—but..."

"But what, Royal? You're ok, aren't you?"

"Yes, I'm fine. I just found living close to my daughter again, so…I don't know, so right. I'm here to pack up everything. Chloe and her friends have added a mother-in-law apartment to her house. It should be finished by the 15th, so I can take a couple of weeks to finalize things here."

"I'm stunned. We've all counted on you returning. I mean, I'm glad for you and Chloe, but, oh Royal, everyone will miss you so, me especially."

"I'll miss seeing all of you too, but it's time for a change. Anne, I have faith in you. I'm sure you've managed well these last three months and will continue to do so."

They heard some noise outside the office and went out to find several seniors coming in for the day. Hilda turned the lights on and began straightening the chairs, emptying the ashtrays, and lining up the card tables.

Royal visited with the group while Anne went back to finish up her work.

Royal stuck her head into the office. "Anne, I'm going over to City Hall to hand in my resignation. Why don't you meet me for lunch at Las Enchiladas, say about 12:30? I'll ask John if he can join us, too."

"Sounds good. I'll have Agnes cover the office and the phones until Fay gets in."

"Fay? Is she coming in for a special occasion? No, tell me at lunch. See you then."

Anne had a busy morning. She reviewed lunch plans with Mary and Brenda and told them she'd be going out.

Emma and Phil came in and set up for his painting class. He'd taken over for Anne when she stepped in for Royal.

When Fay arrived, Anne told her in confidence about Royal's resignation, and the two of them started planning a farewell party for her. What a blessing it was to have Fay working at the Center as the part-time Activities Director.

At 12:15, Anne left the Center and walked over to meet Royal and John at the restaurant. Royal and John were already seated, and she joined them in the booth.

"Anne, I asked John about the grant, but he said to wait and ask you. So what has happened?"

"There's not much to tell. The class was a bear, but surprisingly, Mr. Tabor ended up helping a lot. As required, I submitted my proposal to J.D. Butler at City Hall for review. He's looked it over, but said he won't comment until the new mayor sees it."

Royal interrupted, "The *new* mayor? John? Are you quitting?"

"As you said, Royal, it's time for a change. Eight years as mayor is plenty. I've been asked to run for county commissioner in November. I think I have a good chance, since so far I'm running unopposed. And, well, with Anne and me...I mean, well..."

"Royal, what John is trying to say is—we've been dating. So far, we haven't told anyone. But, if he works for the county, then there'll be no more conflict of interest being my boss. Then we won't have to keep it a secret any longer."

"Perfect! I always thought you two would be good together. What are your plans? When are you getting married? Make sure you send me an invitation."

"Not so fast, Royal!" John interjected.

"John and I are taking it slow, Royal. It's been less than two years since Terry died. We need to take time to really get to know each other and enjoy dating. Besides, John is busy with the campaign, and the Center takes a lot of my time."

"You don't need to tell me how busy it is! So, what have you done to handle all the Center's demands without me?"

"Anne talked the City into hiring a part-time activities director, just for the duration of your leave."

"Fay has taken over planning and leading the monthly

field trips, bless her soul. She also schedules guest speakers and special events. She even found a replacement for Dr. Foot Care—a sweet, helpful nurse who comes when scheduled and even likes being at the Center."

"Sounds good, Anne. How is the nutrition program going?"

"Officially, I'm still the nutrition director, but with Mary handling the kitchen, and Brenda taking money, it's a cinch. We're still having lunches three days a week and potlucks on Thursdays. My church oversees another potluck on Sundays from two 'til five. That's going well. Several ladies stay afterwards for a quilting bee, and some of the men work on their wood carving projects from Janet Nemmers' class. That, by the way, is also going very well."

"Royal, I think it was a wonder that day you found Anne for the nutrition program. She has done a wonderful job. Attendance is up fifteen percent for meals," John noted. "I'm sure the grant will be approved. I'm keeping my fingers crossed that we'll have a new Center in two years. You'll have to come up from New Mexico for its opening."

"I'll do that," Royal responded. "I know the Danville Senior Center is in great hands.

ABOUT THE AUTHOR

 **Jean Young** was born in Wenatchee, Washington, and currently lives in the Seattle area in the log home she and her husband built fifty years ago. A retired senior center director, Jean fills her time with volunteer work, gardening, writing, reading, spending time with her family, and travel. Trips she has taken included a year in Japan and a summer in Ghana teaching sewing at a high school.